Hitmen, Gangsters, Cannibals and Me

• • • • • • • • • • • •

Hitmen, Gangsters, Cannibals and Me

• • • • • • • • • • • • • •

Donal MacIntyre

First published in 2010 by Y Books
Lucan, Co. Dublin
Ireland
Tel & Fax: +353 1 621 7992
publishing@ybooks.ie
www.ybooks.ie

Paperback	ISBN: 978-1-908023-00-1
Ebook - Mobi format	ISBN: 978-1-908023-01-8
Ebook - epub format	ISBN: 978-1-908023-02-5

A CIP catalogue record for this book is available from the British Library.

10 9 8 7 6 5 4 3 2 1

Typeset by Y Books
Cover design by Graham Thew Design
Front cover image courtesy of Peter Evers Photography
Back cover images courtesy of Five TV, BBC and David Wootton Photography
Printed and bound by CPI Mackays, Chatham ME5 8TD

To Allegra,

my princess – for her sparkly turquoise heart.

ACKNOWLEDGEMENTS

I owe a great debt of gratitude to all those who have worked with me on the hundreds of hours of television and radio, and on the acres of newsprint to which I have contributed over the years. Thank you for your tolerance and forgiveness of my many limitations.

Grateful thanks to the Tanner and Binns families, who hosted the Insect Tribe when we travelled outside London. Thanks to Tigress Productions, Five, the Discovery Channel, Sky and the BBC for their support of my work. Also to Bravo, National Geographic, ITN, Granada and ITV for our ongoing work together. Prof. David Wilson, Prof. Howard Tumber and Peter Salmon have been important guiding figures in my career, as have my former colleagues at *World In Action* and the *Irish Press*.

Thanks to Gerry Easter, Ms Nydiger, Shane Timlin, Susan Feldstein, Robert Doran, my editor, and Chenile Keogh, my publisher at Y Books, for all your patience. Thanks to photographers Dave Wootton and Robin Culley. Thanks to all at Dare Films and True North Productions. Thanks to Vincent Browne, the late Michael Hand, Mick O'Hare, father and son, and to 'Braveheart', Michael Mendelsohn.

It goes without saying that I owe a great debt to those who have protected me and my family over the years. Mitch, Clive Driscoll, Gerry Hamilton, Eddie Halling, Ginger, Tony Gilbert and Gemma Smith and the Metropolitan Police – it's your fault

I am still alive. For my sanity (what's left of it), thanks must go to my assistant, Lloyd Page. Thanks to Nick Armstrong, my lawyer, for keeping me out of jail and to my colleagues, Steve Cooper, Michael Simkins, Paul Samuri, Martin Hickman, not forgetting my creative wingmen, Mike Turnbull and Nick Manley. I could not let the chance pass without saluting all at Guilford Spectrum – Andy, Melissa, Ruth and Stewart, my ice angels.

Special thanks to my family: Darragh, Deirdre, Tadhg, Desmond and of course my mom, Peggy, for being unstinting in their support. My mom is a most remarkable woman, and I could not wish for a better mother.

Finally, my love and gratitude to my wife, Ameera, who encouraged and cajoled the best out of me and gave me my reasons for living – my beautiful princesses, baby Tiger and Allegra, my proudest and greatest accomplishments.

There are so many more I could mention, and I apologise for not being able to thank all of you. But you know who you are, and I hope you know that your support and efforts are what have made the adventures on these pages possible. I remain eternally grateful.

CONTENTS

Introduction

The Accidental Journalist

Our standard-issue Bakelite phone rang. 'Hello, is that Darragh?' asked the man with a Belfast accent at the end of the line. It was 1984, and my journalist brother, Darragh, had gone to the US to work for the *New York Daily News*.

He had previously been a regular sports freelancer for the nationals, and, unaware that he had left the country for pastures new, editors were still calling the house, looking for him to cover stories. This was long before people were in the habit of announcing their whereabouts and state of mind to the world via Facebook and Twitter!

'I'm afraid he isn't here. Is there anything I can help you with?' I asked.

'Could you let him know that we need him to cover the Kildare match in Athy this weekend? Four pars and results, please,' said the man from the *Irish News*.

'He's in the States, but I'll do it for you,' I said, trying to sound older than my 17 years.

There was a sharp intake of breath.

'No, that wouldn't do, sorry.'

I insisted that I was the man for the job, but he said: 'I appreciate your offer, but we'll get someone else.'

I got the feeling that my interlocutor wanted to commission someone who didn't have to finish his homework before going to cover the story. I had no intention of doing my homework anyway, so I persisted, and he eventually relented somewhat and said he would check with his boss and call me back.

And, to my surprise, he did. He had been mysteriously unable to find anyone else to cover a Kildare hurling match (if you had seen Kildare play hurling in those days, you would understand why), and offered me the princely sum of IR£4.50 to turn in four paragraphs, the team sheets and the results by early evening on Sunday.

After attending the match, I phoned the news desk and proudly read them my copy, eager to see my words in print for the first time. And that was it: I was suddenly a journalist!

What follows are some of the highlights in the career of an accidental journalist and the adventures of a boy who covered a Kildare match and never looked back.

1

Lying for a Living

My career as a 'professional liar' began at the age of seven when I made my first confession at St Brigid's Primary School in Celbridge, Co. Kildare. In preparation for this momentous event, we were given a list of indiscretions to rattle off to the priest, so as not to leave him underemployed. 'Bless me, Father, for I have sinned. This is my first confession but I have remained without sin since my virgin birth,' was not likely to go down well with the nuns, or indeed the priest.

So our teacher wrote a selection of 'Tesco own brand' sins on the board, so that we could repeat them verbatim to our holy confessor, the local priest, Fr Eugene Kennedy. For weeks, we practised and practised. 'I have been disobedient to my parents and mean to my brothers and sisters,' was one that could be safely assumed to apply to all of us. Now this convenient mantra meant that some of my classmates were confessing to quite a caseload of the Devil's works. Some had 15 siblings (contraception was still an alien concept in 1970s Ireland), and I feared that their first confessions would open the gates of hell after years of disobedience, pinching and kicking. It seemed entirely possible that the heavenly accountants would do a quick tot and send them directly from the confession box to eternal damnation.

I had three brothers and a sister, so I certainly had a few sins to confess myself, but I was left more confused than most in the class of 45 pupils. Seeking forgiveness for sinning against my Dad was problematic because he wasn't around. My father had left the family home when I was four, and although I did see him in the following years, there was little real opportunity to sin against him. However, because it was written on the board, I was required to accept the sin as my own, on the teacher's orders.

The issue of an absent father didn't weigh too heavily on my mind apart from the odd occasion when an older kid called me 'a little bastard'. Of course there were plenty of times when I *was* a little bastard, but even at the age of seven I knew when it was meant literally. A broken family was not something that the church wanted to engage with in those days and I was not going to be indulged with a bespoke set of sins tailored to my domestic circumstances.

When the priest came to check on our progress as pious young Catholics, we tried to impress with our clasped hands and bowed heads. My Act of Contrition was word perfect and I could reel off my sins like my 10 times tables.

On the big day we were divided into two queues, the boys in one line and the girls in the other. This military configuration did nothing to encourage military discipline and the excitement of being out of the classroom meant that I was soon adding to my list off sins.

'MacIntyre!' came the hushed admonishment from one of the nuns – even she wasn't allowed to shout in God's house. I protested that I hadn't done anything and maintain to this day that I was innocent. 'But you were thinking about it,' she shot back, and in that she was probably right. I had my knuckles slapped with a ruler and was placed in the girls' line, which was the ultimate humiliation for a seven-year-old boy.

My first confession was heard by the aforementioned Fr Eugene Kennedy, a handsome priest who always seemed out of place in our village parish. A more sophisticated city congregation would have been better suited to his debonair manner. If James Bond had found God, Eugene would have been called up for audition.

It seemed a terrifying experience, or at least it did back then. We were under the impression that unless we were suitably contrite for our sins (by 'our sins' I mean the ones we had learned off by heart), the Devil would be rubbing his hands with glee, ready to take our souls to hell. Remember that at the time we were still donating our pennies to pay for the 'little black babies'' souls to be lifted out of purgatory. There was a recession on then, too.

The time came to meet my confessor and I recounted my sins verbatim to the priest. He nodded sagely.

'Are you sorry?' he asked.

'Yes, I am,' I replied.

'Will you do it again?'

'No, never,' said I, lying before I was even out the door of the confession box.

An Act of Contrition and three Hail Marys later I was freed of my sins and back in the boys' line. It always niggled at me slightly that maybe I had compounded the sins I had forgotten by telling the invented sins that the teacher had remembered for me. But the joy of Catholicism is that you can return the following week and be absolved all over again. I think it was this facility that turned us all into repeat offenders.

In my teenage years, some of my church-going pals became bolder and turned confession into a dark comedic art. They would compete to see who could construct the most elaborate confession, daring the priest to refuse them absolution. The winner invented an epic of three parts that required separate visits to the confession box on consecutive days. On the first he revealed that he was having an affair with a teacher. The next day he admitted that this was a lie he had told to cover up the fact that he was gay, and on the third day he came clean and confessed that it was all lies. Of course, the confession was interspersed with lurid stories of fantasy sexual encounters, which may have encouraged the priest to indulge the young sinner – or perhaps he was just concerned for the poor lad's soul.

My favourite sin was not even mine. It had occurred in

Economics class, days after the Irish budget in 1982. The teacher was a bright nun, always immaculately dressed and sharp enough to control a 40-strong mob of students who were less than eager to learn the finer points of macro-economic policy. We were asked to offer our opinions on the Minister of Finance's fine deliberations, but when the Sister asked my twin, Des, for his tuppence ha'penny worth she didn't know what she was letting herself in for. Deadpan, he told her that the new budget had made some provisions that could help to bolster the finances of the convent.

'How so?' she enthusiastically enquired.

'Well, with all the new childcare benefits and allowances, I have calculated that if each of the nuns had a child, you would all be substantially better off. And let's face it, in the line of business you're in, you could just pass it off as immaculate conceptions.'

His suggestion did not go down well at all. Funnily enough, Des has ended up working as an economist and I'm sure the school is delighted that his early promise has been realised, even if it didn't meet with their approval on its first outing.

Another thing that would meet with the nuns' disapproval and that would have come as something of a surprise to them would have been the news of my consistently outstanding grades throughout my secondary education. I was an average student, as my official school records will testify, but that's not what my mother was led to believe. On the first day of school I stumbled across a box of blank report cards in the schoolyard. They had fallen off a pallet of stationery on the way to the principal's office and I, naturally, couldn't pass up an opportunity like that.

Deft handling of the post meant that my mother didn't receive a single genuine report card from the school for me in the five years I was there (sorry, Mum!). I usually gave myself A's across the board, but occasionally added that 'Donal could try harder'. The oddly juvenile handwriting might have been something of a giveaway, but my mother never said anything.

She might have turned a blind eye to my forged report cards – bringing up five kids by herself meant that she had other, more pressing priorities – but if she had found out about another one of my porkies there would have been all hell to pay. Being the products of a broken home, we were something of an anomaly in the holy Catholic Ireland of the seventies and eighties. Divorce was illegal and separations were still frowned upon. But I was a shameless opportunist and was determined to turn the social stigma to my advantage. My lesser sins involved refusing to wear the school uniform and blaming our domestic circumstances for my inappropriate attire. Politely, the school authorities didn't want to intrude, and, more often than not, let it go, while I lorded it over my classmates in my jeans and trainers.

But our Christmas whopper was my most shameful lie. Every December without fail, Des and I would take the month off school to go turkey plucking. We would tell the school that we had to go to work because we couldn't afford Christmas otherwise. Well, if my mother had found out, she would have plucked the hair out of our heads. While she went out to work as a schoolteacher in Walkinstown every morning, we left the house, schoolbags on our backs by way of camouflage, and went off to the turkey farm a couple of miles down the road to make our fortunes at the rate of 80p for a cock and 60p for a hen.

'Can any of you feckers pluck a turkey?' Barney, the chief turkey plucker, asked the bunch of ragamuffin truants in front of him. We nodded an emphatic yes, before being let loose to mutilate the dead birds. 'You are plucking the birds – not performing an autopsy, Macker,' he would shout at me when I tore the skin and made it clear that I had no idea how to go about the job. 'For feck's sake Macker, you've ripped another one,' he'd say, the colour rising in his cheeks so that they clashed with his bright-red hair. Shaking his head, he would reach into his pocket and pull out a needle and thread to begin the reconstructive surgery necessitated by my handiwork. For most of the year, Barney was something of a character around Celbridge. He had never attended medical school to my knowledge, but every December he was 'The Surgeon' whose skill saved us all from the wrath of the local shopkeepers.

During the summer holidays, instead of plucking turkeys I plucked wild oats. The oats grew over the crop in the cornfields and contaminated the yield, so they had to be picked out before harvest. At the age of 15, while my contemporaries were sowing them, I was picking wild oats for IR£5 an hour at Farmer Huddleston's, near Barberstown Cross. This was great money at the time, and the job was made even more attractive by the fact that lunch was thrown into the bargain. Obviously, the offer to feed us was made before they had seen us eat. After a week of plundering the farmhouse larder, we were offered an extra pound an hour if we would bring a packed lunch. We must have been like locusts in the kitchen for that to make economic sense.

On the back of my stellar performance as a wild oat picker, Farmer Huddleston offered me a promotion.

'Can ya drive a tractor?' he asked me.

'Of course I can,' I lied, gleefully stretching my hand out for the keys.

In a portent of things to come, I gave the distinct impression that I knew what I was doing. For any 15-year-old who has grown up on a farm, driving a tractor is second nature, but I grew up around farms and not on one, so my confidence in my ability was a little misplaced. After snatching the keys and proudly jumping into the driver's seat, I turned the engine over, waved smugly to the other farmhands and accelerated straight into the ditch. After he pulled his shiny new Massey Ferguson out of the flood drain, Farmer Huddleston sent me back to the fields in shame.

After that, there followed a brief period as a roofer. My good work can still be seen on the Celbridge skyline, where one or two of the roofs have a distinctive, I would say characterful, concave appearance. In fairness to my work, the slates are still clinging on to the houses – but I try to keep upwind of them, all the same.

My finest hour in the casual jobs market was perhaps as a window cleaner. I worked for Paddy, a good friend of mine growing up, who was a part-time football referee and part-time window cleaner. He was the only referee I knew who red-carded you for bad language and then effed and blinded you off the field as you went. As a window cleaner, Paddy had something of a professional handicap – he was afraid of heights. I wasn't aware of this when I lied about my own fear of heights to get the job. This presented us with quite a predicament, until Paddy threatened to fire me if I didn't 'get up that ladder and wash the bloody windows'. I had a few terrifying moments three storeys off the ground, but in the end my lie paid off as I found my fear of heights dissipated and I had gained an unexpected new skill. The real danger lay in Paddy being engrossed in the racing pages while he was supposed to be holding the death-trap ladder. Every step of that ladder looked ready to snap, but Paddy, not having to use it himself, refused to accept that it needed to be replaced, and left me to risk life and limb while he chose his bets.

Next came my Jackson Pollock period, made possible by my newfound ladder-climbing skills and a little well-judged bluffing. A group of us styled ourselves as painters and decorators by buying new overalls and splattering them with paint samples to make it look like we had been doing the job for years. This touch of authenticity got us several jobs. We would generally last a couple of weeks before being sacked amid accusations of dripping gloss and ruined carpets.

No one found me out quite as quickly as the inner-city kids who I taught during a stint as an arts and crafts teacher while I was a student. They would listen to *Rum Sodomy & the Lash* by The Pogues as they built churches out of lollipop sticks. These kids spent their time out of school robbing cars and breaking into houses and they cut me some slack when they figured out that I knew less about arts and crafts than they did – but only as long as they could choose the music.

*****

Later, when I met the serious gangsters, I would fall back on these experiences and I have found them more useful than any state exam or university education. By accident, I had discovered the art of lying for living, and living other people's lives became my occupation for nearly 15 years, on the back of saying 'yes' when the answer was really 'no'. It was a little over 15 years ago that I sat in a room full of producers in the *World in Action* offices at Granada in Manchester. 'Has anyone here ever done any security work?' the editor asked. Of course, I said yes, as if stretching my hand out for the keys of the Massey Ferguson all over again. This time, though, I couldn't afford to end up in a ditch.

2

My Life as a Headhunter

Jason Marriner held his audience in rapture. He wrapped his arms around his rotund frame to mimic a belly laugh, though his ample waist was big enough that he didn't need to exaggerate. He was telling a story about him and his mates going to Auschwitz, pissing on the graves of Holocaust victims and mocking their remains with goose steps and Nazi salutes. I looked on smiling, part of the accepting throng of hooligans and England supporters who were relishing the horrific story. We were in Copenhagen. Chelsea F.C. were on tour, and leading their travelling army was their hooligan firm, the Headhunters.

'So, they're having this tour thing,' Jason painted the scene animatedly, 'and they're talking to all these Jerries about what happened … blah, blah, blah.' Marriner describes dismissing the tour guide's measured words and instead deciding to photograph his friend, Andy 'Nightmare' Frain, making a Nazi salute.

'All the Jerries started going mad. Nightmare's response was, "Fuck off! This is what I believe in,"' Jason said, wiping his eyes mockingly. 'Next he's up on the roof acting like he's having a David Gower [shower] where they put the gas in.' Jason acted it out like he was in an Ealing comedy. 'I think I put the final nail in the coffin when I was in the gas chamber and I was trying to get in the oven,' Jason said, to roars of laughter.

He told his drunken audience that this is what he believes in, and that is that. 'And they all come to Auschwitz to work their bollocks off and they wind up with fuck all,' he laughed. 'I don't care – all the Jews that didn't get gassed, they moved to North London.' Lovely chap! And he was my new best friend.

*****

It all started in an office at BBC White City. The series producer, Pip, an old colleague from Granada's *World in Action*, suggested that the world of hooligans deserved an in-depth undercover look. Bizarrely, he suggested that I was the man for the job.

'I know undercover work is risky, but there are limits,' I said. 'You want me to be a raving England supporter [heresy for any Celt], a Chelsea supporter, a neo Nazi and an ultra-right-wing UDA/Johnny Adair sympathiser?' That's what he wanted from a 'Paddy' who was a BBC journalist and a non-practising Kildare fan. This was surely a stretch.

The year was 1998 and England was in the World Cup in France. Desperate to avoid this rather impossible gig, I said, 'Isn't this all a bit eighties?' Pip disagreed. He is an award-winning current affairs veteran, who has risked his life on stories in places like Columbia and Nigeria, so he wasn't going to let me wriggle out of this one.

He showed me a rogues' gallery of Police photographs of some of Britain's most dangerous football supporters. The scars, the tattoos and the shaved heads all looked familiar and dangerous.

'Why the Chelsea Headhunters?' I asked.

'They have been causing trouble for decades. A major undercover Police operation against them in the late eighties failed. They are still active and 'at it', in hooligan parlance.'

He explained that Andy 'Nightmare' Frain was something of a recidivist offender, with more than 30 convictions for violence and public disorder. His most recent convictions included a three-and-a-half-year sentence for threatening a victim with assault if he didn't drop charges against one of his associates. I think Pip must have seen the colour drain from my face.

'Oh, you'll be fine,' he said, laughing. 'Don't be such a wimp.'

To ease my concern, he repeatedly slashed his hand back and forth across his neck, showing me just how my throat would be cut.

I was brought up to speed on what the Chelsea Headhunters had done to a West Ham fan at the beginning of the 96-97 season. Eight Headhunters were arrested after they slashed a supporter's neck from ear to ear with a knife. His arm was also nearly severed and it took over 360 stitches to save the man's life. Unsurprisingly, the victim did not turn up at court.

* * * * *

The decision was effectively taken out of my hands and it was agreed that I would volunteer to go to the World Cup in France for my induction as an England supporter and a hooligan. Nothing like being thrown in the deep end, I suppose.

My first day as an Englishman abroad saw me in Marseille, surrounded by French riot police hoping to round up English hooligans. It was 35°C outside and the sun was beating down on the masses of pink-skinned tourists. There is something about the cocktail of alcohol, football and sunshine that is toxic and contagious. One England supporter caught everyone's attention as he ran semi-naked towards the policemen, rubbing an Irish flag on his backside.

His affront to the Irish, bizarrely outside an Irish bar, got the backs up of the local Police, and they went in to sweep up the miscreants who had begun taunting them too. It was not a particularly well-targeted swoop – it seemed that anyone with an English accent or in the company of English supporters was going to be dragged in. The provocation towards the French Police was escalating and they weren't going to mess about.

It looked like I was going to be arrested. About to be carried off, I protested: 'Je suis journalist, je suis Irlandais!' On my first day in the field, I had to break cover to avoid spending a night in a prison cell in Marseilles. Thank God hooligans can't speak French.

It wasn't quite a strip search but I was well patted down to ensure I didn't have a concealed weapon, and I may as well have been naked. My legs were shaking with nerves. It obviously didn't help my case that I was dressed like a hooligan, in the company of hooligans and chanting with them; I was essentially part of the angry mob. A French policeman looked me up and down suspiciously and took out the handcuffs. As a last resort, I took out my Irish passport and within minutes all was forgiven and I was allowed to go.

My apprenticeship as an undercover hooligan was not going well and it wasn't going to get any easier.

*****

This day was a long time coming. My team and I had moved in next door to Jason Marriner, the football hooligan who, very appropriately, lived in Chelsea Close in Hampton, West London. The glorious moment when we had driven past his flat to see a 'For Let' sign in his block was the day we knew the gods were with us and that we might very well get close to this hooligan and use him to get close to the rest.

We had been tickling the belly of this beast. For weeks and months we had Marriner under surveillance as I slowly introduced my world to his. First it was the Chelsea insignia in the car, then the requisite Stone Island gangster-chic clothes, then the wads of flash cash, which painted the picture of a criminal doing well. Over a period of about six months, we became well acquainted and he allowed me into his world. 'The first time I seen you, I thought you were "at it"[i.e. a criminal],' he told me.

I was about to pick him up outside his tyre replacement centre in Feltham, near his Hampton Hill patch. He rented the property and ran a pretty shambolic business there. He was also in the car recovery business, so he was kept reasonably busy when he wasn't being a football thug.

We were going to a Leicester v Chelsea game. The Headhunters already had a history of trouble with Leicester fans. The match was to take place in Leicester and my producer, Paul, and I were going to drive Jason there.

In this job you live on your instincts. My gut instinct that day was not good. There was something not quite right. We were due to pick up Jason alone: there were no other players in mind, but with Jason, you never knew. 'Will there just be three of us in the car?' Jason had asked me previously. I wondered why he had asked that question. It had stuck in my mind and made me slightly nervous. It was beginning to dawn on me that he might be considering bringing another hooligan along on the trip.

When I pulled the car up at the garage, I checked obsessively to make sure that there were no camera remotes in the door pockets, or BBC paraphernalia, or exposed wires that might betray my real reason for being there. All was well. Jason's Vauxhall Vectra pulled up and, sure enough, he was not alone: there were two men in the car with him. I hoped that they weren't coming with us.

I turned to Paul and saw his face blanch as he recognised one of the men.

'It's Andy Frain,' he said.

I had seen his face on photo-fits of hooligans, and I recognised it when I saw it. He was dangerous and capable of extreme violence. Knowing no limits and acting like an animal, he was a real gutter street fighter who would use any weapon at his disposal without a care for the consequences.

Andy 'Nightmare' Frain is close to the heads of the right -wing terror group, Combat 18, the National Front and the BNP. He is a major figure and is all over Police records. He is known to have been heavily involved in the Nazi hate rock scene as well, and has the dubious distinction of being a former Grand Hawk of the Ku Klux Klan in the UK. He was once a National Front election candidate for Feltham. With more than 30 convictions he has certainly earned his 'Nightmare' nickname.

His arrival was a shock of seismic proportions. I was chain-smoking and so was Paul. When I saw Nightmare's face, I nearly sucked my fag in and swallowed it whole.

The advice I have always been given for these situations is that less is more: keep it low key to start; be excited to see them, but not too excited. I warned myself not to use bad language. I have an Irish predilection for cursing, but in this situation, using the wrong bad language could blow our cover. It is difficult to use it for emphasis when you are undercover, so it is best not to use it at all.

We had to be very careful. A misplaced word could have got us killed and that is no exaggeration. Psychologists who have debriefed me after undercover stints describe the skill you use in these situations as 'Formula 1 concentration'. This is a state of mind, an acute awareness that the slightest error could have fatal consequences. We were about to spend a day in the company of very dangerous men and there had better be no slip-ups.

I was no better prepared for this job than the man on the street. I have no military training, no surveillance courses or modules on covert tactics from City University. My real skill is the ability to feel the fear after the event. I break down and shake after days like this. And then I do the same thing again the next day and the next day.

But there I was in Feltham, in an alien world in dangerous company. And then I remembered when I had most recently heard the nickname 'Nightmare'. He was the guy who had gone with Jason to Auschwitz to make Nazi salutes and urinate on the graves of victims. I couldn't believe it. He would be sitting within a foot of me in the car. I would be new to him and would be under his scrutiny for at least three hours. Any sign of weakness, vulnerability or of my real reason for being there, and there was no telling what could happen.

We had been wrong-footed: this man arrived looking for a lift when we had expected to be dealing with Jason alone. Things could go horribly wrong, and, in these uncontrollable situations, they often do. I rushed back to the car where we had left some blank tapes in the pocket at the back of the front seat. We had left them there because we thought we would put Jason in the front. I frantically removed the tapes and the spare recording disks and put them in the driver's door pocket. I threw a cigarette packet over them, hoping they were out of sight.

Should we let Jason in the front or should we impose ourselves on the situation and put the guys in the back? 'I think I should sit in the front,' Paul said. We agreed that Paul should sit in the front for the first part of the journey while things settled down, and, when the mood was good, we whould put Jason in the front seat for optimum footage. This exchange was happening in quiet whispers as our hooligan friends got out of the Vectra and approached us. The boys loaded into the car. They were joined by a third hooligan, Ian. The three lined the back seat, with Nightmare in the middle where he could happily hold court. Introductions were made and I delivered a handshake to Frain, robust and firm to the end. 'All right mate?' I said. I held his gaze just a little longer than normal as a trust-building exercise. I hoped he didn't think I was challenging him. In this world, handshakes are measured. They have a value and can help place you in the pecking order.

'I can't be doing with those black man's slap and high-five, whoop-and-holler shit. I hate them fuckin' wankers. Me, I like a good English handshake, a man's handshake,' Jason had said to me previously. I overcompensated. Frain's hand was smaller than mine and he had a firm and measured grip, the grip of a man who was not sure of the person he was meeting.

I drove off with three hooligans in my car, knowing – but not much reassured by the fact – that there would be a car following us and filming from a distance. I was equipped with a covert camera in the middle of my T-shirt. The dark designer top had a pin-prick in the middle of a letter of the brand name. That was the lens. Behind that was a small computer board and microphone. At the time, the technology was still quite bulky. The wires for sound and pictures went to a small DV recorder that was packed into a money-belt style wraparound holder, which also had pockets for batteries and spare tapes.

Our very own 'Q' had provided me with a remote control fob that allowed me to turn the camera on and off. The moments when you turned it on and off were the ones when you were most likely to be caught out. Your body or your hand gestures might betray you, questions would be asked and things could spiral out of control very quickly. This is what's called a 'choke point', a point at which you could crash and burn.

There was also a camera hidden in the clock in the dashboard of the car. This gave a perfect view of the back seat and provided a great shot of Nightmare. On that day, however, I wasn't too concerned about the shots. In these investigations, it's the evidence and the words that are most important. The pretty shots can come later.

It was a little quiet in the car. Instinctively, I went to turn on the radio but then remembered that the noise would interfere with the recording. The silence put even more pressure on the conversation and more pressure on me not to mess it up.

Eventually, Jason and his pals started chatting in the back. The talk was of passport restrictions that the Police had put on football hooligans after the 1998 World Cup.

'They took mine away. I still had to sign on when fucking England were playing abroad. I didn't even have a fucking passport and I still had to go to the Police station,' Nightmare complained.

He was happy to take control of the conversation and it was clear that he was the leader of the pack. Putting on a mock PC Plod voice, he scoffed at the authorities' efforts to eradicate hooliganism:

'He's the brains behind the outfit,' he said, speaking about himself. 'We've arrested them many times but they keep escaping our clutches.'

I had a stand-up comedian in the back, and a dangerous one at that, so I had better laugh at his impression of the bumbling copper. He was funny but there was a note of menace that undercut his humour. He was quite clearly letting me know his status – he was the boss and I had better not forget it.

Andy continued the parody, warming to his theme: 'They dress in suits and go to a pub, start a bit of action and then sit back and watch it happen.' He curled his lips to enhance the caricature. 'They're so highly praised by their moronic followers that all they have to do is shout the word and they steam into battle for them.'

He told us that he had read the report of a recent Police press conference on hooliganism in the *Star*. The headline was 'Jet-set Sickos'. Andy said his mates were still buying him drinks to celebrate on the back of this publicity.

I was feeling rather sick myself at that moment. Andy 'Nightmare' Frain loved the notoriety that these headlines gave him. He appeared to be unconcerned about jail, but, as he relaxed, I was hoping that he would make an admission that would send him right back there.

He boasted at length about his well-earned reputation, saying that one policeman had described him as 'brutal'. Mimicking the policeman again, he said, 'He can fix anything, from a bar room brawl to an international riot. This man's ruthless and won't stop at anything. £50,000 robberies, and all that violence.'

'He seems to know you well,' Jason responded, laughing.

I laughed too, for appearances. I smoked another fag and wondered if this posturing was a not-so-subtle warning to me. Andy revealed that he had spent nine of the previous 13 years in jail. Well, he was certainly sending out a message that he is not to be messed with. The conversation continued: 'Black c**ts! Do we like niggers? No! We hate niggers. In fact we hate any c**t who ain't British,' Nightmare said.

'Krauts. Like their political views, don't like them,' Jason chimed in, eager to please.

'Tell you what annoys me as well: Reading [Frain's hometown] seems to be a fucking dumping ground for all them fucking Bosnians and that. Every afternoon, they get about five or six of them out of the back of a lorry. I'll have to get the boys out on the streets.'

Lovely. Sometimes I guessed that I was expected to nod and laugh and at other times supposed to appear disinterested. It is very difficult for a normal person to keep their mouth shut in the face of such prejudice.

We were about halfway to Leicester on the M1 and there was

sweat dripping down my face. I was wiping it discretely, trying not to draw attention to myself or to my nerves.

Concentration is key in this job and I was struggling to hold it together. I had to drive with these lunatics in my car and I'm a bad driver to begin with. It took me four attempts to pass my driving test and then it was only after over 100 hours of lessons – and none of those lessons gave any hints on how to drive with dangerous hooligans in the car.

Amid the banter, Frain's phone rang. After a quick conversation he told us that there were three coaches of Chelsea supporters on the M1, all up for action. Other Chelsea fans were already on the rampage in Hemel Hempstead.

'We are up to full strength. The boys are swigging beer, snorting charlie and eating sandwiches!' said Nightmare, painting a pretty picture of his friends preparing for a riot.

'Today's the day,' said Jason excitedly.

'And you've brought the new recruits out,' said Nightmare, finally anointing us.

'Maybe we've cracked it. Keep cool. Hold it together.' I told myself.

Just as I was beginning to relax a little, my precarious situation was driven home to me by a story about an encounter with a police officer.

'He had his throat proper cut,' Jason told us with a smirk.

Nightmare took up the story: 'We was laughing at him, we was. He [the policeman] says, "You can't do that, I'm an off-duty policeman." I said, "SHUT UP! It's one o'clock in the morning. Nobody can see us." [He made a slashing motion across his throat.] His bird ran off hysterical. We was just laughing.'

The police officer needed 68 stitches to his face and throat after the violent knife attack by Nightmare and his mates.

As he proudly told his story, I was watching him in the mirror, and the camera in the dashboard was whirring away. Normally, I cannot hear the recorder turn on, but on this occasion, I swear my senses were so acute that I could hear the cogs click into action. Nightmare's story was like a perfect piece to camera. He might be a thug but he was also a performer in search of an audience. He didn't know when he recounted his sick tale that he was in fact performing for an audience of eight million.

The closer we got to Leicester, the more excited they became. Phone calls were made and arrangements put in place. This is the way violence is organised: in advance, between rival firms who agree the rules of engagement and the meeting place. The Leicester boys had already agreed to organise a ruck in Narborough, a small village not far from the Leicester grounds. It had been specifically chosen to avoid Police attention. Nightmare's hands were sweating in anticipation.

Rival firms meet by agreement to settle their differences by fist, bottle, baton and whatever they can gather by way of street furniture. We were keen to witness and film the violence, but, unless we could duck out, we would be under Nightmare's watchful eye when the ruck broke out and would be expected to get stuck in. Besides, I can't fight, so we hoped that there would be enough distractions for us to slip away from the violence unnoticed.

We arrived at The Narborough Arms, which was packed full with Chelsea fans. Jason was still 'Man United excited'. I recognised a few faces and I hoped that they might recognise me and the company I was in. We were with hooligan royalty and I wanted everyone in the firm to know it and to clock us. I bought the boys drinks and then withdrew to give them room to mingle.

Within minutes, the Police raided the pub and the immediate threat of violence was quashed. The Police have informers everywhere, but gossip never got a conviction: that was my problem with how the situation was being handled. We needed evidence to put them away. I was hoping that the tapes in the car would do the job. Jason reckoned that he had it all figured out.

'I don't care what they say, some of our phones are tapped, man. The cops do their homework about you,' he said, sagely.

Well yes, we had done our homework, but we weren't the cops.

'You've got to be careful, mate,' we advised him.

The Police made it clear that they intended to escort the crowds to the game. Thankfully, Jason and his pals decided to continue their journey on the bus. 'I don't want to bring down the Old Bill on your car,' Jason offered, generously. He told us that they might be staying up for the weekend, so we said goodbye, telling them that we would phone after the game.

Despite the massive Police presence, trouble broke out around the ground and dominated the airwaves in the hours after the match. The Chelsea Headhunters seemed unstoppable.

*****

Nearly two years after the investigation started, Judge Charles Byers told Backfriars Crown Court that football hooligans had brought the country into disrepute, as he sentenced Andrew Frain and Jason Marriner to seven and six years respectively. The evidence we had gathered on tape proved crucial in securing the convictions. They were both banned from attending football matches for 10 years. The Judge had initially banned them for 20 but was told by the Court clerk that the maximum allowable was a 10-year ban. He said that football hooliganism was 'one of the most horrifying and frightening spectacles of recent times'.

Frain has continued to work on the fringe of the far right, with Combat 18 and the BNP. He remains a threat to law and order. I spoke to one prison worker who said that in jail he was a lovely chap. I hope so, but I am well aware of the potential for violence that lies behind the cheeky-chappy façade. He was released in 2003 and it's hard to believe that he will put this behaviour behind him. Having already chalked up 35 criminal convictions, it seems unlikely that his rap sheet will stay at that.

Jason Marriner's ban was lifted after eight years, but he has continued to associate with football hooligans. He has carved out a career of sorts, speaking about his adventures as a football hooligan on the one hand, and claiming that the BBC stitched him up on the other. I met him subsequently at the funeral of a mutual friend. 'You fucking grass,' he said, ready for a fight. I reminded him that we were at a funeral, but it didn't stop him from trying to resort to fisticuffs.

Afterwards, we came close to agreeing to put the past behind us, and even considered making a documentary together, reliving some of the past, but then something happened that made that gesture unthinkable for me.

Throughout the case I had Police escorts to the Court and bodyguards at home. Safe houses and security detail became part of my daily existence after this investigation, as regular death threats were made against me. My friends were afraid to have me to dinner. TV studios put on extra security for my appearances, and sometimes would only announce me as a last-minute guest. Richard Madely and Judy Finnegan were particularly nervous on *This Morning*, but gave me a warm welcome on set.

But it was 10 years later, when I thought everything had settled down and I was living a normal life again, that this investigation really came back to haunt my family and me.

It had been a busy evening. I had been in Camden presenting awards to the winners of the MENCAP photography competition and had dashed off to meet Ameera and the kids for a feast of Mexican food. After that, we went home and got the kids to bed. Ameera was feeling stressed, and with good reason. She has a brain tumour and she was due to go for a scan the next morning. We were hoping for good news, but her headaches and nausea had been getting worse and there was a genuine concern that the tumour might have grown. When we got home at about 9.45 p.m. we decided that we would call the babysitter to watch the kids, and go for a quiet drink to calm Ameera's nerves about the scan.

We went to a nearby wine bar and had just ordered two glasses of plonk and had a few sips when I noticed some trouble developing to our right. There was a party of revellers who were getting louder and drawing attention to themselves. We were a little out of the way, keeping a low profile, when one of the men came over and pointed at me.

He accused me of being a grass and a snitch and of setting up his mate, Jason Marriner, all the while pointing agressively at us.

For Ameera this got too much. She ran to the toilets in tears. I followed her but stopped to try to reason with the group of men. 'Guys, give us a break. My wife has a brain tumour and she has a brain scan tomorrow. She is very stressed. We're just out for a quiet drink. Give us a break.'

They continued their aggressive posturing and there seemed to be no talking to them. I escaped to the toilet to try to comfort Ameera. There were other women there, wondering what was going on. A girl who was there for her birthday approached me and said: 'Why is she upset? Does someone want to beat you up?'

'It appears so,' I answered.

'Is that because you put someone in jail?' she asked.

'I guess so,' I replied.

'Then you deserve it,' she said.

Her friend suggested that I leave the ladies' toilet. I went back to the bar area, where the men continued to abuse me. As soon as they saw Ameera appear from the toilets, they attacked me, and in the melée Ameera was badly assaulted and beaten up. I later collapsed unconscious while the Police were taking my statement. The brain scan was cancelled.

For the first time, my work had come to haunt my family. There is nothing I wouldn't do to take those moments back. Ameera needed counselling to cope with the incident, which left her suffering from panic attacks and feeling vunerable and suicidal because she felt that she couldn't protect the children. We were constantly looking over our shoulders in fear of attack. The assault on Ameera is my greatest regret. No exposé is worth that.

During the course of the investigation, I got a Chelsea tattoo to help me pass as a genuine hooligan. Ludicrously, I fainted while it was being done, but the technician continued, on the insistence of the producer: nothing would give me away more than a half-finished tattoo. After the programme went out, I had considered getting it removed and had endured one laser removal treatment, courtesy of the BBC. It didn't bother me much then, so I never went back for more painful treatments. It bothers me now.

3

MacIntyre of Arabia

I was in Oman as a guest of the Al-Amris, a Bedouin family living halfway between an ancient world and the encroaching modern civilization. They were good people who lived for the camel. I was about to die for it. The genesis of this mad adventure lay in a series I did for the Discovery Channel, where I lived with tribes around the world from Borneo to Bolivia. For me the series afforded the opportunity to get a snapshot of these societies before they changed into something unrecognisable.

This was a *Boy's Own* opportunity. I had to open myself up to any and every experience, and be ready with an upbeat smile even when I was feeling like a deadbeat. For me this is the essence of the good traveller: an open heart and an open hand will open doors locked to others. As I travelled the world from culture to culture, continent to continent, I was left with the enduring impression that however differently we live our lives, we are all intrinsically the same. We have our hopes and dreams, fears and stresses, and we have a fundamental belief in family and community.

This adventure brought me to the Arabian Desert, to the ocean of sand dunes that looks like it could carry you off the edge of the earth. This was my journey with the Bedouin, which immersed me in an alien culture, a foreign land and an inhuman climate.

It hadn't rained there in the previous six years and the

temperature was regularly hitting 50°C. It's one of the harshest environments on earth and it felt like it. The Bedouin tribes call this land their own; for a light-skinned Irishman, it's an oven-like hell. For thousands of years the Bedouin have lived in the Arabian Desert and I had travelled 5,000 miles to live as they do, to breathe their air, eat their food and walk their land – but definitely not to race their camels.

I was in the heart of the Middle East. Over a three-week expedition, I walked the line between an ancient culture and the modern world. Despite the temperature, I felt strangely at home in this part of the world. My mother was brought up in Saudi as part of the American expatriate community working in the oil industry. The place was in her blood and she had immersed us in it with stories, art and books.

My journey to the Bedouin commenced from the Oman capital, Muscat. From there I headed south to the Sharqiyah Sands, a vast expanse of desert which was to be my unlikely home for three weeks. It's easy to understand why man has such a slim foothold on this corner of the earth. Just 3,000 Bedouin manage to survive there. With extremely high temperatures and very little water, it's not an environment that welcomes the novice. On the final leg of our journey, we left the modern freeways behind and ventured out onto the sea of sand. I stood in the back of the pick-up taking the breeze and held in my tummy as the cameras rolled. Vanity is a sin that doesn't last long in this climate, though.

The Bedouin culture requires an arrival gift, so I came prepared with fruit and a goat, affectionately named 'Number 37', which we had bought at the local market. I tried not to get too attached to our new friend, as he was not long for this world. I was bristling with excitement at the thought of spending time in a culture so removed from my own. Traditionally, the Bedouin have lived a nomadic existence, migrating with their herds in search of what little pasture the desert provided. Their lives are defined by a strict set of rules, stressing the values of loyalty, honour, obedience and hospitality.

Finally, we arrived at the home of the Al Amri family, my

hosts for my stay in the desert. It was a mixture of ramshackle wooden buildings, with some iron sheeting and carpet ceilings. From the outside, it had all the appearance of an allotment with some random huts built out of mismatched materials that had been salvaged from the desert. But inside, every wall space had a traditional Arabian carpet draped on it, protecting those inside from the heat of the day and the cold of the night. There isn't a tree for miles, just great mountains of sand on either side of a flat valley floor. Somewhere in the dunes, coarse grass grows and there is some vegetation for the goats to feed on, but none of this is visible to the Western eye. I was expecting that there might at least be some palm trees.

The first to come and greet me was the eldest son, nineteen-year-old Siad.

A traditional Bedouin greeting can take a while. You kiss on the left cheek and your host asks you: 'Have you brought any news?' You are not necessarily required to give all your news at that moment, but you must reply with: 'Have you any new news?' When you're with a group and somebody actually has news, the procedure can go on for a bit. Siad looked at me in a geeky kind of way, said 'No', and went to move away from the greeting, lest I have too much news to bore him with.

There are nine in the family, with 50-year-old Salim at its head. They're a traditional Bedouin family, with three generations living and working together. Bedouin women are reticent about meeting strangers, but eventually I was introduced to Samta, the mother of the family. In my head I had a vision of the submissive Arab woman, a second-class citizen in her own home and beholden to the patriarch. But I was soon disabused of this notion. Samta was sparky from the outset. She was the boss and playfully let me know that she was in charge.

The family keeps four camels and 40 goats, and they rely on these animals for food and income. They used to be nomadic but now the flimsy encampments are here permanently.

In Bedouin tradition, hospitality is an obligation. It's said that any stranger, even an enemy, can approach a settlement and be guaranteed food and lodging. A family is even duty bound to slaughter their last goat to welcome a visitor. There is a custom that when a visitor arrives, all the neighbours for miles around are invited to a feast. And it didn't take long for the enthusiastic first guests to come and welcome me. Some had travelled for days to meet the strange foreigner, others had travelled for five hours in the blistering sun that day. The food was soon bubbling and enticing smells wafted round the compound. I was given quite a welcome and an impressive feast was laid out for all the visitors and me. The high point of the meal was a goat stew, prepared in time-honoured fashion. The men ate together, while the women retreated to a back room where they ate the meal but did not partake in the group discussions. Local Islamic custom and Bedouin traditions are still strong here, and no exception would be made for our arrival.

'Do you have any children?' I was asked by one of the guests.

'No,' I replied, 'I am not married.'

Shocked, they immediately insisted on finding me a wife. I bring a goat to dinner and go home with a wife – now that is hospitality.

Our worlds are very different, and, not surprisingly, they were as interested in me as I was in them. Well, maybe not quite as interested, but they were polite enough to ask me about where I am from and what I do. I was impressed by their confidence: they didn't seem at all threatened by the modern world. All was, as it had been for a thousand years, until we heard the ringing of a mobile phone belonging to one of the visiting guests. While much of their tradition harks back to ancient times, they are not averse to technology and have embraced it faster than many in the West.

It had already been quite an eye-opener, and in one of the most inhospitable landscapes on earth, I had been treated like a king.

But, as you can imagine, this treatment was not going to last. I had to earn my keep and was expected to join the women in their chores early the next morning. At dawn the women of the Al Amri family were already hard at work. I was supposed to join them and I knew that they were looking forward to giving orders to a man. Samta, who wears a burka that resembles a medieval battle facemask was definitely the boss and took charge of organising everyone. The women have a lot on their plate. Cooking, cleaning, weaving and childcare are exclusively women's duties. Samta and her daughters are also responsible for taking care of the small herd of goats which provides most of the family's food. Nothing keeps long in the desert heat, so milk is made into cheese and every week or so one of the goats is slaughtered for meat.

It was not yet six o'clock and of course I was late for my first day. The goats were already off to graze, and I reckoned I might be in trouble. Samta gave me a ticking off. Most of the hard work had been done and I had failed myself and my tradition. 'You are lazy and fat,' she scolded. 'The Bedouin people eat less and they work hard. You eat more, sleep more and work less.' She had a point.

Bedouin women start to wear the burka in their teens, and remain veiled to all but their immediate family. Tashla is 25 years old and is Al-Amris' eldest daughter. She is very beautiful and beguiling, maybe more so because of the veil, but good manners forbade me from making any comment on her appearance.

Although her life sounds quite restrictive, she takes a different view: 'I have more freedom here than the women in the city. They are just sitting, watching TV. It's a very boring life compared to ours.' Certainly, compared with the life of an urban Muslim woman in many Arabic societies, she was right. Tashla is already married with one child, but is happy to continue living with her parents and siblings, and they are delighted to have her and her young family with them.

Perhaps the person who said the most about this family was nine-year-old Salima. She has Down's syndrome and was fully involved in family life, an integral part of their daily activities. She is cared for and celebrated for everything she is and everything she wants to be. It was uplifting to see that a big heart in a big family can go a long way. They may have had little in the way of possessions, but they still had great riches.

I wasn't the only one avoiding the chores that morning. The other skiver was the youngest in the family, little Mohammed, who, at age 12, drove their truck around the desert and was easily a better driver than me. From behind I could hear a car horn excitedly hooting to get my attention. It could only be one person.

Mohammed loves the desert, and which 12-year-old wouldn't, if it means that they are allowed to drive the family's prized pick-up truck? He sings while he drives, and I was glad to spend only a little time in the car with him: he is a better driver than singer. A cheeky, outgoing chap, he would be well able to handle himself in any playground from L.A. to Lisdoonvarna.

'In town the Police would catch me, but here in the desert I can do as I like.' Here, Mohammed has a degree of freedom afforded to few. It occurred to me that, in a society that I had perceived as oppressive and restrictive before I arrived, the dominant theme appeared to be the liberty afforded by their lifestyle.

The family cooks on an open fire and the task to find wood generally falls to Siad, the eldest brother at 19 years of age. I joined him on his search. As far as the eye could see, there was only sand, and yet Siad assured me that there was wood out there. I couldn't believe the effort involved. We spent two hours hunting for sticks, just to cook a single lunch. When you do come across scrappy pieces of wood, they splinter easily and are so dry that they seem already barbecued. The wood fires in seconds. 'I don't think my body was made for this,' I told Siad as we trudged on through the sand, each of us with a camel on a leash in tow and a stick whip in hand. It was like climbing in deep snow high up on a mountain, but the temperature was oh so different.

Siad gave me my first lesson in camel training: 'Salivate, and then, from the bowels of your mouth, deep from your throat, utter a guttural spit – Hiccccchh.' And, lo and behold, the camel knelt on command. Race meetings tend to sound like a gathering of emphysema victims.

After my roasting in the midday sun, Siad's father, Salim, invited me into the main room of the house for a traditional

Bedouin power snack of coffee and dates. We exchanged world views. He is a wise man and every opinion he expresses is considered and delivered slowly and calmly. He is, in essence, very cool.

Salim earns extra money from breeding and training race camels. They can be worth a fortune and are a big investment for the family, so they are very well looked after. We went to see one of the family's prized camels, who had an irritation in a delicate area. Mohammed tried to hang on to one end of the beast, while his dad attended to the other with a special ointment. I had heard that they feed the camels honey, quite a delicacy in these parts, and I expressed my surprise to Salim. He explained: 'The diet that we give to our camels is much better than we give to ourselves. It is part of our culture. You're not a real Bedouin unless you've got a camel.'

And of course I wanted to experience life as a real Bedouin. So, Salim had a plan: he would going to take me to the sea to trade dates for dried fish, and on the journey he would train me in the art of camel riding, so that I could say I had experienced the authentic Bedouin lifestyle. Although, to be honest, to this day I have a feeling he might just have done it for his own amusement.

But the idea had started to take root in his mind, and I was powerless to stop it.

Every so often, the Bedouin gather for camel races. These huge events, often attended by thousands, are a celebration of their culture and a chance to show off by displaying the latest fine specimens for sale. These gatherings are big business and a great chance to socialise and share gossip. Samta had decided that to become a true Bedouin, I needed to race a camel in a real race. I thought that this was moving the goalposts a little. Perhaps it was revenge for my earlier laziness. But it was a huge honour to be allowed to race one of their camels and I'm a sucker for races anyway. If I didn't destroy the family's pride or kill myself, it might just be my moment of triumph! That's what I told myself.

I think they really wanted me to succeed as an ambassador of sorts for them, but that was before they saw me on a camel.

It took nearly two days of trying before I could even get on one properly.

Training began with the basics:

'To go straight, just do nothing,' I was told.

'It's hurting in all the wrong places,' I shouted back, as my camel took me in circles. 'I haven't had children yet,' I pleaded.

Two-year-old children ride camels here and my performance didn't even match that of a toddler. If I was to immerse myself in Bedouin life, then this had to be my lot and the camel would have to become my friend. In the end they lifted me onto the camel and pointed me in one direction. One camel will follow another, so there is only so much that can go wrong.

My intensive training as a camel racer would come in the form of the week-long trek to the sea and back to trade the family's dates. This would be a challenge for me in so many different ways and for so many different body parts. Not many have crossed the Arabian sands relying on a lavender pillow for salvation, but I confess that I did. Now I am keen on my pastels, but lavender was in fact a random choice of colour. The pillow had been left in a car by one of the film crew. As my need was greatest, I commandeered it. It was the only relief I had for my backside, which would be brutalised by an over-acquaintance with an uncomfortable camel over an unforgiving terrain.

Irish men of pale complexion are not built for 50°C and indeed have no place travelling in the company of anything lavender, but this was my lot and I was beginning to savour it. I felt there was a little hint of the Special One, Lawrence, in the deserts of Oman as I travelled with the Bedouin on a hallowed camel trek to the sea, to trade dates for fish and gossip. Clearly, I was getting carried away with the romance of it.

The sight of it was less romantic – a red-tinged white Irishman with a lavender pillow, slumped over like a drunk on a menopausal camel. My eyelids were sweating and my bum was still unforgivably sore. There was no relief from the sun, the camel or for my posterior for eight merciless days. We slept in tents and warmed ourselves at makeshift fires. The backdrop was stunning as the wind blew the sand, shining like crystals, into the light of the crescent moon.

For days the traveling continued. The sun's intensity was crippling. I would have had my bum amputated if it had been possible. Physically, I was just hanging on. Psychologically, the disappointment of seemingly getting nowhere for hours on end was very difficult. I was certainly holding up the journey to the sea, but they were a forgiving bunch.

I think Salim was beginning to regret his decision to train me for the race, though.

'You,' he said, laughing, 'would make a very good camel.'

He was referring to my sense of direction. Left to their own devices, camels will wander aimlessly, following each other to nowhere in particular. They don't have a compass in their heads and they don't sense that they have lost their way. Instead, they will continue wandering on the same path until they are rescued by a herdsman. Although I try to pretend to my kids that I have an 'explorer's gene', that I would have been at home with Shackleton in the Antarctic, the truth is that I am lost without sat-nav. This was the one thing I finally found I had in common with the camels.

'You see, Mr Camel, we are like brothers: you are lost without the Bedouin, and I am lost without my producer!'

Camels also have poor sight and smell. Often, they can be practically standing over food and water and not notice it. I don't share this trait with them, however. No matter how lost I get, I don't miss a meal!

Eventually, Salim announced that we were not far from the sea, and that there was a Bedouin camp close by. We couldn't get there soon enough for me. A ramshackle Bedouin encampment appeared on the horizon out of the desert. I felt like we'd just discovered the Emerald City. We were obviously a bit of a pull for the local kids, not many of them having seen a delirious Irishman before.

While we stuffed our faces with dates, an old man told us how their traditional way of life has been improved by technology. In oil-rich Oman there is now access to fine medical facilities and most of the water close to the towns is supplied by public hoses and is transported to homesteads in barrels. The Bedouin have mobile phones and even satellite TV in some parts. The window onto the wider world has opened more than ever for them, but still their daily chores and simple lifestyle remain largely unaltered.

The dates were covered in a carpet of flies, but I was obliged to eat them as a mark of respect to our hosts. I drank more coffee with three sugars, and took four paracetamol to dull the pain. I could have done with a drink but there was no alcohol openly on sale within a thousand miles. In its absence, the only kick to be had in this abstemious area is from tea or coffee, which in desperate circumstances, is sometimes made with camel urine. Alternatively, if you cannot find a co-operative camel who will urinate on command, a fine brew can be still be had by removing well-masticated cud from the camel's mouth and squeezing the water out of it to get some liquid.

Once more we headed off in the direction of the sea, now just a couple of miles away. We've all heard of the mirage that magically appears out of the shimmering desert to tantalise the unfortunate delirious traveller. As we ran down the hill towards the beautiful blue ocean, I was half expecting that it would evaporate before my eyes. But we had in fact arrived at our destination and the sea was real and reassuringly wet.

Just reaching the sea was enough for me, but the reason for coming was to trade our dates for fish and it was getting late. Salim looked after the business and we loaded up our bounty of fish to take back to the family.

That night, we were treated to the greatest light show the ocean has to offer. As billions of plankton crashed onto the shore, they glistened and shone, turning the barren and naked coastline where the Arabian sands meet the sea into something more like the electric Miami shoreline.

Days later, smellier, hungrier, sunburnt and very saddle-sore, we finally made it back to the compound with our consignment. These days in the saddle had boosted my confidence hugely. Even so, I still wasn't keen on the idea of racing a camel. I dropped hints to the producer, but he wasn't unduly concerned about the health and safety risks involved, and my pleas fell on deaf ears. Pride wouldn't allow me to duck the challenge, so my fate appeared to be sealed.

The Al-Amris wanted to make an impact at an upcoming festival and I had to do them proud. If I could at least stay on the camel for the duration of the race, I hoped that I could earn the Bedouins' respect, and in some small way say thank you to my hosts.

In many ways, the desert doesn't allow you to get stressed. Everything is as everything was and you simply have to deal with it. But in this instance I felt entitled to panic, as the madness that had possessed my producer, consumed my hosts and horrified me was about to culminate in the humiliation of race day.

Thousands had gathered for this camel-racing jamboree: women in burkas, children running among the camels, and Sheikhs out for the day on this key date in the camel-racing calendar. This race meeting seemed to be a huge event: there was a band, and hundreds of spectators. Guns and swords were on display and there was a carnival atmosphere. Siad told me to do some warm-up exercises. He got me to lie prone. 'Stretch out,' he said, 'and then, while fully extended, roll and stand up. It's good for your joints.'

I needed more than help with my joints but I did as I was told. A small crowd had gathered and there were giggles as I tried to limber up. I surveyed the scene and discovered why: in the background, there was a group of camels doing the same thing as me and it looked like they' were imitating my pathetic attempts. (It seems that when the heat of the day becomes too much for the animals, they roll in the dirt.)

Score: Camels 1, MacIntyre 0.

I was beginning to worry that the camels and spectators had all come to watch me fail. I tried to remind myself that this wasn't about me racing: it was about selling camels. Traders come from far and wide to see racing camels in action and often base their decision to buy on how the animal moves. Buyers come here to do deals on camels for breeding, for farming and to supply meat and milk. But the main attraction remains the spectacle of men on camels racing across the desert sands.

Many of the creatures on display were being treated better than the humans. Around me there were camels enjoying a high-protein food mix, a concoction of honey, dates, milk, corn and cardamom. They often vomit up this 'go fast' food before the race, but trainers actually consider this to be an indication that their speed machine is raring to go!

Camels have four distinct gears, each of which carries its own distinctive characteristics, none of them remotely elegant. These are easily recognisable to the experienced observer, but were of course invisible to me. At their fastest, camels can exceed 60 mph. The female is the boss of the track and the faster of the sexes.

Champion camels can sell for up to €1 million, as it takes years of training for them to be able to maintain a racing pace so out of sync with their natural gait. The camels become celebrities in their own right and when the four-legged racing legends are flown into the country for events, the local headlines report on the arrival of VICs, or Very Important Camels.

I was so nervous before the race that I couldn't even get on the animal without assistance. I didn't ride the camel so much as mount it, my thighs gripping its behind, trying desperately to steady myself. Trust Siad to give me the grumpiest camel in his troupe. It was frothing and salivating and clearly unhappy at having an Irishman clinging to its hindquarters. It was either in heat or had a migraine, either way it wasn't good news. It is not unheard of for people to be killed by camels, and I wouldn't have put it past this one to trample me underfoot, given half a chance.

The camels rolled and lurched as they raced, jostling and bumping into each other. At full tilt, they never really appeared to be contained or fully containable. Groups of cars followed the race, with spectators hanging out of the windows and cheering after the animals, fuelling the mayhem and chaos. Camel racing was once the preserve of young Pakistani and Indian boys, aged just six or seven, who were bought or stolen from their parents and brought to the Middle East to begin new lives as jockeys. After an enduring scandal, this practice was ended, and they were replaced with over-18s and, wait for it – robots. Developed in Japan, these remote controlled robot jockeys have now become widely used and accepted. It is quite a spectacle to see a robot straight out of *Buck Rogers*, riding a camel at high speed in the sands of Oman. They, of course, have no fear; I am unfortunately not programmed that way.

Throughout the race I clung on for dear life as my nether regions slipped closer and closer to a certain camel exit point. This was starting to look like a very strange act of bestiality, so I tried to pull myself up, to ride a little higher. Then the distinctive rocking motion settled in and my beast really took off. Suddenly, we were bounding ahead and before long I was in the lead. 'Go on, MacIntyre, you were born to this!' I said to myself, suddenly feeling like a professional. 'Lester Piggot, eat your heart out; robot jockeys, eat your hearts out!' I passed the Sheikhs' stand and there was bewilderment at the fat, lobster-coloured Irishman haring down the course, out of control. Some spectators scrambled up the bank of the course for safety, and I didn't blame them one bit.

Siad was slightly perplexed by my performance. He had forgotten to tell me that winning is considered crass in this culture. It is how the camel runs that really matters, and it is almost considered bad sportsmanship to win. Siad, nonetheless, wouldn't give me the victory and he chased me down, whipping his beast into a nuclear reaction. We hit the notional finish line together, and a draw was declared. The crowd cheered and there was celebration all round at the gentlemanly outcome. I was just glad I hadn't killed anyone.

The camel was still spitting and frothing, but I was off and I didn't care any more. I had seen into the abyss: the green-drenched mouth of a camel. I had smelt its breath and its hair oil, and its sweat had congealed on every part of me. We were as one, but no more, and I can't pretend that I wasn't happy to see the back of my camel friend.

*****

The next time I saw a camel, it was well-done and between two baps. I know that might sound odd but I was attending an Edwardian-themed evening with Michelin-star chef, Heston Blumenthal, celebrating the daring age of exploration and the achievements of Scott, Shackleton and T.E. Lawrence. He put a modern twist on it with the 'Humpy Meal', which consisted of camel burgers and a rose petal and sand-salt accompaniment. There were even little burger boxes. As I bit into the Humpy Burger, I savoured it much more than Heston or my dinner companions could ever know. 'This is for the welt on my bum,' I thought, biting into the succulent meat, 'and that is for the third-degree burns on my hands.'

Revenge, as it turns out, was a dish best served warm, with fries. And far from being sweet, it was in fact pleasantly savoury.

4

The Dog's Head

'This is Manchester: by day it's run by police, by night it's run by gangsters. Manchester is where I was born, where I live and where I'll die.'

Dominic Noonan

I hadn't intended to spend five years filming with a major criminal. As with all great adventures, it was an accident; I was going to say 'happy accident', but 'disturbing' is perhaps more appropriate. It was 2003 and I had spent 11 years as an undercover journalist. I had had enough of it and it had had enough of me. I was on the hit lists of right-wing terror groups, crack dealers and gun-runners because of various operations I had been involved in, and my face was too well known for me to continue doing covert operations in the UK or Ireland. Ironically, my success as an undercover reporter had made me unemployable. My job as covert crime fighter had evaporated before my very eyes as the investigations were broadcast.

The truth is that keeping your sanity while at the same time trying to maintain three or even four identities is a difficult task in itself. It's a pressure-cooker kind of existence and you're constantly aware that your cover could be blown at any time. It was time to move on.

While I was figuring out what to do next, I decided to do some research at Belmarsh Crown Court, one of London's most secure courts, used for the trials of major terrorists and gangsters. I wanted to make a very aggressive, confrontational series on serious criminals. My plans were dependent on the cooperation of a very uncooperative gangster class.

In the dock of Court 3 stood Dominic Noonan, a large bulldog of a man, over 20 stone at his heaviest. His shaven head, thick neck and grave-digger hands gave no hint of a man who speaks Urdu and has experience of running a multimillion -pound crime empire.

Dominic is a member of the infamous Noonans, a well-known criminal family from Manchester. He changed his name to Dominic James Lattlay Fottfoy by deed pole while in prison, where he has spent 25 of his 44 years.

Every day in Court, the judge would struggle with the name before eventually asking Dominic if he would mind if he abbreviated the name to Mr Fottfoy. Dominic nodded his assent. The judge then asked Dominic the derivation of the name.

'Many years ago my dad used to say to me, "Just look after those that look after you, fuck off those that fuck off you." So I changed my name to Lattlay Fottfoy: that's what the initials stand for.'

The Court, including the jury, collapsed in laughter.

Dominic had been caught more or less red-handed with over half a million pounds' worth of heroin. He told the jury that he was under the impression that he was providing security for a shipment of foreign currency. Imagine his shock when Customs and Excise arrested him and told him that he was in fact transporting a class-A drug! The handover of the consignment to a major London criminal gang was filmed by Her Majesty's Customs and Excise. It did not look good for Noonan or the other defendants on trial.

By some quirk of fate, Dominic had been granted bail and was free to chat with me outside the Court. There were few who could envisage a not-guilty verdict for the charismatic gangster, but those who had followed his criminal career wouldn't put any Houdini-like act past him.

Every time he appears in the dock, the Court is inevitably surrounded by a platoon of armed police and marksmen. His last conviction saw the judge lament that he could only give the Manchester godfather a maximum of nine and a half years in jail. The Judge sounded crestfallen as he told the Court of the limitations of his sentencing powers and said: 'This man is a menace to society. He is one of the country's most dangerous criminals.'

*****

I first met Dominic Noonan, the head of the notorious crime family, in a circular corridor inside Belmarsh Crown Court.

'Everybody I know wants to kill you. My brother was asked to whack you; I can see the job isn't done,' he told me.

'He's obviously not very good, then,' I replied, holding my ground.

As I chatted with him, I realised that we had much in common. He was facing the very real possibility that he would spend the rest of his life either behind bars or under threat of a rival's bullet in the head: either way, he was facing a sentence every day he woke up. Such pressure creates a vulnerability that is easier to share with strangers than those close to you. I had had to face down kidnapping and death threats and some days I felt that same fatalism that Noonan lived with. He looked into my eyes and recognised that we had both experienced terrible things. Indeed, Dominic had been both perpetrator and victim of 'experiences' that are far too graphic to write about here.

He believed that we were born on the same side of the street but had chosen different paths in life: his was a life of crime and mine was one of exposing it. I was a little uncomfortable with his assessment but I was glad that he felt we had something in common. Added to this was our shared Irish background and an obliviousness to danger that had threatened to end both our careers and our lives. I think these are the reasons why one of the UK's most dangerous criminals decided to invite me to spend five years filming him and his criminal network.

The six women and six men of the jury spent four days deliberating on the verdict. We were taking bets on Noonan's fate in the production office.

'Five pounds says that he will be sent down,' I said to Sam, one of the producers.

'He's the Teflon Dom,' said Sam, 'I wouldn't put anything past him.'

As we waited for the verdict with Dominic, the stress in the courtroom was palpable. Occasionally, the jury would return for guidance. There would be a flurry of excitement and then they would return to their deliberations and we to our tea and coffee. On one occasion, we were joined by a senior Customs and Excise officer. Dominic and his adversary were polite to each other, almost to the point of playfulness, and it was obvious that there was an element of gamesmanship to their relationship. Eventually, the moment of truth came and the verdict was given: 'On all four counts, we find the defendant not guilty.' Just one defendant in the multimillion-pound trial was convicted, but he had already skipped the country. Dominic would remain a free man.

When I asked him for his reaction to the verdict, he was pumped up on adrenalin and could hardly believe that he had escaped the jaws of jail.

'It was the right verdict to come back with. At the end of the day, my solicitors and my barrister did the investigation for my case to prove that I was innocent, nothing else, nothing short, nothing less.'

He was feeding me a line. Looking on, I felt that a guilty man had walked free and I don't think Dominic would mind me suggesting that he was more shocked at his acquittal than anyone. Justice is not always about guilt or innocence. Convictions are lost as defendants bob and weave and demonstrate acting skills that create just enough doubt in the jury's mind to secure their freedom.

'What now?' I asked him.

'I'm going to go back [to Court] because they're sorting out my expenses. It's cost me a lot of money, this trial.'

The Teflon Dom had got away with it again, and he was going to ask the taxpayer to sweeten his acquittal with a honey pot of cash. You would expect no less from Mr. Fuck off Those That Fuck off You.

My new best gangster friend celebrated in swashbuckling style. Champagne and chips were the bill of fare at his local pub back in Manchester, where friends, family and criminals gathered to celebrate his victory and welcome him home.

From the stage, Noonan addressed his posse: 'To British justice! To British justice! Thank you everyone for coming tonight. As you know, I was on a very serious charge down in London.' He went on to explain how there had been confusion over what was contained in the shipment: 'I went down there as security; someone else was picking up some drugs. I never knew about it; I thought it was a load of money.' But he didn't need to fool this audience and admitted: 'I'm talking a load of bullshit, but who gives a fuck?!' Away from the Courts and amongst his own, he felt comfortable enough to taunt the prosecutors with a pretty frank confession.

'Enjoy yourselves! Eat the food; don't wait for me, cos I just had some chips on the way up. This is dedicated to the Customs and Excise,' he said as he launched into the Elvis classic, 'Caught in a Trap'.

*****

Dominic Noonan is an unusual cocktail: dangerous, brutal, amusing, smart and devastatingly cruel. His character has been influenced hugely by his Irish family and background. Born into abject poverty, they lived in a two up, two down house in the Harpurhey area of North Manchester. All 14 of the siblings have Christian names beginning with the letter 'D'.

'Me family all came from Dublin, and so the kids were all named after the capital of Ireland, Dublin. There is Derek, Delia, Damien, Diana, you get the picture.'

The Noonan kids would rob the stick fences of neighbours for firewood. In an effort to get a bigger house for her family, their mother once set fire to their home. 'I remember seeing the firemen in the backyard,' Dominic told me. 'I was just eight at the time.' Despite their home being badly damaged by the fire, the council refused to move them from the cramped two-bedroom house. It was a dysfunctional home and Dominic mother turned to alcohol to cope. 'Me dad was soft as fuck and my Ma was the boss. He was never in trouble with the law but Ma was often brought home drunk in the back of a police van.' The police often called to the house to arrest or question one of the seven boys.

But it was the death of Noonan's younger brother, Damien, in a motorcycle accident in 2003 that brought the family's influence and power to public attention. Large parts of Northwest Manchester were brought to a standstill during the funeral. Ten police riot vans supervised the wake. One hundred policemen blocked the roads for the cortege. Five thousand people lined the streets. These are impressive numbers and give some idea of the Noonans' influence in the area. Greater Manchester Police asked the family to contribute to the cost of the operation. The Noonans, to no one's surprise, refused.

The family had become well known in Manchester as a kind of 'Murphia', or Irish mafia. Dominic himself had worked his way up to being the number one target of the Manchester Police. He is a cross between an Italian mafia-style criminal with deep-rooted connections in the community and the steely British gangster of old black & white movies, and he and his gang dress to match. However, they lack the Italian accents and their suits never seem to quite fit. They have stolen their swagger from American crime movies and have even been known to steal some of their stunts. Dominic told me about the 'Dog's Head' incident, which took place when he was providing security to the Hacienda in Manchester, one of the world's first superclubs.

'We just went to the pub; one of my lads had a shotgun on him and I had a machete. One of the other gang-lad's dog was about, so I just chopped its head off, carried it inside the pub, put it on the pool table and more or less asked them, or told them, to stay away from the Hacienda, or the next time it would be a human head. They never came back. The Dog's Head was the nickname for the pub after that. Everyone used to say, "I'll meet you down at the Dog's Head."'

These words were spoken matter-of-factly as if he was reading the contents on the side of a pack of cornflakes. Men who deal with their enemies in this manner have no need to impress or exaggerate: their deeds speak for them.

Dominic was one of the architects of the Strangeways riots in 1990 that resulted in two deaths, 200 injured and £50 million worth of damages, as a thousand inmates took over the prison and staged a rooftop protest that lasted days. This protest inspired others around the UK and Ireland, including one at Mountjoy Prison in Dublin. I was a young cub reporter for the *Irish Press* at the time and I remember ringing in my copy to the office: 'The Strangeways choreographer is on tour,' I told them. I didn't know at the time that 15 years later I would be that choreographer's new best friend.

Dominic is still a Tony Soprano-type figure in Manchester and that's what attracted me to him as a film subject. With his strong base in the community, the racketeering business came easy to him. He took a percentage from many businesses, from car parks to pubs, and the rumour was that there were millions of pounds at his disposal.

'How much money do you think has gone through the hands of the Noonans over the last 20 years?' I asked him at one point.

'Allegedly, *allegedly*, we've made £5–6 million. But where's the money?'

'That's the question I'm asking. Where's the money? Is it in property? Is it in horses?'

'No, it's behind the bar in landlords' pubs.' Dominic would never give a straight answer when a funny one would do.

'So, even with all the money that you've made, you're still out making money, you're still active. Is that the message that's going out?'

'I'm still dangerous. Anyone's dangerous, but there's some that are really dangerous.'

'Are you really dangerous?'

'Yeah.'

'And the next generation is ready and waiting?'

'Yeah, they're already primed. There's about 20, but I always keep the young ones around me because they're more loyal, more trustworthy. And I've got a lot of respect for them and they got a lot of respect for me. I know that they will watch my back and I will actually respect them and watch their backs, and they know I've had their backs many times for them.'

Dominic would travel the streets in his ex-police cars with a posse of young men, many homeless or from very difficult backgrounds. He was a kind of criminal Pied Piper of Manchester and there was no shortage of youngsters happy to dance to his tune.

'I know that they would die for me and I would die for them; they shoot for me and I shoot for them,' he said, speaking of the loyalty they showed him.

In the community he was the gangster social worker to whom everyone brought their problems. I went with him to meet Mick, who had got himself into debt with a London gangster and found himself being threatened to pay up, or else. In desperation he had attempted to rob a corner post office, armed with just a towel wrapped round his forefinger. He had called upon Dominic for help. In his red-walled sitting room, bare except for the big sofa and obligatory widescreen TV, Dominic presided over proceedings.

'Just for the record, what possessed you to go into a post office with no weapon and expect to walk out?' he asked Mick.

'Fucking stupidity, I suppose. I walked in, put the bag through the tray and said, "Put the money in the bag and don't do anything stupid." He went, "What?" so I repeated myself. He went, "Fuck off, poof," and pushed the button. I was like, "Fuck" cos I've seen it on TV where the shutters come down and trap you. Then the shutters came down. I thought, "Fucking hell, I'm well stuck here!" I turned round, looked at the door, I could see the shutter was still slightly open, so I just fucking ran for the door and out. Bam, in my car, I was gone.'

'Was the alarm ringing?' Dominic wanted to know.

'Oh fuck yeah, that's loud that. That were loud, that. I'll remember that fucking sound for ever: it was fucking horrible.'

'So how were you caught?' I asked Mick.

'I did it in me own fucking car. Me own car! No fucking false reg plates on it or nothing. I parked the fucking thing outside,' said Mick, not quite believing his own foolishness. He was not by any stretch of the imagination a criminal superbrain: he was poor and desperate and he had come to Dominic for help.

'And you're coming up for trial shortly? You'll have to plead guilty, I suppose?' I said.

'Can't fucking deny it really, can I?'

Despite Mick having been caught red-handed, Dominic, who had been there before many times and been acquitted, felt that he could still get away with it. He probed Mick's defence.

'What have they charged you with?'

'Attempted robbery.'

'Without firearms, though?'

'Without firearms.'

'Did they have any CCTV?'

'No.'

'They can't really prove it was you then.'

'I've admitted it now,' said a crestfallen Mick.

'You shouldn't have said anything: no comment,' advised Dominic.

'That's it now. Nowt I can do about it. The only reason that I went in there was through fear. I've got to get this fucking money; my time is running out. It's like, I had to do what I had to do.'

Dominic took this on board and sorted out the debt with the London loan shark. Problem solved, except for Mick's court case, which would be outside Dominic's circle of influence, mostly.

*****

But Dominic was famous for exerting influence in the most unlikely of places. On one April Fool's Day, he organised for superglue to be smuggled into a number of the UK's biggest prisons. In unison and on command, all the locks in the jails were glued shut. It cost millions to undo the damage. As a result he spent extra time in jail but he felt the laughs were worth it.

On another occasion he arranged an escape on the way to a court hearing. While he was being broken out, he pretended that he was in fact being kidnapped. 'Don't let them take me,' he pleaded with the terrified prison officers. Meanwhile, his brothers, Desi and Damien, let off a round and bundled their brother into the back of a stolen car. In the following three days, they robbed two cash-laden security vans. In true Dominic style, he then presented himself back at the prison as if he had just been released by his kidnappers. The Police were searching all over Britain, because, despite the ruse, they rightly suspected that he had arranged his own escape from custody to go on a spree.

Granada News reported:

> *Police in Manchester say they're baffled by the apparent kidnapping of a remand prisoner. They are not sure whether he's been abducted or whether it was all part of an elaborate escape.*

Dominic takes up the story: 'We had two security vans to rob the same day: one in the morning around about 10 o'clock, and one around 4 o'clock. We was going for the double. No one had ever done a double before. So we just thought we'd have a go.'

My fellow Granada reporter, John Molson, told the ITV viewers:

> *Two masked men ran up to the car at these lights. One had a hammer, the other a gun. They threatened the police officers and forced them to release Noonan. In the struggle, the gun was fired but no one was hurt.*

> *Noonan was bundled into the back of a waiting car. Police say they are now afraid for Noonan's safety, if he's been abducted.*

I love that last line of the report and have never heard the like of it before or since. But there are few gangsters like Mr Lattlay Fottfoy. I asked Dominic what fear did to the officer with him in the van when they were held up.

'He admitted in Court that he pissed his pants. He said, "I just pissed my pants in the back of the car." I could hear him pissing anyway. I remember saying to him, "Don't let them take me; don't take the cuffs off!" and he said, "I can't, I can't stop them, I can't stop them," because he had a gun pressed against him.'

Here is the raw brutality in this man: a matter-of-fact display of sickening terror. And yet it was partly comical in a *Keystone Cops* kind of way, with the Police and Dominic testing each other's wits.

*****

Dominic has two children by two different women and has had relationships with strippers by his own account. Initially, he may give the impression of being a ladies' man, but I had a suspicion that his sexuality might not be what it seemed. The posse of young men following in his wake made me wonder if he was gay. Understandably, I was reticent about raising the subject with him. How could I ask a man, who by his own admission has been implicated in at least six gangland murders, about being gay? Well, the answer is, very carefully. Despite having prepared it in my head, it came out all wrong.

The scene was right out of the movies. This was very appropriate because in Dominic's case, it was sometimes hard to see where the crime classics he watched ended and his own life began. We were at the Salford Lads Club, a boxing club and community centre that has been sponsored by the Noonans over the years, in fine gangster tradition. It is in fact an old church with thick walls, 1950s flaking paint and the smell of a spit-and-sawdust gym that owes more to Charles Atlas than Duncan Bannatyne.

'I've always thought, I hope you don't mind me asking you this, that ... erm ... that there's a hint of lavender about you, Dominic,' I said nervously.

'Lavender? Why's that? Because I've got a bald head?'

'Put it another way: are you gay?'

'Yeah, of course I'm gay; everyone knows I'm gay,' said Dominic with equanimity. After all my anxiety about getting shot for the intrusive question, he didn't seem one bit bothered.

'My family knows, brothers and sisters, best mates,' he told me.

'How did you first become aware that you were gay?' I asked him, hoping I wasn't pushing my luck now.

'I went to a boarding school just a day after my thirteenth birthday. I was exactly 13 years old and I was sat in the bedroom upstairs in the dorm and when the night-time came, I sat on the bed and just got punched straight in the face. I saw a white flash and that, got told, "Do what we tell you to." Got told to take my clothes off, start playing with them, sucking them off, and then they raped me, about six of them. It went on all night, went on for weeks. Every night they'd take turns with me, staying in the bed all night: two at a time, they raped me, and then they just went on to the next one, the next one, the next one.' Dominic was totally frank about what had happened to him and I was shocked by what I was hearing. Suddenly this self-styled Robin Hood with a cruel twist was revealing where some of the cruelty had come from.

In true Noonan style he had tracked down everyone who raped him and gave them it all back and more.

'It just went on and on and on: laughing and joking and making me do dirty things that I wouldn't wish on anyone. I've caught up with every single one of them and I've severely hurt them,' he continued.

About ten years later, he met the main perpetrator in the gay village on Canal Street in Manchester. He didn't recognise Dominic, but Dominic recognised him.

'I dealt with him severely: I really, really hurt him. I tortured him proper, the best quality torture we could do. Knocked the fuck out of him. I did things that he wished he never did to me.' I tried not to imagine the revenge that was exacted.

The Godfather was speaking with an honesty I had never expected. It was an almost solemn moment.

After this conversation, Dominic took his men to church. Despite his criminality, Dominic regularly visits his local Catholic church. In prison it was a place to meet and arrange trouble both inside and outside of the joint, but, on this occasion, it was time for some slightly twisted reflection.

'Dominic, you've done some terrible things. How do you square that with being a Christian and a Catholic?' I asked him.

'I get satisfaction from coming to church and asking for forgiveness. I believe I've just been forgiven for what I've done and I can walk out of here and probably do the same again and just come back here. Obviously you can't do that in Court: say, "I'm sorry", and expect to walk away.' That was Dominic's very bespoke interpretation of the rite of confession.

'Do you have any consideration for victims?' I pushed him.

'I do, yeah. On quite a few, I look back and think, "Should I have done that? Should I have handled that a different way?" and sometimes I think, "No, they got what they deserved. They did it to someone else and they get back what they've done."'

Hoping the sanctity of the church would protect me, I looked for more confessions. In the background a woman with an apron and brush was sweeping the floor, oblivious to the unholy conversation taking place on the hallowed ground.

'Did you ever kill a man?'

'No.'

'Did you ever order a man to be killed?'

'I can't answer questions like that, can I really? You can't answer questions like that: I'd be arrested. It's been alleged that I have.'

'If you allegedly ordered the execution of a man would you allegedly feel guilty about that?'

'If I was going to do something like that, that person would have to have done something really bad. Not a silly thing, something really, really serious. Then, yeah, I wouldn't think twice about it,' he admitted.

'How do you sleep at night?'

'Laid out on my bed, straight.'

*****

I had initially planned to spend six months filming the Noonan family, but things just kept happening and I continued filming. I started the project as a single man and ended it married with kids. I remember on our wedding day, during our reception at Slane Castle, Dominic phoned from prison and told my new wife: 'If he ever gives any trouble, you can always count on me to sort Donal out.' With friends like that, as they say.

I knew that to know someone's world you had to live in it and, although this was not undercover, I had become as embedded in the Noonans' world as much as I had in any undercover operation. I cared for them, was disappointed by them and had hopes for them. But in my filming I had to remain neutral – as neutral as any human can be in this dangerous and cruel cartoon world.

While my time in Dominic's world may have appeared to be focused on the Godfather himself, in truth it was the children in his life that drew most of my attention and concern. In his motley crew he had a range of lost souls, including Bugsy, his nine-year-old son, red-haired Paul, who was also nine, and Sean the nightclub singer, who was 14.

Sean Noonan was a Frank Sinatra style crooner and sang at 'funerals, baptisms and acquittals, mostly acquittals'. He was a good kid and a talented boxer. He didn't really get into trouble and I thought he might escape the fate that had been laid out for him by the rest of his family. He may not have had Sinatra's looks or cool but he was a decent singer and would keep a good pub crowd on their feet with ease.

Paul, was a nine-year-old smoker to whom Dominic acted as

godfather. 'He got a bad habit. I don't know, maybe he needs nicotine patches.' Bugsy, Dominic's son, seemed to have the heart and face of a choirboy but, according to Dominic, he was a 'little bastard'. I thought Bugsy was a delightful kid. He had a cherubic face, dark-brown hair and brown, soulful eyes. His mother, Mandy, was like a character out of *Shameless*, but provided Bugsy with a loving environment despite the crime surrounding them. Already, Bugsy had lost three major role models to crime, and he had seen Dominic for just two years because of all his time in jail.

The question was whether little Bugsy would follow in the steps of his father. I desperately hoped not, but I wondered what chance he had. I found myself offering avuncular support to the young kid, hoping that something from the normal side of my own abnormal upbringing would encourage him down a road less fraught with danger. It was a difficult thing to do: his father was a gangster and his uncle a hitman. I asked him what a gangster was.

'Well, they go round killing people, but not for no reason, for a reason; there has to be a reason, like you owed them money or something like that.'

I wondered how he felt about his dad's crimes and all his time in prison.

'Well, I love him of course, cos he's my dad, and that's it, really, cos I love him and that's it, no matter what he does. I can't help it, can I? He's a gangster: that's it, really.' This was a terribly sad moment. There was an acquiescence to his circumstances that I felt foretold his future. Dominic was struggling with fatherhood and I feared for the rest of his son's childhood.

A couple of years later, a similar question was asked of Bugsy, this time by his crooner cousin, Sean, as they were fishing one afternoon.

'Do you want to be like your dad?' Sean asked.

'Me dad? No, because he's done armed robberies and stuff like that, hasn't he?'

'Would you ever go to prison?' Sean takes over my role and does a very good imitation of Jeremy Paxman.

'No, cos they spit in your drinks, and how would you know? They could piss in your drink, you wouldn't know; spit in your food and mix it all up,' replied Bugsy. It was as good a reason as any to stay on the straight and narrow, and, as his father has spent more than two decades in prison, the point was well made.

'I bet he's been eating all sorts,' he continued innocently.

While this pair, the next generation in the crime dynasty, fished on the banks of the Grand Union Canal, they pondered jail and their own futures.

'I'd do it to try and get one of my mates out of trouble. I'd go into prison for that, but ...'

'I'd go in prison for my family,' Bugsy interrupted.

'Yeah, so would I. But I wouldn't go and do something off my own bat,' said Sean, 'like an armed robbery, for example.'

'Yeah, yeah, I couldn't do that. I'd prefer to get other people to do it for me, if you think about it.'

'I don't want to die anyway, don't want to die young.'

'Neither do I,' replied Bugsy. They both seemed aware that it was a distinct possibility in their world.

'No, I'm going to be a singer, become a millionaire with my voice, and then I'm going to buy a pile of pubs and clubs in Manchester. And then I'm going to design my own train, design my own plane, buy a pink Hummer, a Porsche 911, a Range Rover and my very own boat - like Abramovitch with his big fucking Russian yacht!' Sean was, at least, thinking big.

*****

Meanwhile, I was following Dominic as he bought a London taxi, a red double-decker bus and three ambulances, all for his own amusement and as a macho display of his strength. 'And if the cops give me any hassle I'm going to buy a tank.' This was a man who was judge, jury and executioner on his own patch. His fleet of vehicles hinted at his ambition to 'actually police the law' – not in some underground sense, but in a very obvious and cheeky way, to put two fingers up to the establishment.

It wasn't like Sean's ambitious desire for an Abramovich-style yacht: this was about power and making sure people knew you had it.

Dominic had recently set up his own 'community police station', with safe deposit boxes, community alarms and its own quasi-police force. It was located in a disused pub that was being completely renovated for the purpose. Each window had metal shutters and the basement was being carved out for security storage facilities. It was an imposing building, enclosed with iron fencing. For the first time the Godfather was making public the community secret that he considered *himself* to be the law, and not the Greater Manchester Police Force.

Since coming out of prison in 2002 after a ten-year stretch, Dominic had styled himself as a security expert and developed an unhealthy interest in uniforms and security vans.

'There's going to be 11 of these [vans] in the next few weeks. We're going to convert them into cash-carrying vans. These back doors will be sealed up … One man will remain in the back of the van, one man gets out, lifts up the shutters, drops the money in or out, puts [the shutter] down. We're offering a cheaper service because I think Securicor and Group 4 are too expensive.'

During this time Dominic was at the height of his powers, but his older brother, Desi the hitman, was on a downward trajectory when I met him on the family's old stomping ground in North Manchester. A huge bear of a man, he was wearing a balaclava that revealed only the touch of madness in his eyes. He was possibly the scariest man I had ever met: a monster that had brought many lives to a sharp end wearing the same balaclava.

Desmond Noonan was a serious criminal and he was staring me in the eye, holding my gaze with determination. He had a long track record as an armed robber and a reputation as a gangland executioner.

'My mates asked me to whack you for them,' he told me matter-of-factly.

'Did they?' I replied.

'Yeah, in front of the camera,' he revealed. 'Believe it or not, we're a nice family. We don't do everything nice, but, you know, we do look after each other; we look after our friends. We come out at three or four in the morning. We stop all the burglaries, we stop most of the fucking filthy drugs hanging about, you know what I mean?'

This was slightly ironic, because those in the know were aware that, against all family tradition, Desi had been dabbling with crack cocaine. But I decided not to draw his attention to the contradiction at that moment in time.

He slowly rolled his balaclava off his head.

'You still seem to be very strong in Manchester,' I said, keen to get on his good side.

'Yeah, we're still strong. It's not just that we're strong, we've got strong people around us ... we've got lots of strong, loyal people around us. We'll always have that. If you think you can take just one of us out and it's over, then you're really silly people, very silly people.'

When we were all back at his house, with the camera battery crashed, he threatened the Dutch cameraman for no apparent reason. 'I killed a Dutchman once. Make sure you are not the second,' Desi warned, before making the tea. During a quiet chat he told us that he had been involved in the INLA, in the Warrington bomb, and that he would never be caught for murder unless he was caught directly at the scene. He had never been convicted of murder but had been charged and arrested for the crime many times, he said.

He was, however, convicted for witness intimidation, which might give some insight into the low conviction rate for murder. Was this simply bravado to show off to the media? Well, not according to the off-duty police officers and other gangsters I spoke to in Manchester and beyond.

Desi continued wise-cracking jokes and making implicit threats. He may have been high; I don't know. With a Noonan, you never knew. They are fast-witted and clever enough to know how to keep you on the edge, if that's where they want you.

Out of the blue, the brothers started talking a strange language. Was it a dialect or a patois? No, this was a special language that the Noonans had constructed and crafted over the years to avoid the attentions of covert Police recordings and to allow them to speak on the phone in safety. I asked for a translation and was told, in no uncertain terms, where to go.

A couple of weeks later, I met Desi again. The mood was darker this time, and the conversation was more prophetic.

'I'm a Catholic: I don't believe in a life for a life, I don't believe in taking life,' Desi told me with a wicked grin. He sipped his pint of Becks. His son was slouching on a nearby chair in the lobby of a Manchester hotel. I had wanted to meet in public this time: it felt safer and the situation would be more manageable.

I suggested that he was lucky to have got off so many charges.

'It's not that we have luck – it's just that the jury believes we are innocent people and, you know.' I had a fair idea.

'Would anyone ever take out a Noonan in Manchester?' I asked him.

'I hope so and I hope it's me. I'm fucking fed up, fed up of life. No money, not got a pot to piss in. Shitty car, marriage, kids, mortgage – fed up. If there's anyone thinking of taking the Noonans out, can you take me first, please? But please do it as quickly as possible. In fact, I'll even come to you if I have to. Just give me a phone call, I'll meet you anywhere you want, make sure it's round the back of here and it's fucking clean,' Desi said, pointing to the back of his head.

Dominic looked on laughing and encouraging, as he had done for 40 years. His brother was wise-cracking again but it was hard to separate this from his serious side. He was heavily into crack cocaine at this point according to reports, but still active. He had recently stolen a £300,000 load of cigarettes from another gangster family and had been given a warning that his life would be in danger if it happened again.

'Don't let me linger, for fuck's sake,' Desi cointinued, 'I am a whinging bastard. Please make me the first. But in the meantime, if you want to take Dominic first, you can have him! You can't take out the Noonans: we've not done anything to be took out. No one wants to hurt us at the end of the day. And if they did, by God, there'd be some fireworks. I've got a bigger army than the Police; we've got more guns than the Police. I'm down for 25 murders! Well, load of bollocks, innit?'

I asked him how many he had killed and he indicated 27. I ran the figure past some of the main heads in Manchester and it seemed to be a realistic figure.

Less than eight weeks later, a drug dealer who he had fallen out with killed Desi Noonan. The man who lived by the sword died appropriately. ITN reported:

> *Medics were called to Merseybank Avenue in Chorlton, where they found Desmond Noonan with two stab wounds to his abdomen. [He was] stabbed in the stomach near his home in Chorlton just days before he was due to appear on a fly-on-the-wall documentary. Tonight, Police said there would be large numbers of extra patrols around the Chorlton area over the next few days, to reassure members of the community.*

I was on the scene within hours. I met up with Dominic and he drove us to Chorlton. Very soon, he knew who had done it. He didn't tell me who it was, but he had initiated the manhunt already. The Police had pulled him aside and warned him, but Dominic was not to be advised. There was revenge in the air. Later, outside a fish and chip shop across the road from the mortuary, while his crew ate their fill, he was keen to let it be known that he wanted the worst for his brother's killer.

'If someone whacks him, they whack him [the killer]. Got fuck all to do with me. But good luck to them. The amount of people that have come up and told me how much they want to kill him.'

'You don't think there's been enough killing?'

'It's only just begun, it's only just begun.'

I did not want to be caught up in what was about to happen and went back to London. I returned for the funeral and heard threats issued from the altar by a close friend of the family. The threats were clearly directed at the man suspected of killing

Desi. The 5,000-strong funeral procession closed roads and schools. There were more than a few raised eyebrows among those assembled when the priest delivered the Catholic funeral rite:

> *God of holiness and power, accept our prayers on behalf of your servant Desmond. Do not count his deeds against him, for in his heart he desired to do your will. And may almighty God bless you, in the name of the Father, the Son and the Holy Spirit. Amen.*

Just a couple of months later, Dominic was arrested in possession of a gun and was remanded in custody. The Noonans' chaotic world was falling apart. Death, murder, jail and rape had been part of their everyday lives: it was bound to unravel eventually. I was glad that my time in this community was coming to an end, as I felt sure the Police wagons were circling around Dominic. Whatever happened I was at least sure of two things: He would wind up in jail and he would protest his innocence.

In the event he was convicted of gun possession and sentenced to 16 ½ years. With remission, concurrent sentences and time already served, he would serve just five.

* * * * *

That was five years ago. I remained in contact with Dominic while he was in Frankland, the UK's most secure prison, but he was not allowed by the authorities to see me. As he prepared for his release, his claims that his conviction was on the back of a Police set-up continued, and he was still hoping for a retrial. As ever, he protested his innocence, despite admissions of guilt from two of his junior street soldiers who were co-accused.

In February 2010 Noonan was released on the most stringent licence of any newly-released prisoner in the UK, terrorists included. He has to live in a bail hostel, report in every hour, and is not allowed to phone any number, board any bus or car without first informing the authorities. In addition, he was placed on a 7 a.m. to 7 p.m. curfew. But on a brighter note, he told me recently that he had finally found love.

'Who is he?' I asked.

'It's a she. I'm now bi,' he told me enthusiastically. 'We're in love. Her name is Danielle; she's gorgeous. We are committed Christians and we are going to get married.'

I've kept up with Bugsy, too. He is now 16 and has been to my house to stay and has played with my children. By and large, he hasd stayed clear of the law until recently. But, just as Dominic was released, Bugsy was arrested with 56 rocks of crack cocaine. He was later released without charge but, like his dad, was placed on a 7 a.m. to 7 p.m. curfew by the courts.

Out of all the chaos of the Noonans' world, a sad predictability has emerged. It is extraordinary how their roles are being played out as if they've been mapped for every grid reference and rite of passage. By contrast, out of my comparatively stable upbringing has come a life of unpredictable chaos and flux.

The sadness for me is that the children of that world are living lives foretold. Yet despite the sense of inevitibility that hangs over the Noonans, I'm still hoping that young Bugsy will break the mould.

5

Diet Till You Drop

I have often been accused of being a touch crazy. While there may be some truth in the accusation, I've always protested that I am relatively sane for what I've been through. That is why I am a little reluctant to tell the following story. I feel that it might sway the floating voters and leave me stranded somewhere padded for my own safety.

We were undercover in Moscow investigating the dangers facing foreign businessmen in the city. Over 500 businessmen had been killed in recent years, victims of bribery and corruption. In many ways this was a city on trial. Here the underworld figures have their fingers in many pies, from oil to casinos. My investigation examining this unorthodox business culture wouldn't change the world one jot, but it would change me in one very dramatic way.

In Russia it was nearly impossible to conduct investigative journalism. The culture of surveillance in this society meant that people were very careful about what they said, and were often so fearful about who was listening that they would say nothing at all. This was a world of incredible violence, where life was cheap no matter how much money was sloshing around. Working in such an environment was stressful and the number of issues that we were trying overcome meant that the team often ended up in conflict.

I was going to a strip club to meet a source on the story, who we hoped would be able to give us the breakthrough we needed to crack the investigation. I walked up to the entrance laden with secret recording kit, and there in front of me stood armed guards and an airport-style security scanner. I was doomed. I didn't stand a chance of getting past the burly bouncers and the scanner.

Here was the sticky situation: arriving at a strip club in Moscow armed with covert recording gear can result in a swift one-way trip to the bottom of the Volga, no questions asked, no excuses given.

It was all my own fault. Earlier that day, I had argued that I should go in with my covert camera kit, while Paul, my producer, had suggested I take the safe option and go in clean, to get the lie of the land and consider my options. I was bull-headed and refused to take his wise counsel. I imposed my own will on the situation and naturally it was all going to go horribly wrong. There are some things I can talk myself out of, but a full-body scanner is not one of them.

So here I am, facing the scanner and a couple of Russian heavies who look like they could break my arm between two fingers. 'Where are my fags?' I think. I don't smoke, but in undercover operations, cigarettes can be more useful than an Uzi. They are great for sharing, to break the ice and open conversations or to gain trust.

I take all the time in the world to take out my packet of Marlboro. Every move I make is deliberate and slow: in this world it has the appearance of cool. Of course my head is doing ninety speculating on what is going to happen when these ex-KGB goons find out that I have been secretly recording their friends for the last week.

'Now, who can I share my fags with?' I ask myself, slowing down, trying to appraise myself of the situation. 'Who can I give one to, to buy time? Who can I distract while I figure out what to do?'

I feel that this might be a good time to fake an insulin incident. At times when you fear that your cover is about to be blown, pretending to be a diabetic can be very useful. In the past it has allowed me to buy time, escape via the toilet, arrange an emergency trip to the 'doctor' or just to get a private moment to consider my options. So, out comes my kit: I have a little insulin pack that I always carry with me. Of course I am never going to use it but it is my lifesaver, nonetheless.

But first of all, who do I give the cigarette to? I always try to strike up a rapport with doormen and cloakroom attendants. They are the ones who are most grateful and who have their eyes open to odd behaviour. Let's face it, a foreign bloke with a full filming kit under his jacket can appear a bit odd.

So, time to buy some credits. In front of me are two black-suited crew cuts with square jaws and iron fists, which looked to be permanently clenched. I pick out the one with the warmest eyes. This is a tense moment, as I could be wrong and may simply compound his suspicions. I nod towards the door and tell him about my diabetic predicament. He nods back and takes me to a quiet place where I can inject myself. He's glad of the chance to have a cigarette break and takes out his lighter as he takes me aside. He lights my cigarette and then his own before pointing me to a private toilet. We smoke and chat about football a little, before I flush my covert kit down the toilet. Better hundreds of pounds' worth of equipment at the bottom of the Volga than my dead body! My new friend then escorts me back to the queue and I am able to pass through the scanners without problem.

I was out of danger but I was still keen to defend my rash decision. Now Paul was always the guiding tactician on the team and if I am to admit it (and it kills me), he was the strategic brains behind this operation. He pulled my strings and I moved. The puppeteer was in charge and sometime the puppet – me – didn't like it.

Back at base that evening, I lashed out at Paul over tactics. Really, it was probably more about leadership of the pack than anything else. Notionally, I was in charge, but Paul was really the boss. I was in the infantry and he was the general directing operations.

Well, that evening there was a row in the ranks. We had

a right ding-dong about the rights and wrongs of undercover strategy. I was angry and emotional and, as usual, Paul was cool and collected. Clearly, my working hours were getting the better of me. Just a couple of weeks earlier, I was so tired that I had walked into a glass door. That was in Italy, and since then I had been to Paris, London, and now Moscow. Lack of sleep was affecting my judgment.

The argument left things simmering and unresolved, so over a few drinks that night we stumbled upon a solution. Be wary of the solutions you come up with after a 'few' drinks! In great male tradition we decided that the matter would be settled with a competition. A drinking competition? A contest that would show off our sporting prowess? A duel, perhaps? Well, no, not exactly. It just so happened that both Paul and I needed to lose weight. He was two stone over his ideal weight of 14 st 7 lb, and I was about two stone over my fighting weight of 13 st. Obviously, a 'diet-off' was the only contest that made sense! I can't remember where the idea came from, so let's just blame the vodka.

The plan was this: upon our return to BBC White City on the following Monday, we would reconvene at the gym and have a weigh-in. We would also be filmed and measured, and two weeks later we would be weighed, filmed and measured again. The man who had lost the most weight would be declared the winner. It wasn't entirely clear what the argument was about any more. In fact the entire point of the argument was now irrelevant as we got caught up in the prospect of this testosterone-fuelled competition. It was an idiotic response to a work dispute, but boys will be boys.

And so, on the Monday morning, weighing 14 st 13 lb, I strolled out for a five-miler. I was confident that a few runs around the park, a modest reduction of calories and a ban on alcohol would do the trick. But by Friday, Paul was reportedly down nine pounds and I was down just four. This was not looking good.

On Saturday I stepped up the intensity of my running and went to the gym for a full-on work out. On Sunday I went canoeing and running. I cut my calorie intake down to about a thousand per day, just over a third of the normal recommended intake. I was living on salad for breakfast, lunch and dinner, with the odd Oxo cube thrown in for flavour. Bearing in mind that I was exercising three times more than normal, I was effectively surviving on food fumes. It was purgatory. Physically, I was weak but I thought that it at least couldn't get any worse. I was wrong of course. By Monday I was nine pounds down with a week to go.

But word from Paul's camp was that he had lost a stone. 'I cannot lose this competition,' I kept repeating to myself. For some reason what had started out as a row over tactics had developed into a ludicrous alpha-male competition for Silverback dominance. My state of mind did not allow any leeway: I had to win. God bless my silly, febrile brain. It seemed so important at the time.

I decided to try the black art of propaganda. If I could lull Paul into a false sense of confidence, perhaps he would ease off a little and I could catch up with him. I decided to try to put him off by suggesting that we should back off a little for the sake of our health.

'Ah Paul,' I said. 'Listen, you're going great and I am going great. You're losing weight and I'm losing weight. Let's not get silly! I don't care who wins; we all win if we lose weight.'

'That's very kind of you, but I think I'd rather win all the same,' he replied, flatly.

He wasn't falling for it. I phoned him again but his buddy, Mike, picked up and said: 'He's not here mate; he's gone for a ten mile run.'

'Jesus, I'm a gonner.' I said to myself.

This was not a just a battle to lose weight, it was turning into a game of bluff and counter-bluff between two covert undercover operatives who should know a thing or two about this type of black magic. I chose to believe the stories I was being told, but then I had also chosen to believe that I could survive on lettuce and Oxo cubes. Yes, there was always a suggestion that I was being lied to, but I couldn't take that risk. My pride was at stake, and I desperately needed to win the argument, even if I had forgotten what it was about.

It was time to redouble my efforts and half my intake of calories. I didn't realise it at the time, but my levels of madness appeared to be directly related to the number of calories I was consuming, so this was perhaps not the best move. At this stage I was training two hours a day on 500 calories, and I was still losing to Paul. There was little more I could do without amputating a limb. And I even considered that!

The following Monday morning, the morning of the weigh-in, I was so weak that I couldn't drive. I called a taxi to take me to the BBC and arrived there at 8 a.m. for the 9 a.m. weigh-in.

In order to gain every advantage, I cut holes in a vest to keep my weight down and also wore an unseemly, threadbare pair of boxers to further increase my chances. I was still convinced that I was going to lose. I sat down alone in the gym, feeling that there was no more I could do. Win or lose, I had done my best. I had not weighed myself after the first week because I didn't want to demoralise myself, so the weigh-in would be as much a surprise to me as anyone else.

I put a call in to Paul's camp.

'Is Paul coming in by taxi?' I asked.

'No, he's running the six miles in. He should be there just before nine,' I was told.

'Fuck!' I was panicking.

But it was only 8.30 a.m. In desperation, I spied a plastic bin liner in the bin in the corner. 'Well, needs must,' I thought. In seconds I had it out of the bin and had punched holes in it so that I could wear it as a very fetching vest. I should point out that the bin liner was in fact clean, but I'm aware that I'm grasping at straws if I try to say that this was an indication of a sound mind. I got onto the exercise bike and cycled like a madman for the next 25 minutes, determined to sweat off an extra pound with the aid of my new sports gear. With five minutes to go, I allowed myself a quick shower and towelling off.

The mood was calm when Paul walked in at 9 a.m. Oddly, he was dressed for the office.

'But I thought you ran in,' I said, surprised.

'No,' he said, 'that was a lie. How was your morning?'

I didn't reply but just pointed to the scales.

Paul was first up. I could tell that he had lost just under a stone, and, sure enough, there was whooping from his camp when he came in at 15 st 9 lb.

'Yeah, that's 12 pounds, Macker. Beat that!' he said.

I stepped on the scales. There was silence. 13 st 0 lb! I was declared the winner after losing 26 pounds in just two weeks. I was happy, but my head was fuzzy and my body was exhausted. I may have won the argument but my sanity was slipping away. 'You are barking,' said Paul. 'If it doesn't kill you, it may just be the making of you.'

While I was beating my chest and enjoying my victory by celebrating with a fried breakfast, I had to admit that in the battle of tactics, Paul had proved himself to be more adept than I. Although I won the competition (and therefore the argument, let's remember!), it was Paul who was always in control. He had manipulated me and pushed me into a position where I was able to achieve an impossible weight loss in two weeks.

Looking back now, I am aware that my behaviour was a little psychotic and I find it hard to understand the headspace that I occupied for that fortnight. But I wish I could draw upon that kind of focus at will and use it more constructively. Paul just laughed at how I had taken the bait and allowed vanity and dogged determination to drive the diet home to its slimline but slightly unhinged conclusion. I think, however, he was making another point, too: left to my own devices, I can end up in uncharted and unlikely waters.

6

Dead Men Walking

The fishing on Lake Killarney is among the finest in the world. The fish grow to huge proportions because only a favoured few are permitted to fish here among the cypress trees. Access to the lake is through a security detail of armed guards, who are constantly on the look out for escaped convicts. The lake of course isn't situated in the beautiful Co. Kerry in Ireland, but in the heart of Angola Penitentiary in the middle of the Bayou, in Louisiana.

There are few prisons more remarkable and notorious than Angola, Louisiana State Penitentiary. 'The Alcatraz of the South' is an extraordinary complex, built on a loop of Mark Twain's great Mississippi River and spread over 18,000 acres. It houses nearly 5,500 inmates and employs 1,800 staff. The prison is a commercial entity in its own right and self-finances many of its activities with income from its prison rodeo and farm produce. It is one of the few places where cotton is still picked by hand and you can buy golf tees made out of handcuffs at the Prison View golf course. Thoroughbred draft horses and wolf dogs are bred and trained as Police animals with the help of inmates.

As a film-set location, Angola has been used for movies such as *Dead Man Walking*, starring Sean Penn and Susan Sarandon. It has its own *American Beauty* style suburb, which is home to 200 families. Generations of prison workers have lived here and it is famously dubbed the safest town in America.

It is the only prison to have its own federally licensed radio station, KLSP 91.7 FM, nicknamed 'The Incarceration Station'. There's no gangsta rap here, though: jazz and gospel music are the order of the day. And it has its own award-winning newspaper, the *Angolite*, which naturally has a death penalty columnist.

The inmates are nearly all destined to be here for life, as a life sentence in Louisiana means just that: there is no prospect of parole. The death chamber, where state-ordered executions are carried out, may facilitate an early release of sorts, but some prisoners entering as 15 year olds face the prospect of 70 years here. One prisoner has spent 37 years in solitary confinement. 'You can go a bit crazy,' he explained with some understatement. The longest serving prisoner, Sammy Robinson, inmate 78589, arrived here in 1953 and has served 57 years. He came as a 17 -year-old and is now 74.

I was here on a crash course in prison life. My work over the years has been a factor in sending many men to prison, and I wanted to experience for myself what it felt like to be denied freedom. I wanted to know if I would feel any guilt or remorse for what I had done, even if it wasn't a crime. So I was certainly curious – that's the stock of my trade. But I have to admit that there was also a voyeuristic element to my stay here. I knew I would be leaving, and in many ways I was no different to the tourists on buses who come to this prison to get a flavour of life behind bars and perhaps congratulate themselves on their own righteousness.

I became acquainted with its lush, wooded landscape as I fled the prison grounds with Leroy Cutwright, who is serving a life sentence for murder. We were being chased by bloodhounds and a specialist human hunt chase team, who were 20 minutes behind us. We were going for it. There is no clear path through the dense woodland, where wild hogs and bears roam free. Snake-infested marshes and alligator swamps surround the prison on all sides, making escape nearly impossible, but that doesn't stop people trying. It was hot and humid and I was dripping with sweat. The dense swampland was increasingly difficult for me to negotiate. Leroy, however, was used to the oppressive climate and was making steady and easy progress. He had a silver watch and two rings on his left finger and I wondered how long it must have taken to earn the right to wear those. 'Fifteen years,' he replied.

'How often have you done this?' I asked Leroy.

'Practically everyday,' he said, laughing.

Leroy is a trusted prisoner and works with the dog team. He attempts to escape from the prison every day to test the team.

'Do you ever think: "Someday, I'll do this for real"?' I asked him.

'No,' he said, 'it's never crossed my mind.'

'Come on,' I said. 'You're kidding me. Make a break for it now and I'll go the other way.'

This was surreal: I was on the run from America's most notorious prison with a murderer who didn't want to leave. I was determined to see just how long we could avoid capture. First we heard the whistles and then the barking. When we could hear the dogs panting, we knew the game was up. It was all of 15 minutes before Leroy and I were trapped. My efforts at escape were pathetic but I hoped that if I had spent 20 years there, I would have made a better effort, having had more time to think about it.

Colonel Joe Norwood is in charge of the search team. He is a slender man, about 5 ft 10" with a tidy black moustache and church-going hair. 'It's our job to get the bloodhounds out, to get behind the inmate and apprehend them,' he tells me. They have twenty dogs, a helicopter, thermal detectors, night-vision goggles and infrared gun sights as part of their basic bag of tricks. It's not exactly an evenly matched contest.

'What happened to the last person who tried to escape?' I asked him.

'He was caught in about 30 minutes,' Norwood said. 'There is nothing like hunting down a human – a manhunt, that is. It's the thrill of the chase, *mano a mano*.' I was slightly uneasy about the way he seemed to savour the idea. His family has been in the manhunt business for generations and he has followed in his father's footsteps. Joe and his tactical unit were called upon to help return law and order to New Orleans after Hurricane Katrina.

'We are called out for breakouts or chases all across the state. It can get dangerous and people get killed. That's what we expect and that's what we try to prevent.'

This is a man with only certainties in his life. There are the hunters and the hunted, the guilty and the innocent. He is not paid to see grey areas.

Shortly after my visit, an inmate attempted to escape. Henry Smith had been a well-behaved prisoner for years and had earned himself the privilege of a job on litter detail. 'You never know when they are going to run. They can be model inmates for years, decades, and still bolt,' Col Norwood explained.

Smith's escape caused the entire prison complex to go into lockdown. For five days, nearly a thousand correctional police officers and the prison's tactical team searched high and low in the woods and along Route 66, the main arterial route out of the area. After a $500,000 search effort and thousands of manhours, it was Col Norwood's team that caught up with the convicted murderer, who was serving the twenty-eighth year of his life sentence. Smith was found in the woods about four miles outside the prison perimeter, in a dried-out riverbed. He had hidden in a field of briars, which protected him from the bloodhounds and the team of manhunters. He told the warden that he 'enjoyed being out in the woods and hearing the birds sing'. He had survived on berries and some candy he had taken with him from the prison.

It transpired that Smith's only friend at the prison had recently died of a heart attack. He had not had a visitor in about three years and had not had a phone call in three months. It appeared that he was attempting 'suicide by cop', whereby a prisoner tries to provoke a fatal shooting to avoid having to take their own life.

Smith was placed in solitary confinement and it will take him at least 20 years to build up his privileges again. Even if he manages to do that, he is unlikely to be allowed to walk around the grounds without leg irons ever again.

'I want the people of Angola to know that they are not going to get away from us. I want the people out there to know we've never lost one in the 15 years I've been here,' Prison Warden Burl Cain told the media in the aftermath of the escape.

The escape had brought unwelcome media attention to the prison, and Cain was eager to point out that he had the situation under control. He took charge of the institution in the mid-1990s and cut through the prison like a whirlwind. In the previous decades, Angola had been dubbed 'the bloodiest prison in America'. Gangs of armed prisoners ran amok and controlled the penitentiary with intimidation and violence. Prison budgets were cut and regular officers had their hours and duties curtailed. In one three-year period, from 1972 to 1975 over 40 prisoners were murdered. Wilbert Rideau, prisoner and editor of the *Angolite*, wrote: 'The pursuit of survival fuelled a heated arms race among the prisoners for the superior weapon: a sword over a knife, a broad axe over a sword and a gun over everything.'

Every decade or so, some scandal would provoke an inquiry but little changed until Warden Cain took over and imposed his own values on the prison. The key to change was the rejection of the discredited 'trustee system' in which inmates were used by staff to control their fellow prisoners by doling out beatings and worse. Until the 1970s some privileged inmates even carried guns. After legal action, civilian guards were brought in and reform of the prison began apace.

That was then, and it was a world away from the regime in place today.

*****

I had arranged to spend a night as an inmate in the most detested cell in the entire penitentiary: the death cell. My introduction to it was from one of the few prisoners who had experience of it and lived to tell the tale.

Lane Nelson, Prisoner 100076, was convicted of first-degree murder for killing a hitchhiker and spent nearly eight years in solitary confinement and two years on Death Row. A judge later overturned his death penalty, accepting that he had received poor legal advice. He was granted the unprecedented pardon just five days before he was due to be executed and a release date was set for April 2011.

Lane entered Angola as a fresh-faced young man. Now he had the look of a librarian about him, studious and composed, his thick brown ponytail replaced by thinning white hair.

'I was on Death Row in the Summer of 1987 when eight guys were electrocuted in 11 weeks. I was already fasting,' he told me. 'But I wasn't going to walk to my own death [as an innocent man]. I was going to let them carry me. I wasn't going to fight because there was no sense in that. But I wasn't going to walk to my own death.'

He was defiant to the end. Others on Death Row refuse to give the state the satisfaction of killing them. 'I know of a guy who was so serious about killing himself that he ate his veins out – just simply chewed his veins,' said Lane.

He told me about the tiny cell where I was to spend the night. 'You are going to be staying in a cell where guys have stayed for the last minutes of their lives. They knew it and were counting down. Their last breaths were here.' He suggested I get into the role: 'Make it meaningful, and also think about staying there for decades! Take care.'

Lane's words had quite an impact on me. I imagined what it would be like if I only had a few hours to live. A prison guard brought me into the cell. It is the most basic of accommodation: there is a concrete-framed bed, a single mattress, a pillow and a white sheet. There is a sink and a toilet and a single shelf for books and toiletries. That's it. No TV, no radio, not even a window. If this was my last night, it would be a terrible send-off, but the thought of spending years in solitary confinement here was simply unthinkable.

I was jet-lagged and exhausted, yet I couldn't fall asleep on the narrow, uncomfortable mattress. Men have been known to hang themselves on the leg of a bed in these cells. The desperation to avoid death by someone else's hand can inspire great ingenuity. To face a lifetime here would be very bleak prospect and I can fully understand how suicide would seem like a release. I lay awake for hours, thinking about my family and how they would feel if I was condemned like the others who have slept here. I finally managed to get some sleep, but at 6 a.m. I was abruptly awoken. Breakfast was served. My 'last meal' was a veritable feast of porridge, eggs, cornbread with jam, and coffee.

After breakfast the charismatic Burl Cain walked me to the death house, where prisoners are killed on the State's orders. What shocked me was the banality of the building. It looked for all the world like an old folks' home or a social security office. Inside, the walls were a tired magnolia colour and there were Formica tabletops and Radio Shack speakers. I had expected the place to look more significant, to express the gravity of its purpose in its architecture. But the building failed to impress, much less intimidate.

At the time there had been six executions on Cain's watch and over 80 men remain on Death Row in Louisiana.

'I think they think it is not going to happen until it does. They keep thinking they will get a stay or something,' Cain told me. He was rather matter-of-fact about it. 'Every person we executed here has been guilty,' he said with certainty. I wondered how he could be so sure. 'Well, God help us if they weren't,' he added, eventually.

I asked him how executing the men had changed him.

'It made me hate crime and made me want to rehabilitate these guys.' His tone was sincere. You get the impression that Cain wants to improve people, to morally enhance them, if only so that they are sent to heaven rather than hell.

In 1991 Angola replaced the electric chair with the lethal injection. Once the condemned man is settled on the leather gurney in the shape of a cross, two intravenous tubes are inserted into each arm to inject three drugs. The first acts as an anaesthetic, the second stops breathing and paralyses, and the third induces a heart attack.

A group of six senior officers called the 'strap-down team' escort the condemned man to the death chamber. The death gurney has five lock-down points: two leg and two wrist manacles, and one crisscrossing leather strap around the chest. If the prisioner has to be carried, each member of the team takes responsibility for a body part during the short walk to the gurney. There is safety in numbers; the group can share the psychological burden of carrying a man to his death between them. One veteran member of the team said: 'We each have a small role to play. We have a duty to do it as efficiently as we can.' Efficiency is not something I had associated with capital punishment but it is a way of coping for those involved in the process, and, at the end of the day, they have a job to do. 'My goal is that we don't have to carry him in there. We want him to walk, because it's more traumatic for everyone [if he has to be carried],' Burl Cain told me.

Shortly after I left the prison, Cain presided over his seventh execution. Gerald Bordelon had kidnapped, raped and murdered a 12-year-old girl, and his punishment was a lethal injection. He had waived his right to appeal his death sentence. His last meal included peanut butter and jelly sandwiches and cookies. He apologised for his crime as the victim's family looked on and saw him take his last breath. I wonder if it gave them any real satisfaction.

*****

Although Angola is chiefly a prison, it is also a working farm. Every day a thousand, mostly African American, prisoners are marched out with hoes and buckets to work the fields, picking cotton, squash and corn. It's the first job inmates are assigned when they come here, but some have chosen to continue doing it for over 20 years. They earn four cents a day for doing this backbreaking work in the heat of the Louisiana sun. The preferred inmates get to drive the tractors.

I headed out to one of the farm lines. The inmates begin work at 7 a.m. and work until 3 p.m. I was paired up with Roy Morgan, who was sentenced to life on a first offence of rape when he was 22. He was resigned to spending the rest of his life in prison and had already served 27 years here. 'Have you served your time for your crime?' I asked him. 'Over and over,' he said.

Historians note that many old plantations in the South

became prisons after the Civil War. It was seen as slavery by another name, a way of continuing a tradition that was supposed to be dead. In the years after the Civil War, convicts were brought in to replace one imprisoned workforce with another. Between 1870 and 1900, inmates were regularly tortured, beaten and maimed. Over 3,000 were killed during this period.

Today, the black prisoners mostly work the fields under the gaze of armed white guards on horseback. Over 80 per cent of the inmates are African American. At the end of each the day, they are marched off to their modest cells, just as they were 200 years ago. It leaves a bad taste and it disturbs my social conscience. It's easy to make the leap from one era to another because the images remain the same.

At the prison golf club, lunch is served by shockingly servile inmates who pander to the predominantly white diners like silver service waiters. The wardens and deputies can call upon these 'trustees' to cook and clean in their own homes on the prison grounds. The lifers are expected to be grateful for the opportunity to do this work.

You can see how easily the slavery model fits in with that of the prison. The inmates do have a choice: they can stay in their cells for ever or they can work and engage with the community. If they choose to work, they at least get to build a life that involves some sort of reward and social interaction. If they choose to stay isolated in their cells, suicide is often the only option left to them. The prison farm, it seems to me, has originated as one way of perpetuating slavery, but today the economics of prison management make the prison farm a necessity to provide for the running of the whole enterprise.

*****

Angola is a reservoir of extremes and perhaps the most potent example of this is Jon Barry Simonis. A former high school athlete with an IQ of 128, Simonis is one of the most prolific sexual predators in US criminal history. He is one of the most notorious inmates in the US penitentiary system and has admitted to raping over 130 women. His sentence amounts to over 2,500 years. I wonder if the caution of the US court system is designed to punish the perpetrator or comfort the victim. It seems to say: 'Should he live and live, we will still have him inside, don't you worry.'

An entire wing of the prison was locked down for my meeting with Simonis. Extra officers were drafted in and the atmosphere was tense. He is known as the Ski-mask Rapist, because of the distinctive disguise he wore when committing his horrific crimes. He is about 6 ft tall with greying hair and deep-set blue eyes, and appears to have changed little since his arrest in 1981, at the age of 30.

Soon after he arrived at Angola, the former Public Enemy Number One found God. Adopting a strong religious belief here is encouraged and is the easiest way to escape the reality of what you have done. Once you find God, you can treat your past as an irrelevance. Your present comes out of a rebirth and is completely divorced from everything that went before. Certainly, religious conversion is one way for the prisoners to make life easier for themselves. It is a way to earn more credits and to gain valued privileges. Warden Cain is explicit in his support of religious practice: 'The choice is: do the men become better people here, or not. We put religion at the forefront of personal rehabilitation here and make no apologies for it.' The New Orleans Baptist Theological Seminary has 12 full-time pastors working on-site, and there are ministers of other faiths, including an Imam. While this philosophy had clearly worked for some, I wonder how appropriate it is for a state penitentiary to reward religious practice.

When I met Jon Barry Simonis, Prisoner 95868, he had already served 26 years in solitary confinement, locked in his 7 ft by 11 ft cell 23 hours a day, seven days a week. The bare cell had one small table, a bar of soap, a slim mattress and bare concrete white-washed walls and floor. A CCTV camera monitored his every move. His little luxuries were a bible and Fox News. I asked him how he had endured such austerity over the years.

'People were never a necessity in my life, so when I was

isolated, it wasn't that traumatic for me living in the cell. My cell is the equivalent of a small bathroom. Instead of a tub you have a bed. Life is as good or as bad as I want it to be. I had to accept that, and that this is where I will live and die. Once I did that, life became easier.'

Simonis' preference was to rape women in front of or within earshot of their partners. He sometimes acted with random accomplices, sometimes alone, but always with a viciousness that ruined lives forever. It takes a certain kind of arrogant pathology to pursue such a campaign of destruction, yet for Simonis it was only a game. His spree came to an end after an off-duty police officer noticed his red Pontiac Trans Am and realised that it was similar to the vehicle spotted near a number of the attacks. Simonis was put under surveillance for five days before being arrested and charged.

When I asked him what drove him to commit these crimes, he said: 'Some people are into sports; I was into excitement and adrenalin. Crime was my drug of choice. I could have done the same thing if I was into racing cars or climbing mountains.' Taking occasional sips from a tall vanilla-coloured mug, he continued: 'Crime had so much more to offer in terms of the different excitement.' It was disturbing to hear him explain his crimes as being the result of some kind of deviant adrenaline addiction.

He was a gambler playing a game of chance with the Police as he raped and brutalised his victims in a sexual blitzkrieg. I'm against the death penalty, but as I looked at this man I thought I could do the job myself. He was so matter-of-fact about what he had done. He told me that he has regrets, but that it doesn't do to dwell on the past. 'I have remorse for my victims but at the time you don't care too much about the consequences or the victims.'

And it wasn't just the victims who suffered because of Simonis' crimes. 42-year-old Clarence Von Williams was convicted and sentenced to 50 years in prison for an aggravated sexual attack on a 40-year-old Bridge City woman and her teenage daughter. When the Police caught up with Simonis two months later, he admitted that he had carried out the crime alone, and Von Willaims was released.

In that instance, the victim, Sally Blackwell, awoke to find Simonis at the foot of her bed. She tried to speak but was warned that if she made any noise he would kill her children. Over the next two hours he raped and abused Sally and her daughter, Janet, while they were blindfold and bound.

In 1981, aged 30, Simonis was sentenced to 2,527 years in prison. In addition he was given 20 life sentences (just in case he survived the duration of his initial sentence). He will spend the rest of his life and more in Angola, as he has chosen to be buried here, too. He escaped the death penalty because rape did not become a capital offence until after his conviction.

'I probably deserved to die,' he told me. 'I am guilty of these crimes. I knew extremely well what I was doing beforehand and while I was doing it, throughout. I have found a place now where I can be at peace. I have already filled out a will to be buried here. This is where I came when I was 31. I figure this is an appropriate place to be when I am dead. When I'm dead, I'm dead.'

*****

Point Lookout Graveyard, which will be Simonis' final resting place, is a beautiful little cemetery overhung by trees and carefully tended by the inmates. Simple white crosses mark the graves and American flags blow in the wind. A white picket fence surrounds the area and a simple ironwork sign indicates that this is the prison cemetery. The dead murderers are treated well in their final repose and are laid to rest in coffins crafted by fellow inmates.

The coffin makers operate out of a rustic barn a few miles from the cemetery and well away from the main prison blocks. Outside, there are thoroughbred horses in the fields and a pet dog running around the yard. The scene could be out of a tourist brochure. Indeed, tourists are allowed here on supervised visits.

Joseph Greco and David Bacon are the craftsmen who work

I can't say who was responsible for the haircuts but she was a dab hand with a pudding bowl.

Tadhg and me at home in Kildare in 1975.

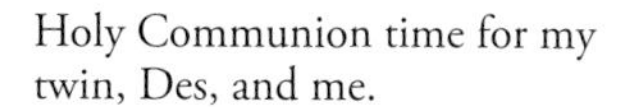

Holy Communion time for my twin, Des, and me.

Tadhg, aged six, and me, aged ten, in 1976. We would work together undercover nearly 30 years later.

Chelsea Headhunter, Andy 'Nightmare' Frain, filmed covertly as he holds court in the back of my car. He would get seven years in jail following my undercover investigation.
© BBC

Ten years after the investigation, Ameera and I were attacked by thugs sympathetic to the Chelsea Headhunters' cause.
© Dare Films

My time with the Bedouin and the Al Amri family. There are good reasons why an Irishman and a camel should not spend any time together!
© Five TV

Dominic Noonan watches over his territory with his henchmen in Manchester.

'By day it's run by the Police, by night it's run by gangsters.'
© *David Wootton Photography*

I filmed Dominic and his gang for over five years.
© *David Wootton Photography*

Noonan walks the streets with his posse of young men in their ill-fitting suits.
© *David Wootton Photography*

Graham Johnson and I display our haul of Semtex. It was all going to plan until we were told that we had buried the explosives in the middle of a minefield.
© Sunday Mirror

In December 1999 the *Radio Times* ended my anonymity with an unusual shot of me on the front cover. Four years later, after my brother Tadhg and I worked together undercover, they reinacted that shot, this time with both of us, wired and dangerous.

© *David Wootton Photography*

My *Wild Weather* adventure sent me around the globe to play guinea pig in the most extreme weather on the planet.
© *Five TV*

On surveillance duty, chasing down the bad guys.
© David Wootton Photography

An X-ray image of my covert recording kit. I wouldn't have a chance of getting through an airport scanner.
© BBC

My worlds collide: skating to bring attention to the plight of the mountain gorilla for the charity, Born Free.
© Born Free

here. Both are serving life sentences for murder. Their output is solely for the prison's needs. 'In total we have made about 70 or 80 caskets,' David told me. He is in good shape for a 40-year-old and has a thick shock of greying hair, parted in the middle as was the fashion when he arrived here 20 years previously.

Because in Louisiana 'life means life', both coffin makers will die here unless the law changes. Their constant hope is that it will, and that they will be given a second chance to contribute something to society.

'I am not the same young man I was 20 years ago. There are so many things that brought us here. It could happen in the blink of the eye. There is a lot of men here, like ourselves, who if given a second chance would be successful in society and would even be an asset in society.'

I turned to his pal and fellow craftsman, Joseph Greco, Prisoner 124401, and asked him: 'What was your mistake?'

'My mistake was going out drinking and taking someone's life. I am ashamed,' he said.

'Who was that?'

'A patron in a bar. I found myself in an 8 ft by 10 ft cell in maximum-security lockdown 23 hours out of 24. I was cut down to my bare soul. I didn't have anyone or anything in that cell, and I realised that that was the end of my life.'

The father-of-one knows that his chance of ever being free is negligible in this state, which is unlikely to repeal its 'life means life' law anytime soon.

'You don't know what you are missing until it is gone,' he said.

Of all the inmates I met, David and Joseph showed the most remorse and regret. Their attitude made me question if 'life' should mean a life without any hope of freedom ever again.

'What sentence would you give yourselves?' I asked.

David Bacon hummed and hawed, perhaps nervous of being too lenient on himself.

'You've had 20 years to think about it?' I added, rather insensitively.

'Twenty years is plenty,' David answered.

'Ok,' I went on, 'but what do you think is fair?'

The grey-haired Bacon, with his baleful eyes, looked like he carried the worries of the world on his slumped shoulders.

'It's a hard answer to give; it's a hard answer. I'm almost getting emotional because a man lost his life.'

On the brink of tears, 20 years after the offence, David seems to be reliving the moment that cost both him and the victim their lives in different ways.

'He had two daughters. He won't see them again. For me to put a number on it …' his voice trailed off for a moment, 'I may be wrong in that respect, because that is a man who is not coming back. But if I am forced to put a number on it, then I would say 20 years is fair,' David concluded.

This was a man who has given an enormous amount of thought to his crime and the consequences of it. This was a man, a murderer, who I would have in my house and feel safe.

Now that a figure had been mentioned, Greco took the baton and ran with it. 'I would say 15 years. When I first came here, I went straight to lockdown. Then I went to cellblock, which is a unit that went out on the line [worked the fields] and stayed there all day. [There were] times when my face done split in half because of the sun done beat me so bad. I stayed out in the field five years before I got my first job. My first one was cutting grass. I worked hard. I don't make any excuses about it because I'm glad because I earned every privilege the hard way, and it's made me the person I am today.'

These men were contrite and were, I felt, the best argument for release before death. Their rehabilitation was revealing and appeared genuine. I began to understand how Angola worked. Take the worst of men who have done the worst of things and break them down through hard labour. When they have lost all hope of release, rebuild them slowly and try to make them productive members of prison society.

*****

'It takes good food, playing, praying and good medicine to

have a good prison,' according to Warden Burl Cain. He has done his best to ensure that prisoners understand that the path to rehabilitation is the path to Christianity. A devout Southern Baptist, he tells everyone who will listen that it is religion that gives the men morality and meaning in their lives.

This prison reserves a special place for prisoners who find God. Religion provides a kind of safety valve that releases the pressure of guilt. For many of the men, God is their only option if they want forgiveness, and forgiveness is the only thing that will allow them a fresh start.

Under Cain's watch, over 150 inmates have graduated as prison ministers and the explosion in religious conversions has necessitated the construction of six new churches on the complex.

'The Bible became the sword in here. Once they took religion into their hearts, then came morality and then care for one's fellow man. We showed the way by building the churches, and they changed the prison,' says Cain.

But Cain's zealous approach to bringing Christianity to the prison has come under fire from the American Civil Liberties Union which said in one statement that, 'Cain's job is to be Warden of Angola, not the Chaplain of Angola.' They believe that the religious ethos put in place by Cain is unconstitutional and they have consistently challenged his management of the prison.

Cain has created a community from the worst of society, out of killers, rapists and paedophiles. My time there left me thinking that if he could do that inside, then surely we should be able to do better outside prison walls. If a prison can rescue those seemingly beyond redemption, perhaps there are some clues as to how we should remedy the ills in our own society.

At Angola I learned that bad men can turn good over time. And if given the chance, they can make a valuable contribution to our communities. Everyone builds their own prison with their habits, peculiarities and thought patterns. I had seen more freedom inside this prison for well-behaved inmates than I have seen in many workplaces where people feel trapped by wages, commitments and expectations. The message that I took from Angola was that we are all free to reinvent ourselves. Sometimes it is not necessary to understand the past to move forward – you can park it and forge ahead with the future if you allow yourself that freedom. It was a striking lesson to me.

But do I feel guilty for putting men in prison? Well, I still struggle with that question. But I do know that it genuinely changes some men for the better. And, by opening my eyes to the reality of the experience, I think that's what it did for me.

7

Dying Ain't Much of a Living

It was 1992, and I was on a military aircraft nose-diving into Sarajevo Airport in the middle of a civil war. I had hitched a lift with the German Air Force into the city while it was still effectively under siege. The Luftwaffe C-160 transporter was carrying journalists and humanitarian aid, but nevertheless had to avoid attacks from the Serbian forces. While en route from Zagreb in Croatia to the stricken city, the pilot was informed that the plane had been locked onto by a weapons system on the ground and was being targeted and tracked, so he initiated a Khe Sanh dive – a manoeuvre named after the US military base in Vietnam, where aircraft would fly in at high altitude and drop sharply from 10,000 ft before dramatically leveling out for a very late landing.

I had been hoping to compete as a canoeist in the 1992 Olympic Games, but I had tragically failed to qualify for the team because I wasn't good enough. As my dreams of representing Ireland faded, I had been offered a chance to report on the Balkan conflict and I dived at the opportunity. The death of one dream had allowed me to pursue another. I had always wanted to be a war correspondent but had never thought that my Olympic odyssey would end on the thousand-metre-long runway of Sarajevo Airport where the fishbowl topography of the area made us sitting ducks for gunners and artillery.

But taking risks had never bothered me. I wasn't afraid to fail and, at the age of 26, I wasn't really afraid of death either.

It wasn't that I had some kind of death wish – I simply didn't believe that the worst could happen to me. I have been accused by many of being slightly unhinged and of being an adrenalin junkie. Indeed, I have had a few close calls in the line of duty. But this has never been my driving force: I have grabbed the opportunities on offer because life is for living, and a life without adventure holds little sway with me. In a way I treated the most dangerous of my assignments as arcade games where the consequences were not real. It is a coping mechanism that has allowed me to deal with the most acute dangers.

It's not that I don't feel fear, but I have the ability to postpone it until after the event and that has kept my mind clear at the critical moment. Flying into a warzone is a calculated risk that can be managed to a certain extent, but the real threat comes when danger takes you by surprise. The unexpected is the greatest of tests and is often the time when you find out more about yourself than perhaps you ever wanted to.

* * * * *

My first significant brush with death came, rather ironically, while canoeing on the river River Liffey. It was 1990, and I was a young reporter working for the *Irish Press*. I was too broke to afford my own car, so I was driving my mother's. I had rather carelessly clocked up £1,000 in parking fines around the paper's offices on Burgh Quay and I was struggling to pay them when the fairy godmother of advertising came unexpectedly to my rescue.

Mars were shooting a commercial to help the transition of the Marathon brand to Snickers in the public's consciousness, and had chosen canoeing as the theme. They had lined up about 40 canoeists including my brother, Tadhg, who suggested I come along to the audition. I got the gig. The fee was £1,000 and I was looking forward to paying my fines before my poor mother ended up in court for my sins in her Ford Fiesta.

There were about 50 people on the set, just to shoot a

30-second commercial. Wardrobe rigged me out in an early nineties day-glo ensemble that was hard to wear with a straight face. The script called my character the 'hero' and I was treated like a star. It all felt a bit embarrassing. I had two assistants and I wasn't allowed to do anything for myself. Instead, I was told to concentrate on learning my line: 'Snickers really satisfies – peanuts, chocolate, caramel – it really keeps you going.' It took me 18 takes to say the line and get the bite into the bar just right. To my mind, all the takes were the same, but the director had a different opinion.

Then it was time for the action shots. They loaded a camera onto the front of my canoe and instructed me to paddle over the weir at full-tilt. I went over the weir with a mighty crash and disappeared under the water. The boat had become trapped in a stopper at the bottom of the weir. A wave had flipped me over, which shouldn't have been a problem, but the weight of the camera meant that I couldn't right myself. I don't remember fighting to escape but it was all caught on camera.

Tadhg saw me get into difficulty and threw his paddle to me as I was washed around and around. But I missed the catch and now we were both up shit creek without a paddle. The camera was still rolling as I was drowning. It wasn't a terribly unpleasant experience: something like gradually falling asleep. Then, as I lost consciousness, my body relaxed and I slipped out of the boat. I was dragged to the bank, where I spluttered back to life, a little disoriented, but alive.

When they asked me to do it all over again 10 minutes later, I did as I was told. This time I managed it without capsizing and they called it a wrap before there were any more near-death experiences. That was my first foray into the world of television and perhaps I should have taken the money and run at that point. If I nearly got myself killed canoeing down the Liffey, what chance did I stand with gangsters and drug dealers?

Well, I would soon find out...

*****

Badger was a Liverpool drug dealer and one of the first to

put crack cocaine on the streets of Europe after it had swept through the ghettoes of the America's inner cities. We were on a simple research trip to meet him at his tiny two up, two down terraced house in the shadow of Anfield Stadium. There were no cameras, no wires and no disguises – just old-fashioned pen and paper and one unstable crack addict. Badger had the look of a lithe rock climber, without the healthy complexion. He had been on a crack cocaine bender for three days straight and there was a wildness in his eyes that should have forewarned me that this was an unpredictable situation.

We had come looking for information on another major gangland figure. Badger knew everything about everyone on the Liverpool scene, and was a tried and trusted informant for crime journalists.

We entered his sparse living room, where I was directed towards an armchair in the corner and my colleague, Michael, was told to sit on the sofa with his back to the window facing the street. Michael is the father of three kids, and is very-laid back. He has worked in warzones and nothing fazes him. He is exactly the type of person you want by your side when you are meeting strung-out drug dealers.

Like the Police, journalists need informers – tipsters who will give us the low-down on their criminal colleagues in return for a few drinks or a couple of hours of feeling self-important. We were doing a story about a supergrass who had shopped his own son to the Police, along with one of the UK's biggest gangsters, John Hasse.

Badger knew all about Hasse and the drug trade in Liverpool and had volunteered to give us a briefing on the underworld landscape there. Michael was leading this investigation and I had come along for the ride.

There was a constant flow of smokers through the house. They would come in, light up crack pipes and then leave, promising to pay later. The air was heavy with smoke and Badger's kids came in and out of the room, oblivious to the business that was taking place in their home.

Badger was telling us about the early days of crack on the

streets of the UK and had started to ramble a little. I was doing my very best to appear interested and respectful, but, much as I tried to hide it, my distaste for him and the environment he provided for his kids must have permeated my façade. We had been there for about an hour and the smoke was already giving me a headache; I couldn't imagine what it was doing to the kids. Badger's behaviour disgusted me and, even through his three-day crack haze, he knew it.

'You don't like me,' he said, out of the blue. He stared at me with his piercing blue eyes, his pupils scarily dilated. His forehead was scrunched up as though he was trying to work out a complex maths equation. He was prison-hardened and feared nothing – not jail, not the Police and certainly not me.

'You don't respect me,' he said, raising his voice.

'I do, mate. I do,' I said, desperately trying to placate him.

'This is my house and you're fucking disrespecting me,' he said, this time more coldly and more slowly than before.

Abruptly, he stood up and left the room. I looked at Michael.

'There could be trouble ahead,' said Michael.

'Oh, it'll be fine,' I said, ever the optimist.

We heard a rush of footsteps going up the stairs, the sound of doors and cupboards being opened and shut, and then footsteps racing back down the stairs. Badger burst back into the room and headed straight for me. He leapt onto my chair and wrapped his thighs around my hips and his arm around my neck. Sitting tall above me now, I saw his hand rise in an arc and then swing back down with force against my neck. I felt metal against my jugular and it was only then that I realised he had a gun in his hand.

'Whoa! Badger, take it easy – easy,' said Michael

'You c**t! You don't respect me. Eh? In my house? You motherfucker!'

He increased the pressure, drilling the gun into my neck.

'Respect! Respect!' I shouted.

'I'm going to fucking kill you, you c**t.'

'There, there, Badger. If we're not careful, someone will get hurt,' said Michael calmly. He could have been talking to his four-year-old child. For two minutes Badger ranted, Michael cajoled and I pleaded, as he buried the gun into my neck, drawing blood. It took a lot of convincing, but Badger finally got off me and took the pistol away from my neck. I held my sweating palms up and out and retreated into the cushions of the armchair.

He sneered at me, cocked open the gun and let a bullet fall to the floor, as if to show me he hadn't been joking. I watched the bullet as if it was in slow motion. I heard it hit the floor and bounce. He then sat down on the sofa, threw the gun behind him and continued his story, as if the previous three minutes had never happened.

Few words were exchanged as Michael and I drove back to the hotel. I went to my room and ordered a bottle of wine to calm my nerves. In between gulps I cried like a baby.

The following morning we went back to Badger for clarification on a number of points. This time he was the epitome of the good host. The events of the previous day were never mentioned, and I certainly wasn't going to be the first to bring them up.

*****

My favourite near-death experience was the Semtex incident. We had been investigating the proliferation of weaponry on the black market after the collapse of communism in Eastern Europe. We had travelled all over the former Yugoslavia and eventually to the Kosovo-Montenegro border, where we were conducting business in the immediate aftermath of a bloody civil war. The UN had come into Kosovo to impose law and order, forcing Serbs out of the country in line with the wishes of the Albanian 'ethnic majority'.

In the messy aftermath of the war, there were all sorts of things for sale. I managed to buy over one hundred sticks of Semtex from a wheeler-dealer in Pristina, the capital of Kosovo. We were staying at the Grand Hotel, off Mother Teresa Road, in the heart of the rundown city. The hotel was full of UN officers, spies, drug dealers and arms merchants. It was the kind of place where lives and fortunes were lost in the blink of an eye, and I was there posing as a representative of a fictitious Irish Republican splinter group. I was acting as a sort of quartermaster, supposedly looking to replenish munitions for this terrorist organisation. We had made contact with 'Sinbad', who was a middleman for anything you wanted here. The whole place had a hint of Cold War Berlin about it and even the most mundane of people and places had an air of intrigue and mystery about them. I met Sinbad in the hotel garden. The lush fake lawn and white plastic garden furniture provided a grand backdrop to an illicit arms deal.

'There are spies everywhere,' Sinbad told me. His contact in the Kosovon Liberation Army, Hugli, had agreed to do a deal, initially for a haul of Semtex, and much more if all went well and I proved to be a reliable customer.

I had never met Hugli, but I had seen a photograph of him holding aloft the severed heads of two of his Serb enemies, so he was clearly a man not to be messed with. But I couldn't help myself. He knew that I was Irish, and I had arranged for him to receive an appropriate gift to sweeten the deal. Knowing him to be a huge fan of U2, I had sent him a signed copy of their album, *The Joshua Tree*. The inscription read: *To Hugli – I hope you find what you are looking for – Bono*. Bono's handwriting bore an uncanny resemblance to my own, but nobody remarked on this and the gift seemed to do the trick. Sinbad asked me to pass on Hugli's thanks for the touching gesture and I promised I would do so the next time I met Bono and the lads for a pint.

And so the deal for the Semtex went ahead. One hundred sticks of plastic explosive is enough to cause wholesale devastation, and, as a general rule, Irishmen abroad should not get caught with it in their possession. I had been posing as a dissident Republican, so, if we were discovered with the goods, it would take some explaining. We hatched a plan to hide it for a couple of days while we got the Channel Five lawyers to contact the UN and arrange a handover.

On the advice of my producer, the aforementioned Michael, we buried the Semtex in an empty field well out of harms way about 20 km outside Pristina. We painted an arrow pointing towards the hole on a nearby rock and marked the spot with an 'X'. We figured there was little chance that we were being watched and that it would be safe there.

Well, we were right in that respect, but we were clearly not well-informed about the area. A couple of days later, when we met in the UN explosives unit to hand over the Semtex, the Finnish officer said: 'Thank you. We'll make arrangements to take your statements and consider the evidence against the arms dealers. Just one thing, though. Why did you bury it in a minefield?'

The road to Semtex is paved with good intentions, it seems. In the end the UN managed to convict our middleman, Sinbad, with illegal arms dealing and he received three years in jail.

*****

These risks were all taken with some degree of calculation, and I always felt as though I had some control over the situations. They were self-inflicted moments of danger, I confess, but it was in a Wimbledon hospital bed where a cancer scare left me feeling at my most vulnerable.

For about six months I had had reason to believe that all was not well, and that is why I found myself in a room affectionately nicknamed the 'Colon Suite'. I knew that, of the group of people on the ward, some would get good news and some would get bad. I hoped that I would be one of the lucky ones, but knowing that I could do nothing to change the outcome made this one of the most difficult situations of my life.

The concerned consultant put a latex-covered finger up my bum and as he withdrew it with an unfortunate sound effect, he said, 'My kids loved you on *Dancing on Ice*.' He then scheduled an emergency colonoscopy and more probing procedures for the next day.

As the moment drew close and I was reaching my lowest

ebb, a nurse came in and raised my spirits:

'Today, Mr MacIntyre, we are putting cameras up places where not even you have placed them,' she said, deadpan.

'Touché!' I laughed.

The natural justice of it was not lost on me but the revenge of the covert camera stopped there, and I was given a clean bill of health. It was another escape from fate's worst offerings, and the only conclusion I can draw from all this is that it is always better to be lucky than to be right.

8

Suffer the Little Children

The dormitory held about 30 beds, packed in so close together that there was hardly a hair's breadth between the bare metal frames. Apart from a few religious icons and pictures of 'Our Blessed Mother', the white walls were bare. The torch swept across the faces of children sleeping, screaming, laughing and sobbing, and finally rested on the hunched figure of a boy in a white vest. He was obviously distressed, and rocked back and forth, his ankle tethered to his cot like a goat in a farmyard. This scene was reminiscent of the worst of the Romanian orphanages that caused international outrage in the 1990s. But this wasn't Romania and the 'Great Mother' was not Elena Ceausescu – this was India and the 'Great Mother' was Blessed Mother Teresa.

Mother Teresa was educated at the Loreto Abbey in Rathfarnham in Dublin, and is still held in extraordinary devotion in Ireland and around the world. The last thing I thought I would be doing is investigating this much-lauded woman. Critics of mine have been known to say, 'N[illegible]hing he'll be undercover with Mother Teresa.' And funni[illegible] that's what came to pass.

I had received a tip-off from workers who h[illegible] with the Missionaries of Charity at several of th[illegible] in India.

The volunteers felt very uncomfortable with much of what they had witnessed there. According to them, the local workers and the nuns were often cruel or indifferent to the children in their care. Children were tied to beds or abandoned in soiled clothes for hours on end. One volunteer reported that at another of the charity's homes, she had seen a mentally ill female patient shackled to a tree.

Such treatment of the most vulnerable was beyond my comprehension and while the aura that surrounded Mother Teresa had deterred other reporters, I felt that this was information that needed to be acted upon. The issues surrounding care homes have been close to my heart for many years. Where I grew up, in Celbridge, Co. Kildare, the St John of God religious order run a home for learning-disabled adults where they take care of over one hundred residents. I remember the whole community being involved in the care culture and, even in the seventies, the home was decades ahead in terms of the treatment and management of mental health issues. Everyone considered the residents to be part of the community and they were included in every aspect of village life. Many worked in the pubs and the shops, and every Sunday one of the guys would come to our house for lunch – we all had our regulars. This wasn't seen as some kind of charitable duty: it was just the way things were done, and we were all richer for it. Looking back, I feel it represented the best of Ireland in the seventies.

Over the years I had built my reputation on – and nearly lost it to this cause – My first major investigation in this area was in 1999 at the Brompton Care Home in Kent. I went undercover there and reported on the disgraceful conditions that the most vulnerable in society were expected to live in. I witnessed physical assaults and humiliations of all sorts. On one occasion I saw a worker pull a resident to the floor by the hair and then kick her in the head. Her colleagues looked on and did nothing. Residents were marched naked down corridors at the end of a mop, as if they were cattle on the way to milking. This was normal behaviour at the home.

When the investigation was broadcast, the BBC helpline

received the largest number of calls in the history of the broadcasting corporation. Judging by the response, such abuse was clearly being repeated in other care homes across the UK. There is little glory in uncovering this kind of story, but there was at least some satisfaction to be had from the knowledge that we had protected the 30 or so residents of the home and that we had put the issue of abuse in care homes on the government's agenda.

This story proved to be one of the most challenging of my career and nearly broke me both personally and professionally. About six months after the documentary was broadcast, the Kent Police said in a report that we had made up some of the claims and had exaggerated others. They leaked the report to the *Sunday Telegraph*, which ran the story of our 'alleged deception' on the front page for two weeks running. I was accused of lying about victims of abuse to advance my career. My professional integrity was called into question and it was suggested that I was morally bankrupt. It was a dark time for me and my career was in jeopardy.

The allegations were so serious that they went right to the top of the BBC management. Greg Dyke, the flamboyant former BBC Chairman, initiated an investigation and insisted on seeing the raw footage. He backed me one hundred per cent and I went on to sue the Kent Police for libel.

The Police had confused care in custody suites with that of care homes and would suffer the consequences. They were forced to apologise unreservedly and it cost them £750,000 in legal costs and damages, which I donated to five charities for the learning disabled. It was the first successful libel suit against the UK Police Force in its near 200-year history. Subsequently, I became an ambassador for Mencap, a charity that works with people who have learning difficulties, and Action Against Elder Abuse, and I made a further three documentaries exposing abuse in care homes.

So by the time I got the tip-off about the Missionaries of Charity care homes, I had enough experience in the area to recognise it as credible. We get lots of tip-offs, but this one had the ring of truth about it and I was easily persuaded to take a closer look.

I first learned of the plight of the Kolkata children in 2004 from two Irish international aid workers, both qualified nurses and committed Catholics. They were very well-meaning and genuine in their desire to help. They had worked as volunteers for the Missionaries of Charity in their Daya Dan home the previous Christmas and had been appalled at the conditions.

'I was shocked. I could only work there for three days. It was simply too distressing .... We had seen the same things in Romania but couldn't believe it was happening in a Mother Teresa home,' one of the nurses told me. In January, she and her colleague had written to Sr Nirmala, the newly-appointed Mother Superior, to voice their concerns. They wrote to her out of 'compassion and not complaint' they said, but received no response. Like me, they had been educated in Catholic schools and taught to believe that Mother Teresa was the holiest of women, second only to the Virgin Mary in sanctity. This belief was unwavering and was shared by the media and Church alike. This is what allowed the practices of the Order to go unquestioned for over 50 years. Even when the sister in charge of the Missionaries of Charity's Mahatma Gandhi Welfare Centre in Kolkata was found guilty of burning a seven-year-old girl with a hot knife in 2000 as punishment, criticism remained muted.

So that is how I found myself working undercover at the Daya Dan orphanage for children aged six months to twelve years, one of Mother Teresa's flagship homes in Kolkata.

*****

Mother Teresa founded the Missionaries of Charity in 1950 in Kolkata, answering her calling to 'serve the poorest of the poor'. In 1969 a documentary about her work made her a household name. International awards followed, including the Nobel Peace Prize in 1979 and a Congressional Gold Medal. Her name is attached to some 60 centres for the poor worldwide.

She died on 5 September 1997 and India honoured her with a state funeral. Her seven homes for the poor and destitute of Kolkata were her great legacy. She was fast-tracked to sainthood in October 2003 when Pope John Paul II beatified her.

The road to her beatification was the shortest in modern times. In 1999, less than two years after her death, the Pope waived the normal five-year waiting period and allowed the immediate initiation of her canonisation process. Her beatification followed the Vatican's recognition of her first miracle when an Indian woman said that her abdominal tumour had been cured after she applied a locket containing a picture of Mother Teresa to the area. However, a doctor who treated the woman insisted that the tumour had been cured by conventional medical treatment and not by Mother Teresa's supernatural intervention.

I worked undercover for a week in Mother Teresa's flagship home for disabled boys and girls to record *Mother Teresa's Legacy*, a special report for Sky News. I winced at the rough handling by some of the full-time staff and sisters. I saw children with their mouths forced open, gagging as they were given medicine, their arms flailing in distress. Tiny babies were bound with cloths at feeding time. Rough hands wrenched their heads into position for feeding. Some of the children retched and coughed as rushed staff crammed food into their mouths. I saw learning -disabled boys and girls abandoned on open toilets for up to 20 minutes at a time. They were a pathetic sight as they slumped over unattended, some dribbling, some even sleeping. Their treatment was dangerously unhygienic and was a despicable affront to their dignity.

I heard two young volunteers giggling as one recounted how a boy had urinated on her as he was being strapped to a bed. At the orphanage, few of the volunteers batted an eyelid at disabled children being tied up. They were too intoxicated with the mythical status of Mother Teresa and too drunk on their own philanthropy to see that such treatment of children was inhumane and degrading.

Some of the volunteers did their best to wash the children who had soiled themselves. But there were no nappies, and only cold water. Soap and disinfectant were in short supply. Workers washed down beds with dirty water and dirty cloths. Food was prepared on the floor in the corridor. I saw a senior member of staff mix medicines with her fingers. Some did their best to show some love and affection, at least some of the time. But most of the care the children received was inept, unprofessional and, in some cases, rough and dangerous. 'They seem to be warehousing people rather than caring for them,' said Martin Gallagher, former Operations Director with Mencap, after viewing our footage.

Music has only recently been permitted in the homes as a comfort to the children. It would not have been considered appropriate during Mother Teresa's time. For her, the road to salvation was literally through suffering, even needless suffering.

The most significant challenge to the reputation of Mother Teresa came from Christopher Hitchens in his 1995 book, *The Missionary Position*. 'Only the absence of scrutiny has allowed her to pass unchallenged as a force for pure goodness, and it is high time that this suspension of our critical faculties was itself suspended,' he wrote, questioning whether the poor in her homes were denied basic treatment in the belief that suffering brought them closer to God. Hitchens's lonely voice also raised the issue of the Order's finances. He wondered why the vast sums of money raised seemed never to reach Kolkata's poorest.

Susan Shields, formerly a senior nun with the order, recalled that one year there was roughly $50 million in the bank account held by the New York office alone. Much of the money, she complained, sat in banks while workers in the homes were forced to reuse blunt needles. The Order has since stopped this practice, but the poor care remains pervasive. One nurse told me of a case where staff knew that a patient had typhoid but made no effort to protect volunteers or other patients. 'The sense was that God will provide and, if the worst happens, it is God's will,' she said.

The Kolkata Police and the city's social welfare department promised to investigate the incidents in the Daya Dan home after they saw and verified the distressing footage we secretly filmed. Dr Aroup Chatterjee, a Kolkata-born doctor now living in London, said that if Daya Dan were any other care home in India, 'the authorities would close it down. The Indian government is in thrall to the legacy of Mother Teresa and is terrified of her reputation and status. There are many better homes than this in Kolkata.'

The footage we filmed at Daya Dan was truly shocking and we knew it would help to draw attention to the plight of the children who were living in such difficult circumstances. But first we had to get the tapes out of the country, and this proved more difficult than we had expected.

The Indian authorities are very sensitive to bad publicity and Paul, the producer, and I had worked on the illegal trade in organs in India, so we were on their radar. The Secret Police had become aware that we were filming in the country again. They are a little clunky in their approach to surveillance and we soon realised that we were being followed. It looked like they were after the tapes containing the care home footage, so we ducked out of our hotel early and made a quick getaway. We made it to the airport and checked in together. I checked in all the equipment but I kept the tapes on my person.

Paul had to make some calls, so I said: 'Why don't I go through Customs now, just in case, and you follow when you're done.' He agreed and I went through without any hassle. An hour later there was still no sign of Paul. At this point I noticed a middle-aged man in a shirt and very dark glasses scanning the departure lounge in a very obvious manner. I realised that Paul must have been pulled in and that now they were looking for me.

I couldn't ring Paul, because if he had been arrested I couldn't risk being connected to him. My spymaster friend in the airport lounge might have been a slightly comical sight, but if he pulled me in, he would confiscate the tapes and the evidence would be wiped.

Customs officials arrived on the scene and there were conspiratorial whispers between them and the BA staff at the gate. The only thing going in my favour was that the plane was full and on time and my bags were already in the hold. If they wanted me off the plane they would have to sort through the luggage and that would cost BA their slot and lots of wedge, too. I was sure this would get me through.

But an announcement came over the Tannoy: 'Would a Mr MacIntyre please come to the BA desk immediately?'

I tried to stay cool and casual as I walked to the desk.

'Hello, sir. Did you check in alone?'

'Yes, I did.'

'Are all the bags your own?'

'Yes.'

'Did you check in with a colleague?'

'No, alone.'

'That's a bit odd, sir, because there is a gentleman with a booking reference one numeral different to yours?'

'Coincidence.'

'But both were purchased at the same office by the same travel agent.'

I was running out of wriggle room but I continued with my lies. Paul had clearly been arrested and before the cock had crowed, I had already denied him about five times.

'And all the bags are your own, sir?'

'Yes, they are,' I said.

I returned to my seat. The spymaster was watching my every move. The plane started to board and I could see the BA staff eyeing me closely, as though I was a terror suspect or a drugs smuggler. Eventually, my row was called and I showed my passport and boarding card and walked onto the plane. But I wasn't home and dry until we were in the air.

The most important thing was to get the tapes to London. I quickly made my way to my seat – in economy, naturally. I realised that I had to get rid of the tapes, so that even if they got me, they wouldn't get the footage. I quickly put them in a bag and wrote my address on it, and then, when no one was looking, placed the bag in a locker well away from my seat. Hopefully any argument would be with British Customs and not the Indian Secret Police.

Just as I sat down feeling a little relieved, a text came through from Paul saying that he had been detained and was not allowed to leave the country. He said he expected to be held for a couple of days. They were taking the investigation seriously.

I saw the empty baggage trucks drive away from the plane and it appeared that everything was ready for takeoff, when a steward tapped me on the shoulder from behind.

'Sir, are you Mr MacIntyre?' he asked.

'Yes,' I replied.

'Could you please take your belongings and follow me, sir, as quick as you can?'

'Yes, of course,' I said, heart sinking.

I grabbed my hand luggage and left the tapes behind, hoping that they were safe on their way to London. That would at least be some consolation as I wiled away the hours in an Indian prison, I thought. I dutifully followed the flight attendant through economy and into business class, where I saw that the plane door was still open, with security personnel standing just outside. I prepared to be handed over. As we approached the exit, the flight attendant said:

'I recognise you, sir.'

'Oh?' I said, not sure why that was relevant.

'Here on business?' he asked, raising his eyebrows.

'Something like that' I said,

Then, Just as we reached the exit, he stopped, turned to me and said, 'Sir, will this do?'

He was pointing to a business class seat.

'I think you will find it much more comfortable here.'

'Oh. Thank you very much,' I said.

It took a moment for it to dawn on me that I was not in fact going to be arrested and had instead been upgraded and would be flown home in the lap of luxury.

As I sipped champagne at 30,000 ft, Paul was in custody, being questioned about what we were doing in Kolkata. He was held for seven days and we have both been effectively banned from entering India again.

*****

Mother Teresa remains on the fast track to sainthood. Rarely has one individual so convinced public opinion of the righteousness of her cause. The few who dare to criticise her say that accelerated canonisation is her reward for financing the Catholic Church with huge sums of money that were supposedly raised to help the poor.

Following the broadcast of our documentary, the Missionaries of Charity responded by saying that they welcome constructive criticism. They maintained that the children we saw were tied for their own safety and for 'educational purposes'. Sr Nirmala even welcomed our film and said: 'Our hopes continue to be simply to provide [an] immediate and effective service to the poorest of the poor as long as they have no one to help them.' To me the Order wrote: 'May God bless you and your efforts to promote the dignity of human life, especially for those who are underprivileged.'

For too long Mother Teresa's Missionaries of Charity have been blessing critics rather than addressing the damning indictment of the serious failings of their care practices. They can no longer rely on the aura of holiness and infallibility that surrounded their founder and must be made subject to the same standards as any other organisation working in this sensitive and difficult area. I hope that the Indian authorities recognise this and put more energy into enforcing much-needed standards than into chasing down journalists who dare to cast doubt over the reputation of Blessed Mother Teresa of Calcutta. The only true miracle is that her deft construction of an image over a 50-year period has remained unchallenged in the court of public opinion.

9

The Iceman Cometh

If you are a target, it makes sense to keep moving. I had already moved house several times and was seriously contemplating moving countries. Simply put, people wanted to kill me, and there's nothing like having a price on your head to encourage a little light packing. It was the beginning of the new Millenium, and I was living in a safe house after receiving death threats from far-right groups and football hooligans, and other threats were hanging over me from undercover investigations into drug lords and gangland criminals. If something untoward happened to me, the Police would struggle to know where to start. I had recently dispensed with my bodyguards in an effort to return some sort of normality to my life, but this just left me continually looking over my shoulder. Few people had more reason to leave the country than I did, so an unexpected opportunity to travel the world was an offer too good to refuse. I figured my life insurers would be very pleased, too.

How would I like to be a guinea pig, the BBC asked me. The offer came in between my various undercover lives and would be a welcome break from pretending to be somebody I wasn't. For once I would be over ground and wombling free, and I would choose a cute guinea pig over a violent football thug any day.

'Blasted, roasted, soaked and frozen, you will pit your wits against the last truly wild force on earth. It will be an epic journey from the fastest winds to the hottest desert, from the arctic ice sheets to the biggest rain machine on the planet.' This was how they sold it to me. The mission, should I choose to accept it, was to travel the globe and experience the worst that the weather could throw at me. How could I refuse?

Wild Weather was to be a two-year odyssey from Pole to Pole, and would cover everything in between, from the ice crevices of the Alps, to the lunar landscapes of Hawaii. It was a BBC Science commission in association with the Discovery Channel, which meant that, for once, no expense would be spared. TV budgets are usually miniscule and I had to wonder why such an offer had suddenly come my way. Yes, I was briefly flavour of the month after the success of my series, *MacIntyre Undercover*, in 2000, but football hooligans were a world away from tornados and hurricanes. Best to say 'yes' quickly, I figured, and not ask too many questions, lest the bosses started to have doubts, too.

Inevitably, a long list of preferred talent had turned it down before it reached my desk: Palin was in the Sahara, Attenborough was off filming gorillas again and Ross Kemp was still in *Eastenders*. Robson Green was still singing and had yet to come out of the closet as a fisherman and nobody had heard of Michael McIntyre. On the wall of the executive producer's office was a letter written in elegant handwriting on heavy notepaper. It read:

> *Dear Will,*
>
> *I am sorry to report that, as wonderful a project as this is, I won't be able to afford the time in between being Bond. I wish you every success, and hearty good fortune to my super-sub. I am sure he will do fine, but not well enough that he will take my day job.*
>
> *Regards,*
>
> *Pierce [Brosnan]*

Who wouldn't be happy to feast on Bond's leftovers?

Growing up surrounded by the green fields of Kildare's Liffey Valley, my brothers and I dreamt of such adventures. As nippers we spent our days on the banks of the Anna Livia, around its weirs and the secret salmon pools we were convinced we were the first to discover. We built forts out of bullrushes and ferns in the grounds of Castletown House and spent whole summers exploring the Kildare countryside, making mischief with impunity. Now I was being offered the opportunity to do it as an adult and the world was to become my backyard. Happy days – and not a hitman in sight!

*****

For the first marvellous chapter, I was going to spend nearly three months in the Arctic. I was to be tested to the limit, pushed beyond normal human endeavour. I would hunt polar bears with huskies, brave the ice storms of North America, climb the treacherous glaciers of the French Alps and dive under the icebergs of the North Pole. What I had not counted on before opening the fridge door to my arctic adventure was being thrown into a deep freeze and having my bits lost to frostbite before I even left the comfort of London!

I was brought to a cold store in London's Covent Garden Market where my body was to be medically tested for its ability to endure the worst of the arctic winter. And of course, this being television, my humiliation would be filmed for posterity and public delectation.

This was John Maguire's idea (although he had a few co-conspirators back in the office). He was the unlikely director of the series, who I now saw was taking great pleasure in the sadism it allowed him to express. I say 'unlikely' because in a previous life he had lived in a monastery and had later spent time smuggling extradition papers for refugees across the Berlin Wall during the Cold War. John had been held to ransom in lawless Somalia, flown over the Great Rift Valley through electric storms and had stalled the odd fighter jet at 27,000 ft – all in the name of entertainment. Now that the Iron Curtain had come down, he had abandoned his humanitarian work and turned instead to abusing innocent journalists.

John had already put Jeremy Clarkson through his paces for *Top Gear*, filmed across Africa with Sir Bob Geldof – and I was his next victim. At 41 (going on 21) he had a thick shock of salt-and-pepper hair and a matching goatee. A snowboarding accident had left him with a steel plate and 14 screws in his hip. As a result he walked with a limp, so he was quite the picture of the evil 'Bond' villain as he welcomed me to my trial by icebox and tried unsuccessfully to suppress his glee at my predicament.

It was 4 a.m. on a January morning and I had just arrived outside Covent Garden Market. The weather was miserable and the car was being lashed with rain and whipped by howling winds. This really wasn't a good day to be frozen. Maguire and the crew had been there all night, rigging, lighting and preparing the set. We had to shoot through the night to avoid interfering with the daily running of the business. The approach to the freezer was a long dark corridor lined with hooks and meat rails, the detritus of a previous use. It was all a bit ominous. At the end of the corridor were heavy, overlapping black plastic doors, defined by the shafts of light that crept around their warped edges.

The crew were on the other side, busying themselves with the final preparations. They were all dressed in heavy winter coats and mountain boots to protect them from the cold. 'Hello Donal,' said Maguire, 'we're nearly ready. Can you strip off down to your underwear please?'

Bags of ice lined the inside of the room and there was no comfort to be taken from the concrete floor. My only defence against the cold was a pair of black boxer shorts. I was connected to a body monitor, which was measuring all my core body functions and relaying the readings to a computer outside. Cameras would relay my ever-increasing discomfort to the medical supervisor, Dr Frank Golden PhD. He is a world-renowned specialist on cold and how to survive it. The Cork born doctor and academic has spent his career in the British

Navy and he seemed to have a healthy distain for the ludicrous experiments that television inflicts upon its presenters. I was hoping that he would be the voice of sanity in this initiation ceremony of sorts, as I had already given up on Maguire.

The plan was to immerse my body in simulated arctic conditions. This meant temperatures of -18°C and below. Sensors were placed all over my body to determine my external temperature, while thermal imaging would indicate the temperature of my heart and other vital organs. With the latest technology, Dr Golden would be able to see how the cold affected my body and he could then determine whether I was resilient enough to endure the worst polar conditions.

With a loud thud, the freezer door slammed shut behind me. I was determined to remain in the cold store for as long as possible. I had caught wind that the film crew was taking bets on how long I could last and the big money was on 20 minutes. No one had bet on me overstaying the half-hour mark. So naturally I made that my goal.

Little happened for the first few minutes, but once the cold took grip I did begin to wonder what on earth I was doing in here while the doctor and Maguire sat outside drinking hot tea, occasionally glancing at the safety monitors. The clock ticked by; five minutes passed. I was now very cold but put on a brave face.'Oh, yes, I'm fine,' I replied over the intercom when they asked how I was. Maguire decided to help things along a little by turning on the cooler fans to simulate an arctic breeze. A few minutes later I began to shiver uncontrollably.

After 20 minutes at -18°C I felt like I had the flu. After 25 minutes it felt more like swine flu. I was suffering, but there was a little pleasure in knowing that no one would be getting rich at my expense. Just after the 25-minute mark, Dr Golden came in to examine me at close quarters, hindquarters included.

'Count down from one hundred in increments of seven please, Donal,' he said.

'One hundred, eh, ninety-three,' long pause, 'eighty-six?' I ventured.

It was a lucky guess. I had lost my ability to count. I was

shivering, blue all over and my bones were rattling. But according to the doctor, I was safe to continue for a while longer.

'Have you been circumcised?' he asked me as I stood there with my frozen hands clasped over my frozen manhood. I wondered exactly where this was leading. 'Because if you have , we should get you out right away,' he continued.

Being uncircumcised meant that I had a little more insulation on my most sensitive of extremities, which would afford me a further few minutes of icy pain.

The experiment continued apace as they turned up the fans to the max and introduced a blizzard-like wind-chill factor. The temperature dropped to -45°C. I suspected that this was less in the interest of acclimatisation for my impending trip and more for the amusement of Maguire and the crew. I was not yet a father and feared that after this experience I never would be.

The doc asked me a question through the intercom, but all I could manage by way of reply was a string of mispronounced expletives, as I was unable to control my jaw at this stage. 'Flock! Flecun hell!' was the best I could do. I could hear them laughing over the speaker as I was left to freeze my nuts off. I found out what hell will feel like the day it freezes over.

In the end we were all near collapse: the good doc and Maguire were doubled over with laughter and I was a shivering wreck, my legs barely holding me up. My immediate concerns were focused on the condition of my little fella. It had retreated so much in the freezer that my sex was indistinguishable from that of your average East German lady shot-putter. It looked like the cold had induced some kind of accelerated reverse puberty.

'For feck's sake!' I screamed, 'This isn't a joke!'

Unperturbed by my panic, Golden took out his laser gun, stuck it into my pants and shot me in the shooter. The 'laser' hit my penis and held its gaze on my meat-and-two-veg for longer than I felt comfortable with. Okay, it wasn't a laser gun – the instrument was in fact some kind of space-age thermometer. He took a reading and said: 'Your core temperature has dropped below safe levels, so we need to get you out of the cold store.' I didn't need the *Buck Rogers* technology to tell me that.

'Forget my core. What about my little fella?' I asked.

'There is a hint of early-onset frostbite, eh, eh, ahem,' he coughed, trying to disguise a snigger. 'A hot shower and a cup of tea should perk it up,' he assured me.

What little I could see of it was blue, so I wasn't convinced that I was home and dry. Nonetheless, I had completed just over 30 minutes and survived the training and immersion phase of my arctic odyssey. My initiation as a guinea pig was complete and I was declared healthy enough to embark on my *Wild Weather* adventure.

Apart from serving their primary purpose of proving me fit to have my bits frozen off, the tests reminded me that things were going to get tough for me on this assignment. And the tougher they got, the more Maguire was going to enjoy it.

When the script arrived, one of my lines jumped out at me. It read: 'I am about to be buried alive, frozen solid and plunged into the white heart of winter.' Suddenly filming undercover with football hooligans seemed like a day on the set of *Teletubbies.*

*****

A week or so later, Maguire called me up and asked: 'Can you skydive, Donal? We're planning to jump in a month or so.'

'Of course I can,' I said, lying through my teeth.

My first challenge was to jump out of a helicopter at 15,000 ft, fall through the air at 150 mph and land on an arctic ice cap – with the nearest hospital a thousand miles to the south. No problem. Maguire wanted this footage for the opening sequence of the show and I wasn't going to let on that falling out of the sky wasn't second nature to me. How hard could it be?

I went online and frantically searched for crash courses in jumping out of planes. While Maguire was organising a skydive as close to the North Pole as possible, my internet search threw up a one-day accelerated freefall skydiving course several climates and times zones away on the Florida coast. Well, there was no time to spare, so I jumped on a plane and by the weekend I was at a skydive school in DeLand, Florida, learning the basics of how to fall out of a plane.

'Relax! Relax harder!' the instructor bellowed at me as the plane reached jumping altitude before my first dive. Like any eternal optimist, I talked a great game until I had to actually do it. When the time came to jump, I gingerly stepped back into the cabin, only to be forcibly pushed out of the plane by two 6 ft-something instructors.

'Fuuuuuuuuuuuuuuuuuuuuuuuck,' I screamed, convinced I was on my way to a premature grave. A second later, though, I found myself mellowing into a marshmallow-like state. Everything went pleasantly fuzzy and I felt like I could fall through the air forever. The instructors were so chilled that they jumped in their shorts and they were surfing the thermals as comfortably as they undoubtedly surfed the waves on the nearby golden coastline. There wasn't a cloud in the sky, as I blissfully surveyed the landscape as if it were my own private kingdom. I was thinking: 'Hello birds, hello sky – look at me flying!' and the fast approaching ground didn't bother me in the slightest. I had completely forgotten that my single key task was to pull the chord to unfurl my parachute. They talk in the skydiving business about being 'sucked to the ground', meaning that you lose all sense of perspective and time during freefall. It is a very pleasant experience – until you hit the ground. This is what was happening to me. The problem was that I didn't register the fact. Thankfully, the instructor did, and he was forced to take matters into his own hands. 'Pull, pull,' his semaphore instructions indicated. I smiled and did nothing. As the ground came closer, he became agitated and dived towards me at over 120 mph, pulled my ripcord and dived out again. 'How strange. What was he up to?' I thought. My canopy opened and I was saved from my own squidgy synapses just in time.

Any fantasies about defying gravity had long evaporated by the time I found myself in a helicopter over the island of Spitsbergen in the Arctic Ocean a month later. The island is part of the Svalbard Archipelago and is the last outpost of civilisation before the North Pole. It was summer, so it was bright nearly 24 hours a day. Below me were thousands of square kilometres of ice, a few wandering polar bears, some reindeer and arctic foxes enjoying the midnight sun.

We were waiting for a weather window – a sustained period of clear sky that would allow the jump to go ahead. I was working the odds and the inclement weather was to be my great escape – I hoped. The meteorologists said that it was unlikely that we would be able to go ahead: the forecast was for low-lying cloud, which would prevent any parachuting. I was praying that they were right. Of course I kept those thoughts to myself. Outwardly I was upbeat and gung-ho, but weighing heavily on my mind was a recent sky diving incident in the Antarctic, in which three divers died 60 seconds after jumping from their Twin Otter aircraft. 'They did nothing stupid,' according to a report. 'The three chutes simply didn't open and the trio penetrated 3 ft deep into the Pole's hard-packed crust.'

And trust my luck, a weather window, the likes of which no one had seen in five months, opened up. In an almost biblical fashion, the clouds parted and brilliant sunshine suddenly illuminated the vast expanse of white ice below. Now I know Maguire is still a practising Catholic, but this was taking the biscuit! His God had intervened especially for my discomfort and within minutes I was standing on the cross rail of a helicopter hovering 15,000 ft above the North Pole, strapped to a stranger (this was made a condition of the jump following my private admission to John that I had forgotten to pull my ripcord in Florida), ready to jump.

'Have I lived?' I asked myself. 'If I die now, can I truly say I have lived a life without limits?' My musings lasted all of two seconds because before I knew it I was falling through the air at the speed of a Formula 1 car. If I was going to die, this was as good time as any. And if I did hit the icy carpet below before my parachute opened, I comforted myself with the knowledge that I wouldn't have to live with my decision in any case.

In the end I landed safely. At that moment the aerial crew and I were high on adrenaline, fear and cold. There were high fives all round. 'Wooohooo, did you see that?' I said to the ground crew as Maguire reviewed the rushes from the jump. He wasn't happy.

'Donal, you didn't do the piece-to-camera we discussed last

night. Dude, it's no good just smiling at the camera! I need your lips to move,' he said.

In the excitement I had forgotten that I even had any lines. Maguire wanted another take, and another and another. In fact I ended up jumping out of that plane five times. I thought this was pushing my luck a little. I have never been so happy to see the sky cloud over as I was that day.

In John Maguire's perfectionism lay my misery. After three jumps, the camera crew felt that enough was enough but then they hadn't spent years in a monastery, like Maguire. He had his vision and it was our tough luck that we were part of it.

Five jumps later, it was over. I decided I would never parachute again. The sport has given me more beginner's luck than anyone is entitled to, so I decided to call it quits then and there.

* * * * *

After that I remained firmly grounded at sea level. If anybody was going to keep my feet firmly on the ground it would be the citizens of Ittoqqortoormiit, a tiny, remote Eskimo settlement in Eastern Greenland. The people here were going to show me how they managed to survive in such difficult conditions. Historically, the town had been home to a large Inuit population, but over generations it declined until the Danish helped to resettle the municipality with 80 Inuit people in 1925. Since then the population has grown to just under 500.

The people here are now caught halfway between their ancient ways and the modern world, and alcoholism has become a huge problem in this cold climate. The Inuit parliament banned alcohol from the territory in an effort to protect the community from itself. Alcohol, however, was defined as anything over four per cent proof, so now it just takes the locals longer to get drunk.

The people are, in essence, nomads locked in a sedentary lifestyle. At the time, my own life was so nomadic that I often craved the routine and stability that they were so uncomfortable with. It is a stunningly beautiful place, and away from the death threats and bodyguards of London, I felt myself truly relax for the first time in years. At the end of the earth I had finally found a place where I didn't feel the need to continually look over my shoulder.

The men of Ittoqqortoormiit feel most at peace when hunting for seals or polar bears. From Russia to Norway through to Northern Alaska, the polar bear is a protected species, but here the Inuit are allowed to hunt the beautiful beasts from their sleds pulled by the traditional huskies, and armed with their choice of modern rifles.

Ole Brolund, one of the elders in this tiny outpost, took me out to hunt with him. After travelling 5 km out of the town on the sled, we stopped to survey the scene. For hundreds of kilometres in front of us there was a flat sea of ice. The occasional iceberg punctuated the horizon, creating a scene of breathtaking beauty. While I admired the vista, Ole was on the look out for polar bears. His moustache was already encrusted with ice, but he showed no sign of suffering from the cold. I was wearing four layers of thermal clothing, a balaclava and gloves with a chemical heat pack, and I was still struggling to get my words out through my chattering teeth. Ole, much to my disappointment, was dressed in a blue Northface-style jacket; they reserve the traditional sealskin and fur garb for tourist brochures.

As we glided further out onto the vast expanse of whiteness, another sled passed us, heading in the opposite direction, carrying the carcass of a large male bear. The beast's yellow teeth stood out sharply against the pristine snow. I couldn't help feeling sad at the sight: the great animals seem such easy targets in the vast open expanses. But I'm not in a position to judge the traditional ways of an ancient people.

In a bid to strengthen diplomatic links between Ireland and Ittoqqortoormiit, I politely commented on how well-behaved Ole's dogs were. I was lying. They were in fact savage, snarling creatures that had snapped at me whenever I got too close. I think he knew I was fibbing and, after giving it some thought, he turned to me and said: 'I often watch that programme on the Discovery Channel, *One Man and his Dog*, and I really wish that my dogs were as well-behaved as that.' You know the world is getting smaller when you can share cultural references with an arctic hunter.

When we arrived back in the town, thankfully empty-handed, I noticed a potted cactus in the window of the yellow-painted wooden building that was home to Ole and his family. The cactus looked as out of place here as I did, but it was thriving – and I was loving every minute of my icy adventure. In fact I was beginning to feel very much at home here, and, as we left, I promised myself that I would return soon.

On the way home, we had a stopover in Iceland and decided to make a weekend of it. Before the country went bust, it was a great place to party, and we partied hard, quickly making up for the absence of hard liquor in Greenland!

*****

Back in London, the editors started to sort through the footage, only to find that some of the rushes had been spoiled. This series was being shot on film, which can be vulnerable to very low temperatures. We couldn't do the series without including the Arctic, so we would have to go back and film some new sequences. Well, it was the best bad news I ever got in broadcasting.

But first we had to get there, and there is no way over the thousands of square miles of ice other than by air. We flew into Mestersvig army base, 1,600 km inside the Arctic Circle, on the eastern coast of Greenland. The tiny Cessna plane was struggling under the weight of our filming gear and the kilos of warm clothes we had packed. The runway was a hundred-metre-long strip of flattened snow. At the end of the strip, an ice-covered cliff rose up out of the ground towards the sky. There was little room for error.

I am not a nervous flyer but this was testing. We rocked and rolled like a carnival ride as we descended onto the runway. The pilot, an American, took great pleasure in telling us about the many aircraft that have come to a tragic end in this neck of the woods. Now I like a storyteller as much as the next guy, but I felt he should be concentrating on getting us down in one piece. After two loud thumps and a few panicky 'Oh my Gods' , we came to a sudden stop just a few metres from the cliff face.

This is one of the most remote parts of the world. Satellite phone is the only means of communication and the Danish Navy drops off supplies once a year. The place is so remote that the local population of 40 people produces their own stamps.

I was greeted by Commander Palle Norrit, a Danish naval officer, who sported a fine bushy beard and was built like a Viking. He was in charge of the Serius Sledge Patrol, the navy unit that enforces Danish sovereignty in Northern and Eastern Greenland.

Palle introduced us to Maks and Erik, two Danish elite soldiers who were in charge of the over-laden sled pulled by 13 specially-bred huskies. It was a remarkable sight to see these dogs acting under military orders. They nearly barked to attention, so obedient were they to their young masters. Ole Brolund's dogs could have learned a thing or two from them!

Since Viking days, when the Danes first landed here, Denmark has had a stake in Greenland, but it was in 1933 that the International Court of Arbitration in The Hague granted it full sovereignty, and dismissed Norway's claim over the region. Flying the military flag in this extraordinary territory since then is the Danes' elite Arctic unit, based here in Eastern Greenland. The unit grew out of a group of volunteers that first used the sled dogs to patrol the area during World War II to protect it from the Germans. They used the dogs to locate the few weather bases that the Germans managed to build in the region in the early 1940s. Their success in destroying these bases and fronting down the German threat gave the unit its reputation for stoic tenacity that it retains to this day.

In the last 60 years, the dog teams have travelled nearly one million kilometres, mapping this wondrous landscape, which is more than 50 times the size of Denmark itself.

For four months in spring and two months in autumn, six

sled teams, each consisting of two men and eleven dogs, patrol Northern and Eastern Greenland for the Danish Admiralty. Only 14 men are in service at any one time. The dogs are kept for five years or 5,000 km, whichever comes first. On their final journey, they are taken on board the sled as a tribute to their endeavours. And then they are shot. My sensibilities didn't warm to that. But this region is still about survival, and sentimentality doesn't get you very far.

I spent the next day sledding with Maks and Erik, travelling as Amundsen and the great explorers had under the power of the dogs, surveying the stunning landscape and the animals that have evolved to cope with this harsh environment better than man can ever hope to. In the evening, the Northern Lights danced across the sky for us, sparkling a deep green and taking on the perfect shape of a seahorse. I watched, mesmerized, sinking and slipping on the snow until I gave up and lay flat on my back for 10 minutes, allowing myself to be dazzled by nature's greatest show. Eventually, the wispy green apparition faded peacefully away. Later, we were treated to another light show as the moonlight threw a pink hue on the glossy white landscape, making it glow and shimmer. It was an almost spiritual experience.

Still a little drunk on the Northern Lights and the bottle of red wine I had shared with the irrepressible Commander Norrit, it was time for me to retire for the night and rest my frozen bones. But I wouldn't have the comfort of an army cot – I was going to spend the night in a snowhole. This sounded like one of John Maguire's ideas. A snowhole is exactly what its name suggests. You dig a -30°C hole out of a snowdrift; you then jump into the hole and plug the opening with more snow. This becomes your ice hotel for the night. It doesn't sound too cosy, but it makes for life-saving shelter in these conditions. This kind of survival technique is a basic skill for the soldiers here and I was going to get a taste of it.

It was 10 p.m. and a bitterly cold wind was cutting across the tundra at 48 km/h as I was deposited in my icy home for the night. The only sounds were the howl of the dogs and the muffled whoosh of the arctic breeze on drifting snow. The hole was tiny: maybe a foot taller than me and with just about enough room to turn around if I needed to. After about an hour, it seemed to warm up significantly as my body heated the air around me and the warm air was trapped in the sealed environment. Going to the toilet was a problem – if I left the hole, the air inside would freeze again and I would be back to square one. Also, any skin exposed to the freezing temperatures outside would be at serious risk of frostbite and I didn't want a repeat of the cold store episode. I decided to hold on until morning. I did manage to get some sleep that night, and while it wasn't exactly five-star accommodation, it was a world away from the deadly conditions just a few feet from me.

The next morning as we sped back towards the base, I noticed one of the dogs in the middle of the pack veer left, off the track. His body turned but the momentum of the pack kept him in line. He had spotted an arctic hare sitting tall about 50 metres off the track. Soon the others caught the scent and veered off too in the direction of the snow-white hare. It was discernable only by its dark eyes. As thirteen howling dogs hurtled towards it, it didn't even flinch. It knew that more than any creature, it was perfectly adapted to this environment. It was confident that it had time to outsmart any pack of dogs, and certainly an Irishman who had adapted to no climate except one where there was central heating and a good pub nearby. I hoped that this was something I could take home with me to London: I wanted to learn to live as calmly with the threat of extinction as this little hare did.

*****

At the start of this adventure, I had thought that it would be a huge departure, but in the end it presented me with the same isolation, exposure, vulnerability and danger as my undercover work had done. On this odyssey, however, the dangers were marvels of nature. Hurricanes, blizzards and sub-zero temperatures were undoubtedly more intoxicating and enthralling threats than any hitman or gangster, and, in the end, they also proved easier for me to deal with. Let's face it, no bodyguard or surveillance team can protect you from the power of nature. As I returned home, having survived some of the wildest and harshest conditions the planet could offer, I had gained a new confidence that I could deal with the worst that man could fling at me.

10

Gorilla Warfare

In 2003 I was lucky to follow in the footsteps of David Attenborough on an African adventure that would leave me drunk in a brothel, with only a bible and a gun for company. Well, maybe I added a few footsteps of my own to Sir David's, but we did walk the same ground and meet some very similar and very special characters.

In 1979 Attenborough went to the Virungas, a chain of volcanic mountains, which links the Congo, Rwanda and Uganda. There, on Mt Karisimbi, he met some of the last surviving mountain gorillas. He looked into the eyes of these stunning animals and gained their trust, so much so that they examined him for fleas and allowed him to reciprocate the intimate act of grooming. 'There is more meaning and mutual understanding in exchanging a glance with a gorilla than with any other animal I know,' he whispered to the camera, deeply moved by the significance of the moment. It was a beautiful meeting of minds between one great man of the natural world and a true gentleman of the forest.

Nearly a quarter of a century later, after the horror of the Rwandan genocide and the ongoing civil war in the region, these gorillas were closer than ever to extinction. Their situation was exacerbated even further by the dramatic rise in poaching. Poachers were targeting the gorillas and selling them to unscrupulous collectors, who would remove them from their natural habitat for the amusement of others.

A two-year-old gorilla, a direct descendant of the young male that David Attenborough had locked gazes with in 1979, had been stolen from her mother and sold on the illicit international market, and the BBC had drafted me in to conduct an investigation into her disappearance. The young gorilla had been nicknamed Baby Bibisi (BBC) by the local wildlife officers, in recognition of the corporation's conservation efforts over the years. Baby Bibisi's mother, 11-year-old Impanga, who had lost a hand and a foot in previous encounters with snares, had been killed. Another female, 25-year-old Muraha, was also found dead at the scene of the kidnap. She had been nurtured and named by Dian Fossey and had actually appeared in the film, *Gorillas in the Mist*. Ubuzima, Muraha's 13-month-old baby was found alive, still clinging to her mother's breast, desperately trying to suckle. It appeared that one of the silverbacks (dominant breeding males), Munyina, had attempted to interrupt the kidnap and massacre and had been badly wounded. He was being monitored by local wildlife vets dedicated to the group. Ubuzima was plucked from her dead mother's breast by a blackback (sexually mature male) and brought back into the bosom of the remaining family. In the days after the massacre, the extended gorilla family appeared to grieve the deaths and the loss of Baby BiBisi.

Before I buried myself in the investigation, I had the opportunity to get up close and personal with the same family of gorillas that had fascinated David Attenborough. Each group of gorillas is protected by a large male, the silverback, that weighs about three times my weight. If a silverback takes umbrage, he'll bark at you, I was warned, and I would do well to back off.

It is a 12,500 ft trek up the Virunga Mountains to where the family of mountain gorillas has made their home. Every spare metre of land is harnessed. On the floor is a carpet of daisies, which were introduced here as a cash crop and are used in the production of natural insecticides. Originating in China and traded along the silk route, the pyrethrum daisy plant was used to relieve the itches of civilisations and later to delouse Napoleon's army. Today, they thrive here in the rich volcanic soil, in between Irish potato plants that are specially bred to grow at these altitudes, 7,000 km from home.

I was accompanied by armed wildlife officers to protect me, not just from poachers but also from armed rebels and warlords. The poachers were not far away. They were armed and dangerous, and I was only slightly comforted by the fact that the wildlife officers were also carrying guns. We came across snares, deliberately placed to trap and maim these rare creatures. Many have been mutilated and killed by such snares. They are designed to kill, so that the carcasses can be used in the bushmeat trade. Bushmeat has long been a staple in the diets of forest-dwelling people, but today it is illegal and threatens the survival of many local species. Often, the captured animal will tug for hours, trying to escape the snare. The coil winds tighter and tighter until it locks and begins to slowly kill, as gangrene and septicemia set in.

When we reached 12,500 ft, our guide began his vocalizations to call the gorillas. They have 25 recognisable calls, and the guide produced a guttural coughing sound as if he had TB. It had the desired effect and we soon found ourselves in the company of a group of males. I was captivated by my first glimpse of these extraordinary animals through the tall grass and bamboo. Times have changed since Attenborough's close encounter and we had to keep our distance to just outside seven metres from the gorillas, to reduce the risk of passing on a human disease against which they have no immunity.

They swept around us, curious and wary in equal measure. 'Magnificent. This has got to be one of the most magical sights the jungle has to offer. And in this special moment you just can't help but feel devastated that two members of this small family have been killed, and one is missing. I can't understand why anyone would want to do any harm to these beautiful creatures,' I said to the camera. I caught one silverback giving me a thousand-yard marine stare. He was not happy. It is hardly surprising that there is a degree of mistrust: their only enemies are snares, guns and the humans who use them.

It was clear to the most casual of observer that this was a close-knit family that interacted almost as our own do. Today, the Sousa family population has steadied at around 50, but they remain under constant threat. Nestling close to the silverback, Waninya, we spoted the soft-furred baby, Ubuzina, who had been found suckling on her dead mother's teat. There had been contradictory reports that she had gone missing after the traumatic events, but thankfully she seemed in sound health. Second to the birth of my children this wass the most moving encounter of my life. It was my inspiration and what drove me to help try to eradicate this terrible trade. 'Don't worry; we will get your little cousin back for you,' I said.

*****

There are just over 700 mountain gorillas left on the planet, so even a single death or capture has a devastating effect on the population. The UN tries to control the trade in endangered species but they are fighting a losing battle. Perhaps the most shocking evidence of this was the apparent involvement of a reputable zoo in this illegal trade.

My investigation brought me to Malaysia, where we knew that Taiping Zoo had paid $200,000 for four beautiful lowland gorillas from the Cameroon. Middlemen had been used to hide the fact that they had been taken from the wild and not bred in captivity.

They had bought the apes from traders who claimed to have obtained them from a zoo in Nigeria. Both the Malaysians and the middlemen were claiming that the baby gorillas were recently born in captivity at the Nigerian zoo. A cursory investigation revealed that the only male there was embalmed and that the last female had died several years previously. Given these circumstances, it would have been something of a miracle if the four had been born from this pair.

The zoo in Taiping should have known that the trade was dubious.

This was a well-respected, government-run zoo, but they focused on displaying trophy animals and their acquisition of the gorillas was born out of a desire for high-profile attractions that would generate profit and prestige. The zoo claimed to have had the correct paperwork and the Malaysian government confirmed this. But it was obvious to us that something was fishy and that most people involved in the deal either knew it or should have known it.

We had made enquiries and knew that the zoo had the four gorillas on the premises. They continued to deny that they had been poached but refused to give us access to film so that we could identify them. They had built a $600,000 enclosure for the creatures for public viewing, but this was now effectively obsolete and the gorillas were kept hidden away.

We had managed to get hold of the paperwork from the illegal deal and we were turning up the heat. But we still needed pictures to prove that the animals were actually on the premises. Gorillas are easily identifiable by their very distinctive nose prints. The folds of skin that produce the y-shaped stalk rising above the nostrils make each gorilla very recognisable, once your eye gets used to the different shapes.

So this is why I found myself scaling the wall of the gorilla enclosure of a Malaysian zoo with a mad Australian cameraman called Jay Hanrahan, who later won awards for his work on this film. He was a gung-ho Aussie who was used to filming in warzones around the world and was the ideal companion for a bit of illegal trespass. Even for a hardened news investigator, though, this zoo incursion was outside my comfort zone. At the time the BBC had tightened up their health and safety practices. A colleague had recently had a paramedic and a first aider forced on him as he performed the perilous task of changing the wheel of a car. There was no mention of breaking into zoos in the health and safety manual, but we decided to keep the escapade to ourselves all the same. High walls, armed guards and four startled wild gorillas were all likely to ring alarm bells with the 'elf and safety' powers that be in the UK, who had recently banned a clown from the Russian State Circus from wearing his outsized shoes, which they said had constituted a tripping hazard.

While we were preparing the guerilla style assault on the

gorilla enclosure, the zoo was celebrating the start of its annual festival. We thought that we could sneak in unnoticed while the great and the good of the local political establishment were getting a hospitality and photo-op payback for their generosity. I suspected that the security would be diverted towards protecting the local dignitaries and that this would present us with our opportunity.

'There is a tree stump we can use to get over, but it might be very difficult to get out again. We'll have to improvise,' I said to Jay.

'Sure. No worries, mate,' Jay replied, unfazed by the situation.

'You could get mauled and torn apart by them and then shot by the zoo keepers,' I said.

'I could outrun you a thousand times. And there's enough meat on your bones to keep them busy while I escape.'

I liked his style and I had to admit that the tall, athletic Aussie had the advantage if it came down to a quick escape. I comforted myself with the fact that gorillas are herbivores, but they are still capable of tearing a man limb-from-limb if the notion takes them. Their upper-body strength is six times that of an adult human.

The enclosure was desolate and boarded up: a strange home for the animals who were supposed to be one of the zoo's main attractions. I scrambled over the wall, with Jay close behind me. Our getaway vehicle, an old Transit van, was tucked away around the corner, ready for a speedy departure – if it actually started.

I landed on the dusty terrain first. After helping Jay down with his camera, I quickly surveyed the scene. In the corner of the compound I spotted one gorilla behind a wall. I circled the area and then saw the other three. They looked forlorn in this tired backyard enclosure. This was a world away from the lush green habitat they had been snatched from. Then, in my peripheral vision, I saw a zoo-keeper appear from behind a shed. He clocked me and was obviously startled. At first he was too shocked to think or say anything. Jay continued filming the animals, aware that the priority was to get the evidence. I opened my hands wide, palms up in an effort to demonstrate that we posed no threat. Many Malayasians speak English and it is often the language of authority, so I decided to pretend that I had more right to be there than him. I knew the stages he would go through: stage one is surprise, two is bewilderment and three is panic. Once panic set in, I knew that all hell would break loose. He would be thinking: 'I must get help with this situation', and would go from processing the information to shouting 'Help!' and attracting unwanted attention that could land us in jail. In my head I was treating it as a pantomime and I was just waiting to hear someone shout, 'He's behind you!' This was my way of postponing my own panic and holding my head together.

As I walked towards him, he still hadn't moved from surprise to bewilderment. My hand was extended. 'Hello. We are with the BBC,' I said, in a tone that suggested we might be filming for *Blue Peter*. I acted as if I was greeting him in a hotel lobby. As he moved into the bewilderment stage, he actually shook my hand. 'Hi. I'm Donal MacIntyre; how are you doing?' I went on. Then panic slowly set in: I could see it in his eyes. His hand went limp and slipped out of mine, and then the screaming started. 'I think it's time to go,' I said to Jay, beginning to panic myself. He was standing on a wall, getting as many shots as possible before we were forced to make our getaway. 'Jay, just jump,' I shouted, as the zoo-keeper's screams got louder.

I grabbed Jay's khaki shirt and dragged him back to where we had come over the wall. We used a rock and a tree to perch on and managed to get over the wall before reinforcements arrived. We hit the ground running, laughing like nine-year-olds who had just robbed an orchard. We jumped into the van and sped off. 'Keep your head down,' the driver shouted to us. Just like in the movies, the Police cars raced past us on the other side of the road, oblivious to the culprits making their escape. We were safe and we had the pictures. After the investigation was made public, and on foot of our evidence, the zoo was forced to return the gorillas to South Africa. They continue to deny that they knew it was an illegal trade, a denial that has been treated with some scepticism by wildlife organisations.

*****

A while later, we returned to the area of Baby Bibisi's kidnap in the Virunga Mountains, but this time we were travelling across the border to the Democratic Republic of Congo (DRC), an even more lawless and dangerous place than its neighbour, Rwanda. The DRC has an active market in orphaned baby gorillas, so we came here to search for Baby Bibisi.

The border was heavily guarded by the military on both sides, and customs personnel turned our vechicles inside out to make sure we weren't smuggling any contraband.

This was Goma. If genocide and civil war were not enough for the people to cope with, the city had recently been decimated by a volcanic eruption and there was a tent city growing up around the grass-thatched huts that the permanent residents lived in.

We hadn't travelled far across the border when we received intelligence that Baby Bibisi could be about 100 km away, deep in the middle of a warzone. The area was off-limits to foreigners but I persuaded some wildlife officers to take me in search of the little creature. Looking back on it now, I must have been mad. My head was saying: 'Stop, stop; snap out of it.' Then we heard from a Police source that a trader wanted to do business and sell a baby gorilla for big bucks. My mind was made up. I decided to pose as a foreign buyer and we drove into the unknown, on dirt roads carved out of the jungle. As foolhardy escapades go, this one would take some beating.

Of course, there was a problem. Our guide was a man called Modest, who we had met in Goma. He was a local who knew the criminals, and we had been advised that he would get us close to them and to the information we needed to get to Baby Bibisi. The problem was that we didn't know if he could be trusted. He could have been setting us up and even if he wasn't, life is cheap in this part of the world, so we could easily end up dead on the whim of some warlord who didn't like the look of us. It is no secret that neither foreigners nor wildlife officers are very welcome in the area. Over 190 Virunga park rangers have been killed in the line of duty in recent years. The perpetrators are believed to be members of the militia acting to protect their revenue from bushmeat and other illegal trades.

I was accompanied by Joseph, a Rwandan wildlife officer, who was steady and calm. At 44 years of age, he was already ten years beyond the average life expectancy for a man in the region. In these parts you need an old dog for the long road. I was grateful for Joseph's experience and knew that he could be relied upon for wise counsel.

We found ourselves driving on what is known as an AIDS highway: a connecting road that runs through the heart of Africa and carries trucks the length of the continent. Roads like these provide contact points for drivers and prostitutes and have helped to accelerate the spread of HIV in this corner of the world, where urban antenatal clinics have found that up to 33 per cent of women are infected.

We stopped at a little bar about 60 km from Goma, and waited while Modest drove deep into the jungle to make contact with the seller. We waited and we waited and then, after hours of waiting, we got worried. Modest had gone off in the jeep and we were holed up in this tiny hovel feeling very vulnerable.

I decided to call the team on the satellite phone. We were having problems but I figured they must have been getting worried, too.

I managed to make contact with the producer, who was in a hotel near Lake Kivu. Just as I began to tell him what was happening, my attention was diverted by the reappearance of our jeep. Any relief that I felt was soon quashed by the fact that it was surrounded by armed men and had an angry-looking soldier type sitting in the driver's seat. In any part of the world, this would have been a cause for concern, but here it was a reason to panic.

'What's a soldier doing in our jeep?' I asked Joseph, who was looking very worried at this point.

'The warlord wants to take you to his boss in the region, but I don't know for what reason,' he said, roughly translating.

'Oh dear. Are we being taken on a wild goose chase?'

When I suggested that we refuse to go with them, I was told in no uncertain terms that this was a kidnap and we had better do as we were told or else we wouldn't be doing anything else ever again. Not a wild goose chase then. Message received and understood.

We were bundled into a jeep and kept under the watchful eye of a rag-tag bunch of armed soldiers. I tried to phone my BBC team but there was no signal and the satellite phone was losing power. Things were not looking good. I remember thinking: 'Ok, if this be the time, well so be it.' We were driven at high speed along jungle tracks deeper and deeper into the DRC. We had no idea who had kidnapped us or where we were being taken. It seemed that our friend Modest had set us up. He had disappeared with some of our money and we were now in the hands of warlords – it was difficult not to link him directly to our predicament.

The Rwandan government have notional control of this part of the Congo but the truth is that layers of warlords and rebel leaders are in charge of this volatile region. I was aware of this but put it to the back of my mind and tried to stay positive.

We arrived at a kind of jungle clearing and were kept sitting on the ground in the open. We weren't beaten or threatened, but then we didn't need to be. They could kill us at any moment without consequence, and there was nowhere to run to, even if we chose such a ridiculous course of action. Joseph was translating for me and said that the gunmen were talking about the baby gorilla they were trying to sell. 'They know we have money and everyone in the region is talking about it and us,' he said. The timing of the availability of the animal for sale indicated that it was most likely Baby Bibisi.

I got a call from London on the satellite phone.

'How are you?' the breezy voice asked from the comfort of the BBC White City office.

'Well, I've been better,' I said, with a little understatement. 'I don't want to alarm you, but could you give the producer a shout in Goma and tell him that I'm fine but I'm not, so to speak. I've been kidnapped. Ask him to make some calls to the

Rwandan generals in charge here to see if they can threaten or cajole our release.'

Then the line went dead.

We waited for hours in the clearing. Then we waited some more, before finally getting our instructions – to continue waiting. The frustration was mounting, but there's only so much you can take out on a group of armed rebel soldiers, so we kept it to ourselves.

There was silence for a long time and then a phone rang nearby. There were raised voices. It appeared that the warlord who had kidnapped us was getting a roasting from a more senior warlord. Things could go either way. He could react badly and kick off with us or he could be submissive and do as he was told. The phone call ended and there was silence for 30 minutes. It was a long 30 minutes.

Then Joseph and I were taken aside by two of the soldiers. They took out two AK-47s and loaded them in front of us. I honestly thought that this was the end. The guns would be unloaded into us and our bodies would never be found and that would be the end of it. But things got even more surreal as we were handed a gun each and told to get into the kidnappers' jeep. They then drove us to a motel.

And that was that – we were officially unkidnapped! The warlord had been told that I was not worth the bother and that the Rwandans would be very displeased if anything happened to Joseph and me. So we were free but we were not yet safe.

Although we were just two hours from the comparative safety of Goma, it was now dark and the road was not safe to travel, not for warlords and certainly not for us.

The motel was a filthy but friendly place: too friendly, perhaps. It was what is known locally as an 'AIDS motel' and there were over 50 prostitutes peddling their wares on the premises. Robbers, bandits, killers, girls and us: we were quite a merry band of guests. I figured that we were at greater risk from the food than from the guns, so we ordered a strong local whiskey to line our stomachs.

So, there I was in a Congolese motel room, drunk on local

hooch, with an AK-47 in my lap, a Gideon's Bible in my hand and prostitutes banging on my door. For the first time in my life, there was a queue of women looking to see me. 'Bonjour, Mr Donal. Muzungo, muzungo, you want lady?' The knocks kept coming, despite my polite refusals of the offers of female company.

I remember playing with the gun, entranced by the shiny metallic killing machine and the power to go postal. I read from the Bible as if it were a John Grisham novel, so I must have been really drunk at this point. Outside, gunfire crackled in the air. I didn't know if it was the sound of celebrations or executions, but we had been told that Russian roulette was played at the hotel for sport.

When we returned to Goma, I handed my gun and my stolen Bible over to Joseph. I was upset that we hadn't found Baby Bibisi after everything we had been through. But my mood was lifted when news filtered through that a tiny baby gorilla had been found hidden in a cave in a bamboo forest. It sounded promising. Like our missing infant, it was a female and about two years old, so we were praying that it was her. Whether it turned out to be our lost gorilla or not, it would still be something for all to celebrate. It was a miracle that she had been found. She had been taken off the mountain and was in the hands of the specialist animal ER team at the Karisoke Research Centre, which was established by Dian Fossey over 25 years earlier.

I made my way to the research station and found the baby gorilla healthy and doing well in the care of these great professionals. The camera crew were nearly moved to tears at the sight of the only infant mountain gorilla in captivity in the world. No mountain gorilla has ever survived for long in captivity. Naturally, the vets wanted to reintroduce her to her family, but there was a danger that she could have picked up human germs from the contact she had with her kidnappers. The DNA tests were run and sent to London for verification. Meanwhile, the vets set about repairing her health. Sadly, the DNA results came back negative and so the fate of Baby Bibisi is still unknown.

The new infant was placed back into the group and remains healthy to this day. I am told that there is little likelihood that Baby Bibisi has survived. But the search for her has gone some way to raising awareness about the desperate need to protect the surviving mountain gorillas in this turbulent part of the world, and that is at least some consolation.

* * * * * *

Our investigation brought attention to the plight of this endangered species and mobilised others to do the same. It was exasperating that we could not do more to solve the problem and that simple solutions are not easy to hand. War and famine have made the protection of these animals difficult, but the people of Rwanda have now made the conservation of the mountain gorilla a national priority. Great strides have been taken towards making the Virunga Mountains a safer place for this endangered species.

Future generations should have the right to gaze into the eyes of these great apes and to experience the 'mutual understanding' that Sir David and I were able to enjoy. Five years after my trip to Africa, the charity, Born Free, asked me to help them draw attention to the plight of the mountain gorilla once again. So I found myself dancing on ice with gorilla-suited skaters on an ice rink in front of the London's Natural History Museum to help them spread the message that gorillas are skating on thin ice. I can't think of a better reason to make a fool of myself!

11

Comedy of Terrors

Befriending killers is part of my job. It's not necessarily something I enjoy, and on occasion it has left me feeling dirty. Over time their company often becomes more palatable and that has caused me to question my own morals and motives. However, if I am to reveal anything of these men, I have to get close to them, and I have to reconcile that with my own conscience, both as a journalist and as a man.

I first met with Johnny Adair, the notorious UDA leader and convicted killer, in a very expensive hotel in Glasgow in late 2005. He arrived on time but wouldn't enter the building without first sending in a security detail to clock me and to check for secret cameras.

This meeting followed lengthy correspondence with Johnny while he was in prison and also contact with his ex-wife, Gina. In fact this was a meeting that had been two years in the preparation.

The pocket rocket plastered with tattoos greeted me with a firm handshake. The then 42-year-old had a bouncy, Tigger-like presence that I thought was out of character with his track record. I wanted to film with him over a period of time so that we could capture the real Johnny and get past his PR defences. There would be no money changing hands, but we would be fair and let him have his say, and that's more than most of his victims had.

There was one problem: in another guise, as a football

hooligan, I had pretended to be a devout follower of Adair and his thugs in order to infiltrate the Chelsea Headhunters. Johnny wasn't that bothered about it, but Jason Marriner, the hooligan who I had used the ruse against, was not happy. He considered Adair to be a god, and had in turn gained his trust.

'I've run it by him [Marriner] and he said I shouldn't do it. The problem is that he looks after me and he is part of my followers. It's a problem. He thinks Johnny is a god,' the former terrorist told me, speaking about himself in the third person, much like the Queen and Margaret Thatcher.

While I was there, he phoned Jason and put him on loudspeaker. This was the first time I had heard his voice since the court case in Blackfriars when he was sentenced to six years in jail on foot of my evidence. Adair teased him on the phone:

'Jason, what do you think?'

'He is a grass. He is a Fenian c**t.'

Adair went along with Jason, but roared laughing afterwards. This was as telling a moment about the man as any I filmed with him. He ignored Marriner's advice and agreed to give me access to all areas.

At first Adair was nervous, never having allowed more than the occasional news crew to interview him. But once he understood that there were no covert cameras and that there was no hidden agenda, he engaged fully with me and the process. He allowed us witnesss his extraordinary lifestyle and revealed himself as a troubled terrorist leader struggling to come to terms with the loss of his army.

There is no doubting that the 'Mad Dog' moniker was hard earned: we know that detectives in Northern Ireland link Adair and his gang directly to over 40 sectarian murders (a number that he does not disagree with). Adair was born in 1963 into a working class Protestant family, and during the troubled seventies, his childhood was peppered with riots and sectarian clashes. His teens saw him start a Nazi hate-rock band called Offensive Weapon and he was later drafted into the Ulster Defence Association's (UDA) youth wing. By the early nineties Adair had taken over the leadership of the UDA's notorious 'C' Company, based on the Shankill Road. In 1995 he admitted that he had been a UDA commander and was jailed for 16 years for directing terrorism. In 2002, when he was 39 years old, he was freed from Maghaberry Prison under the Good Friday Agreement. Shortly afterwards, he was briefly returned to jail, but was finally released in 2005.

Now exiled from his Belfast home after a murderous feud with his own Loyalist paramilitary leaders, only Johnny Adair knows exactly how many bodies lie at his feet. He claims that those days are now behind him, and today he's living in Britain, looking for a new place to call home. I found him lying low in the Scottish town of Troon, constantly on the look out for ex-comrades bent on settling old scores. Although he is increasingly irrelevant to the politics of Northern Ireland, Adair is still being monitored by MI5, Strathclyde Police, the Police Service of Northern Ireland, Greater Manchester Police and the National Crime Squad.

These thoughts ran through my mind as I chatted with Johnny in a London pub at the start of the production. I knew a lot about him from books and research, but what I didn't know was that talking about sex and himself was a favourite pastime of his.

Mad Dog once showed me a text he'd received from an Irish girl: *Thx for making a wee Catholic girl very happy.* I suppose we should probably see it as part of the 'peace dividend'. He has been accused in the past of directing his sexual attentions towards his dogs, his male comrades and a litany of women. When he isn't sharing the details of his exploits with everyone else, he is busy sharing his sexual expeditions with his son, Jonathan (affectionately called Mad Pup), and is always happy to show you some recorded highlights on his mobile phone.

Apparently, Adair has recently found love with a glamour model. He has already posed for photographs with the lucky lady and he has declared his love publicly. Naturally, this was done in the third person. 'Johnny Adair has finally found love,' he announced recently in the papers. As openly as ever, but thankfully without the video evidence, Adair declared proudly: 'We have sex all the time: morning, noon and night. Look at the size of her mad puppies!' He is like a love-struck teenager boasting to the boys behind the bike sheds.

Adair is both infantile and deadly, like a child in a killer's body. He is keen to make you laugh, keen to intimidate, keen to befriend, but most of all he is keen to let you know that he is still a king in exile.

'I'm only marking time here. One day myself, my friends and family will return to our homeland. I want to go home to my native Ulster. It may take a month, a year, three years, but I'll be back,' he told me.

'Didn't Arnie patent that line? You can't have it!' I said to him, jokingly.

'Who's going to argue?' he said.

Fair point.

While Johnny plans his triumphant return to Northern Ireland, he is rumoured to be building a new empire under the watchful eye of notorious Glasgow gangster, Mark 'Scarface' Morrison.

'So, what do you do all day?' I asked him.

'Bits and pieces, erm, business interests. I'm kept very busy. Plus I do a wee bit of training.'

He spends his time in the gym building his biceps and casting admiring glances at his scar-ridden body and that of his son, who is also a body fascist. They have both used steroids to help nature along, and it shows.

Adair won't talk about his business interests. He says he survives on benefits and the goodwill of loyal friends. Such friends include major criminal figures in Scotland and the odd Lottery winner.

He claimed to be broke, but appeared always to have money. He claimed to yearn for his homeland, but also that he had never been happier. He claimed to be helping out a friend, but you couldn't help thinking he might have been helping only himself, when he travelled to Norfolk to meet Mickey Carroll, Lottery millionaire to the tune of £9.7 million. Their friendship had begun when Carroll wrote to Adair in prison.

Carroll's parties were legendary, often costing up to £30,000, and, by his own admission, replete with hookers and cocaine on tap.

'In one I had about 200 blokes and 100 women. Most of them call them orgies. It was unreal,' Carroll told Adair.

'How much [cash] did you have in one go?' Adair asked.

'Half a million pounds in cash,' Mickey replied.

'In one go, at your disposal? What would you be doing with that?' Johnny wanted to know.

'I just wanted to see it,' Carroll said.

At the time Carroll had a collection of antique military hardware, UDA flags and a throne in his attic, where he and Adair's boys would play when they got together. The fridge was always full of drink and there was always the sense that Adair had struck gold with his friendship with Carroll. Amid the free flowing-booze at the mansion, Adair anointed his adoring friend as the Brigadier of the Norfolk branch of the UDA.

'Any problem with that, Mickey?'

'No,' said Mickey, delighted.

I asked Johnny if he would be passing on his expertise to the new brigadier.

'No. Mickey will be passing his money on to the Loyalist prisoners,' he told me.

Carroll didn't come across as the sharpest tool in the box: he is a bit soft and is an easy pushover. The six-footer has a mop of black scruffy hair, an ample beer belly and a solid agricultural frame. Despite his size he clearly needs protection from predators after losing over £1 million to extortionists. In any event, when a man needs protection, he should be worried if it comes in the shape of Johnny Adair.

I couldn't help thinking that Mickey might be safer with someone else. I am sure the events are unconnected, but since he has met Adair, his fortune had dwindled to nothing. He has recently declared himself penniless, an extraordinary situation for a man, who until a short time ago had £9 million, to find himself in.

But there were even more disturbing friends to be found in the Nazi wing of Adair's fan club. There had been a long-standing invitation for Adair to visit Dresden to meet a curious group of followers who held him in high esteem. Thirty-year-old neo-Nazi, Nick Gregor, was residing at Hammerweg maximum-security prison after being convicted of bomb making. Gregor had a swastika tattooed over his ear, his head was shaved clean and he was lean and muscled like a frontline soldier. When he wasn't in his cell, he spent his time in the prison gym. He had declared that he and his soldiers were at Johnny's disposal.

I was with them when they met and it looked like the reunion of two lovers. It has been suggested that Adair had gay relationships in the Maze prison but he has always denied this, and I wasn't about to push the point in front of 'Nazi Nick' – that would have been asking for trouble.

The prison authorities seemed unaware that, by allowing Adair and the Nazi to meet, they were bringing very volatile forces together.

'I have all the posters of you in my cell. It looks like the UFF headquarters,' Nick began. 'I thought, "We need someone like Johnny over here to lead us," so we chose you to be our chief. My struggle is to protect you. Should someone shoot Johnny, we will send five guys over. We know where to find these guys [Adair's enemies]. Our guys are very well experienced in punish[ment] beating[s].'

Gregor himself is banned from entering the UK – however, his men are not.

While Nazi Nick languished in prison, Adair spent the night with his supporters, who put on a party for him in a small flat in the centre of Dresden. The guests were all neo-Nazi sympathisers and card-carrying members of the cult of Johnny Adair.

One fan, Christina, admitted to having a shrine to the fallen Loyalist leader in her home. 'I like him and his lifestyle. He's a great man,' she said. Christina doesn't stand out of the crowd, with her dowdy black hair and librarian looks that are a clue to her secretarial job. But she is at least extraordinary in her obsession. 'He smiles all the time and he is so funny,' she enthuses. As she speaks, candles flicker over photos of Adair in various states of paramilitary dress and undress. He is clearly not shy about showing off his honed pecs. Christina is devoted: 'The reason I have a shrine to him is to see him every day, to let him know that he has friends who will stand by him. He is simply Johnny and is simply the best.'

The 'gangster wrapped in a Union Jack' as the Police describe him, is still up for action, but nowadays it is mostly sex with prostitutes. After the party, Adair sought out some female c

ompany on the streets of Dresden. On another night, he had sex with one of his adoring groupies, although he was a little shy about admitting it at first.

*****

Tattoos are the iconography of Adair's world and I went with him and Jonathan when they were adding another to their collections.

'So, what's the tattoo you're getting now, and why?' I asked.

'I'm getting a UFF 'C' Company one. The words in Latin: actions, not words [*factum non verbum*]. 'C' Company was an army – men of actions, not words.'

Mad Pup looked on and winced his way through his own tattoo. What's good for the daddy will do for son! It was obvious that he hadn't inherited his Dad's apparently high pain threshold. He is no stranger to pain himself, however. As a teenager in Belfast, Mad Pup suffered a painful punishment shooting for antisocial behaviour, widely rumoured at the time to have been ordered by his own father.

With his dad beside him, I asked Jonathan about his leg wounds.

'What did they do to you?'

'I was took up an alley and told to sit on the ground, kneeling down with my back against the wall. As soon as they put the bullets in the gun, I told them, "Let's get it over and done with."'

'You said to get it over quickly?'

'I didn't want to be waiting about, thinking about it. Get it over and done with as soon as possible. Before I knew it, I was shot,' Jonathan remembered.

'And where did they shoot you?'

'Both calves. Then they just left me. I tried to get up and walk. I walked a bit, but I ended up falling again. People came out and took me into a house, then took me to hospital.'

'And just to the back of your calves?'

'Just the sides.'

'Any scars?' I asked.

Jonathan nodded.

'Yeah? And the same on the other leg?' I asked.

'Same on the other leg, yeah,' he said.

But it wasn't the mutilation of his leg he was worried about.

'That was through my tattoo, I was a bit raging at that. See it there? To tell you the truth, it wasn't that bad, it was only my calves. It would be different if it was my kneecaps. That's getting off lightly, that. That's only a flesh wound, that one.'

I asked him a question that didn't really need to be asked but I was hoping it would bring out some element of the truth:

'Did the Police ask who did it?'

'I just told them to go away, mind their own business,' Jonathan replied.

For the first time I saw Johnny get twitchy. He was going to make sure there were no direct admissions, so he intervened and took the reins.

'Well, I think Jonathan was man enough to take his punishment, and he realised that he wasn't getting any special treatment because I was his father. He was just treated the same as any other teenager in that area would be treated if they crossed the paramilitary.'

Tragically, despite the old man's best efforts Jonathan was convicted of drug dealing. The court report noted that 19-year-old Jonathan Adair faced 10 different charges of conspiracy to supply and of supplying class 'A' drugs, including heroin and crack cocaine. He was convicted and jailed for five years.

I asked Daddy Adair if Jonathan had reformed.

'Yes, and he'll never do it again. Jonathan quite foolishly got involved in drugs in Bolton and, erm, and as a result he received five years in prison. It's done him the world of good. He's out now. He's clear of drugs and he'll never go down that road again. Neither will his father.'

'You won't be knee-capping him if he gets involved again, will you?' I asked.

'Absolutely not.'

The spectre of drugs has always haunted Adair, his family and his organisation, although he has never admitted to having been involved in their supply directly.

'I don't know if it was the Police or someone in the fucking media who said that I'm a drug dealer. How can someone like Johnny Adair possibly be dealing fucking drugs? How can someone like Johnny Adair possibly be in any way associated with them? Johnny Adair, I have no doubt, is under 24-hour surveillance by the Special Branch, no matter if it's here in Scotland, in Manchester or back home in Belfast. That is a fact. So it would be suicide for me to try anything illegal, let alone drugs.'

The only drugs Johnny Adair would admit to taking are bodybuilding steroids.

'Do I take steroids? Well, does Popeye take spinach?' he laughed. It was common for prisoners in the Maze to use steroids. They were smuggled in to Adair in the false leg of a visitor, who also brought in other drugs and porn.

'It's accepted that your organisation was financed to the tune of millions of pounds to fund military operations by racketeering, extortion and drugs. That's accepted, that's fact?' I asked him.

'That is a fact,' he confirmed.

Once the king of his own little principality with a loyal army and stocks of munitions, Adair was now in Scotland, apparently broke and on the dole. I suggested to him that there were obvious career opportunities there for him should he chose to go down that route.

'Is the next business going to be drugs for you in Scotland?' I asked.

'The people just need to look at my background and other so-called Loyalists' backgrounds and see who has the wealth. Johnny Adair doesn't have the wealth. Johnny Adair was a soldier, a freedom fighter. Money was never his god,' he told me.

'That's true, but nowadays people say you are going to take those big multi-million extortion operations to Scotland.'

'No, because it would be breaking the law,' he said, raising an eyebrow.

Adair's buddy in Scotland, Mark 'Scarface' Morrison, is not a terrorist. He's what police call an ODC – an ordinary decent criminal. His multiple convictions include assault, forgery, breach of the peace and fraud. In Scottish gangland circles, Scarface is known as the A-to-Z of the underworld. Morrison prefers to call himself a 'consultant'. So you do have to wonder exactly what Adair's new 'business interests' are.

* * * * *

Johnny Adair is obsessive. His number one obsession is of course himself, but his Alsatian dogs, Shane and Rebel, come a close second. In 1995, when he was sent to prison for 16 years for directing terrorism, he gave his dogs to his friend and paramilitary associate, Desmond. When Desmond, a convicted drug dealer, left Northern Ireland to live in the North of England he took the pets with him. It seems that while Desmond had tired of people, he had fallen in love with the animals and would not return them to Johnny. Once again, one of Johnny's former associates had become an enemy.

The issue of the custody of the dogs was threatening to further disturb his peace of mind. He phoned Desmond to demand that he return his beloved pets.

'You stole them dogs. You're an evil man, Dessie. I want them back. I've found out where you live and I'm coming to confront you for my dogs, Desmond,' Adair told him.

'Let's see what happens, eh?' said Desmond.

'You see? There you go – "let's see what happens." What are you going to do? Are you going to kill me?'

'Put it this way, Johnny: would you feel safe in my company again? I don't think you'd be safe at all, Johnny.'

'I don't want no violence; I know you're an evil man. I know what you're capable off. But I don't want to confront you to face something like that; I just want my dogs back, Desmond,' Adair pleaded.

'The only time you'll get your dogs back is when I'm six feet under.'

'When you're six feet under?'

'I told you about that time when I was sitting in my Mazda outside your door and I said to myself, "If he moves from that house, what I have in my hand down the side door panel, he's going to get shot with."'

'You see, that's using violence, Desmond. Why?'

'It's not. It's self-defence, Johnny.'

'You're an evil man, Desmond. You're a convicted drug dealer, Desmond. You've stolen my dogs and then you're threatening to kill me if I come face-to-face with you or eye-to-eye with you. I am asking you, Desmond. I'm not threatening you, I'm begging you, Dessie. I'm even begging you. Would you please give me my dogs back? I'm offering you £3,000 for the safe return of my two dogs, Shane and Rebel. The two dogs that I dearly love, Desmond.'

'Can I answer?' Desmond asked.

'Please do.'

'No deal.'

'Well, Dessie, I'm coming to your door. I know where you, live Desmond. I just want my dogs back,' said Adair.

'You know where I live? As far as I'm concerned Johnny, all negotiations are over. There will be no more social. It'll be every man for himself, John,' Desmond told him.

'Well, Desmond, I'll be coming to your door, looking to get my dogs back. I'm not coming with a threat of violence: I'm coming with £3,000 in my pocket now, Desmond. I'll see you soon, OK? Cheerio, Desmond.'

In the meantime, Johnny considered offering a home to a lonely abandoned soul at a nearby dog shelter. Like many prospective dog owners, he seeks characteristics in the dogs that he sees in himself. I couldn't help thinking that perhaps he should have bought a piranha. He prowled around the cages.

He patted a dog and said, 'This one looks very scared.' I don't know why he was surprised.

One of the wardens came over to Johnny to see how he

was getting on. 'Some of the staff seem to think you look a bit like someone – Mad Dog or something,' she said, obviously completely unaware of who she was talking to. There were quiet whispers from her colleagues in the background, who were clearly better informed about his track record. Johnny let it pass and left the shelter, still hoping to retrieve the long-lost Shane and Rebel.

*****

> *Good afternoon, and welcome to this tour of Belfast. On this tour, we're going to bring you through areas that you've probably seen on the news and read about in the newspapers. OK folks, we're just bringing you into the Shankill area. Here you'll see the colours red, white and blue. Now, a Loyalist is someone who is loyal to her majesty the Queen and to the crown of England. This area in particular at one time was run by a man, a man you've probably all heard about – Johnny 'Mad Dog' Adair. Johnny Adair controlled this area with an iron fist.*

Adair enjoys the limelight, but even he was surprised to learn that he's become a tourist attraction. Despite being in exile, he still commands the car-crash notoriety that once filled the front pages of Northern Ireland's newspapers.

> *Now, if you look straight out the window, you'll see a large UFF mural. If there's such a thing as a good mural, this is it. If you watch the gunman's eyes and his weapons as we leave the area, both the eyes and the weapon follow you the whole way round this area. Just to your left-hand side here, you'll see some blank walls. These walls all had murals on them which were commissioned by Johnny Adair when he was the leader of the UFF. When he was moved out of the area, local people had the murals painted over. He actually lived in this street, if you look just down on the left-hand*

> *side here. It's called Boundary Way. They even took the nameplate off the street itself. Since then he hasn't been back again. If he came back to the area, I think there would be a lot of friction.*

The tourists were enjoying their history lesson. They had no idea that the camera that was recording these words would shortly film Adair returning to that very spot.

Just a few years previously, this area had erupted into a chaotic murderous feud between opposing Loyalist factions. Adair's group was ultimately run out of town.

He hated being in enforced exile and still clung to the idea of humiliating those who wanted him dead.

'Six of the so-called brigadiers wanted me dead. To date, two of those are now themselves six feet under, but Johnny Adair is still standing. And Johnny Adair will return home soon,' he told me emphatically. 'What greater insult to them, than to return to their doorsteps and my old haunting ground – they would go fucking mad .... Whoever laughs last, laughs the longest,' Johnny told me. Jonathan joined in on cue to make his own resolve clear: 'And what goes around, comes around,' he said.

I wanted to test Adair on his desire to go home. Was he, despite his new tattoo, all talk and no action? He had said that he wished to return but had made no plans or effort to do so. I suggested that we go in through Dublin Port by car, and drive up to Belfast before doing a kind of dawn raid on the Shankill. This was a dangerous trip but I figured that the Police would get wind of it and follow us, so we would have an unwitting security detail to keep an eye on us.

Over a game of pool, and with military precision, Johnny hatched his plan to complete the 600-mile journey from Troon to Belfast via Holyhead and Dublin. 'Let's hope I don't come home in a coffin .... It could cost me my life if they catch me. I have no doubt that they would kill me if they see me,' he said. We planned to use safe houses and decoy cars but we didn't know if this would be enough.

'If you go back to Northern Ireland you will be shot dead – simple as that,' Former Detective Jonty Brown, the man who had put him in prison years previously, had told him directly. Naturally, this played on Adair's mind, particularly when Brown drove the point home by saying: 'I'd say they'd be queuing up to whack you.'

It didn't halt the march of the plan, however. We were to travel across the border by car and go directly to a safe house. From there, we would organise Johnny's visit to the Shankill.

Adair was distinctly sheepish as we boarded the ferry from Holyhead to Dublin. This was a side of him I hadn't seen before: the bluster and bravado were replaced with a nervous hush.

When we arrived in Dublin, I increasingly saw fear in his eyes. He wasn't cool under pressure and became agitated and twitchy. I wondered if he was feeling the same terror that he had inspired in so many others over the years. In a way it was good to see that he was human, and I was confident that he would escape unharmed. Yes, he was facing death threats there upon his return, but we would be gone within an hour, probably before his enemies even knew he was there.

Before we left Dublin, I decided to bring Adair into the city centre to the birthplace of Irish Republicanism – the GPO, headquarters of the leaders of the 1916 Rising. But Johnny showed little interest and certainly didn't want to linger to soak up the atmosphere.

'How does it feel to be in Dublin?' I asked him.

'Rotten,' he laughed.

'You know,' I said, 'there are 2,000 retired IRA activists here. Is it a dangerous place for you to be?'

'Well, let's get out of it,' he said. And off he scarpered to the car.

He was unmoved when we crossed the border into Northern Ireland. As we drove into Belfast, I said to him, 'Johnny, you're home.' But he said nothing.

Our producer, David Malone, was driving erratically through the streets of Belfast, which were unfamiliar to him. Our retired killer was upset that David wasn't quite following the directions as instructed and became more and more irritated. 'Just to your right. No, no, no, go on round,' he said, his voice rising. The conflicting directions did not help matters. 'Go you round! See, you don't know what you're doing with your driving,' Adair said, becoming really furious with David. I was becoming scared of Adair at this stage and the tension in the car only made David drive even more chaotically.

'You don't know what you are doing. Do what I say. Turn right around,' Johnny instructed.

I spotted a Police car in the rear-view mirror. Adair saw it too, and was beginning to really lose his temper now. 'Just right round. Come on! No, down there!' Adair shouted, as if David was ever going to outmanoeuvre the Police in our tiny rented car.

'See what I mean? You haven't a clue,' he lamented. Young Mad Pup remained silent. 'There's a car following us. We'll go left again and we'll see,' Johnny said, nervously watching behind him. 'If he goes left, go straight up, for fuck's sake.' Adair thought someone was out to take him down.

'I told you to go left, David. Go right!' To give David his due, he remained the coolest in the car. Having a terrorist as a back-seat driver is not covered in the driver theory test. Suddenly, a siren cut through air. 'Who's this? Cops, is it?'

It was the cops. The former brigadier continued his instructions: 'Just drive up there, the further away the better.'

The Police car sped up to us and indicated for us to pull over. 'Just stop here. For fuck's sake, stop!' Adair shouted at David, exasperated at his lack of experience as a getaway driver. I was more than a little concerned by this turn of events.

'Fuck's sake! That's us fucked now,' said an agitated Johnny. I took some little pleasure in seeing him at the end of his tether.

The policemen came to the front of the car. I picked up my camera and started to film, hoping that this might distract them from pulling us all in for a night. Adair was perfectly entitled to be in Northern Ireland. He wasn't breaking any law by being there, but the Police could nonetheless make life difficult for him and for us, too.

'Hello. How are you?' an ever polite David said to the young officer.

'Could you turn that off for a second?' the officer said to me, pointing to the camera.

'I reserve my right to film,' I said, 'as a journalist.'

The officer didn't bother to challenge me. He looked into the back of the car, where Johnny and Jonathan were sitting, but passed no remark.

'Could you step out?' he asked David.

He checked his licence and then allowed us to go. We drove off. If he had recognised the key players in the back of the car, he hadn't let on.

Adair was perspiring.

'Do they know it's me?' he asked.

'Yes,' said David. 'Well, they didn't say, but I think they know.'

'Well, [if] they know, do the UDA know?' Johnny wondered. 'My fear is: will the Police leak to my enemies that I'm in the country?'

Whatever the answer, there seemed to be little fallout. We went to the safe house to gather our thoughts and prepare for a dangerous stroll down Adair's memory lane.

The following morning, three years after his exile, he returned to the community he had once ruled over.

'This is where I used to live, where I was exiled from,' he whispered as we drove into the estate. 'This was an area I loved and a people I loved.'

It was 7 a.m. on 29 December and we hoped that most of the estate would be peacefully asleep. I saw a curtain move but I didn't tell Johnny: I didn't want to spook him. As we moved through the darkness of the post-Christmas morning among the terraced houses and the murals, a pathetic picture began to emerge. 'I used to be a god here – I feel a distance to it now,' he said.

For years he had longed for it, but now this place had left him feeling empty. With his head sunk deep into his jacket, he had the look of a broken man.

He gave it about five minutes and then decided he wanted to visit the Maze Prison, a real home-from-home for Mad Dog. Along the road, graffiti made him wince: 'Adair wife-beater'. Adair had been convicted of assaulting his wife, Gina, who he had been with for 23 years. He had left her bruised and battered, after attacking her in a park following an evening spent at the pub. He admitted his guilt and had been fined for the assault.

With the pressures of his life, they were almost certain to eventually split. In recent years, Gina Adair has battled ovarian cancer and they remain in regular contact.

He spent many years at the Maze and famously even met Mo Mowlam when she was Northern Ireland Secretary. The inimitable Mowlam managed to charm even Johnny Adair and persuaded him to reconsider his opposition to Loyalist political representatives entering the talks that led to the Good Friday Agreement.

Now mothballed and rusting, the H-Blocks were a shadow of their former selves.

'The video of choice [here] was porn. We would view porn movies, get drunk, and the prison authorities would supply us with disco lights,' Adair remembered, almost fondly. He urinated against a concrete prison wall and then took a moment to express an extraordinary thought. 'If I was a Nationalist, I would have probably joined the IRA,' he told me. Naturally, by his own account, he would have been on the Army Council.

This was enough nostalgia for Adair, and there was a sense that time was running out. He made a break for the airport and flew to Glasgow. When he arrived there, he was pulled in by the UK Police and questioned for four hours. They couldn't understand why he would be flying in from Belfast, where the threat to him was so acute. With his record and reputation, this is probably something he has to expect for the rest of his life.

*****

The UDA have now officially completely decommissioned their weapons. However, Adair claimed to me that he alone knew the whereabouts of many weapons and he asked me to contact the arms decommissioning body. I wasn't sure if he was just feeling out of the loop and trying to feel important again. This was certainly not a role I wanted to assume. It was with some embarrassment that I contacted the body and met with them at the most bombed hotel in Europe: the Europa in Belfast. The commissioners were grumpy and taciturn after travelling from all over the world, and they didn't hide it from me. They even thought I was secretly recording the meeting, which of course I wasn't. I played it straight, figuring that more guns off the streets couldn't be a bad thing. 'He claims to have weapons and wishes to hand them over. If you want to play, he will play, but understand that if you don't play ball, he will just say he was confused and you won't get the guns,' I told them.

The commissioners listened and brought the offer from Adair to the Irish and British governments for consideration. Not long after, news came back from the decommissioning body: 'Adair is not entitled to protection under the legislation. If he wants to hand over a gun or guns he would do so as a civilian. They, naturally, would be tested and he might be held liable for any crimes associated with the weapons.'

I told them that I had a feeling that Adair's memory would now prove to be faulty and that he would quickly decide that he didn't know where the guns were. And that's exactly what happened.

*****

I last spoke to Adair on the phone about a year ago. He was well and still spoke about himself in the third person. But my last substantial conversation with him face-to-face was in the window seat of a motorway café in Berlin.

'What's going to happen to the man that takes you out?' I asked him.

'He will probably be celebrated in some dingy pub with about half a dozen drinking in it,' Johnny replied.

'Until Nick the Nazi comes over to take him out?' I suggested.

'Well, Nick says if anything happened to me, he would most definitely come and do something about it,' he said.

I think he is still surprised by the devotion of his Nazi

followers, but welcomes the support all the same.

'What will be on your tombstone?' was my next, rather macabre question. 'Will it be "Johnny Adair: freedom fighter, volunteer, gangster"?'

He took a deep breath and glanced around the room before locking his gaze on mine.

'Johnny Adair: from volunteer to brigadier. *Quid separatum est* – simply the best,' he translated the Latin loosely.

'That's the end of the road, Johnny,' I said, bringing our conversation and our time together to a close.

'The final chapter is yet to be written, Mr MacIntyre.'

I thought there was a sinister emphasis on my name that did not rest well with me then. And it still doesn't.

12

Madame Mac

Answerphone: *Welcome to Sauna Med. We will be opening shortly. If you wish to avail of our services or are looking for work, please leave your details and we will call you back.*

Male Voice: *Do you do golden showers and domination?*

Being new to the business of owning a brothel, I wasn't quite accustomed to the sexually explicit phone messages. In the heart of Camden, North London, I was establishing a bordello, which to all intents and purposes appeared to be preparing to open for business. Sex workers, punters, traffickers, gangsters and even an ad man from a listings magazine came calling to offer their services to me as a new provider of sexual services in the area.

Camden has always had an air of anarchy about it, and so our little business did not look out of place. The building looked suitably seedy from the outside. Inside, we had set up a reception area and a heavily scotch-guarded chaise longue had been ordered. Fruity air-freshener polluted the air to give it the authentic bordello aroma.

On the second floor was a double bedroom, and located on the third floor was a secret studio we would use to covertly film the goings-on and record every word spoken.

It was an uncomfortably proud moment when the make-shift sign announcing our name and phone number was erected outside. The pavement directly outside the door was painted blue and the sign had white text on a sky-blue background to tie in with our Mediterranean theme. As I surveyed my empire from across the street, through the traffic of Kentish Town Road, I felt like a proud business starter, fresh from some government scheme and full of entrepreneurial spirit. What would my old school principal, Mother Perpetua, make of me now?

I couldn't help having a giggle at the inappropriateness of the BBC financing its own brothel with licence fee money. It wasn't quite what Lord Reith had in mind when he created the corporation to 'educate, entertain and inform'. Of course we had no intention of actually taking any paying clients – this was our way of getting the pimps and traffickers to talk to us in person and it would give us the opportunity to film them relatively safely.

This business is a gangster's licence to print money. Another brothel just around the corner, which was open 24/7, was reputedly turning over £1 million a month. It appeared to be easy money, as long as you weren't one of the girls forced to work there.

The point of this investigation was that many of these girls were being given no choice, and were effectively being used as sex slaves. In the most extreme cases, the trafficked women were being bought and sold like second-hand cars and were treateded a great deal worse. They were being forced to have sex with up to 12 men in a shift and often endured beatings and ritual humiliation. Most of the women came from the poorest parts of the world and were easy prey for traffickers who promised a fresh start and a good job in a wealthier country.

Nearly a million women are believed to be trafficked every year. I met Russian-born Sophie on a research trip to Prague. She had been promised a secretarial job in Germany, and the lure of accommodation and a good wage proved too tempting for her to resist. When she met the men at the airport, she knew she had made a mistake.

'As soon as I saw them, I realised they are gangsters. You can tell immediately from the way they look,' Sophie told me. I asked them what kind of work will I be doing. One of them told me I will be working as a prostitute. I said I won't do it.

'They told me that I would have to submit if I didn't want to be beaten up or killed.'

She was beaten and raped and, still only in her twenties, she now looks twice her age. Tears fell down her cheeks as she revealed her pain to me.

Later, I met Tibor. He looked like an ageing nightclub singer in his flared trousers, red smoking jacket and open shirt. The obligatory gold medallion completed the picture. It was a kind of *Goodfellas* chic, if there is such a thing. We were tucked away in the alcove of a seedy bar, surrounded by his gun-toting henchmen. Tibor is one of the biggest sex traffickers in the Czech Republic. He was completely frank about his business.

'Where do you get your girls from?' I asked him.

'All over Europe ... mainly [they are] Czech, Slovak, Polish, Hungarian, Spanish,' he told me in a matter of fact tone.

I could have been asking him how many sugars he wanted in his tea.

'They are being offered to me. We have a meeting, they put some photographs on the table and I choose what I like. It is a kind of network that I have with these people.

'If someone calls me right at this moment to go and get some girls from Spain, I'll send some people immediately and I'm ready to do business,' he said.

He didn't need to let me know who was boss, but he couldn't help himself.

'I work alone down here. I control everything here.'

'If the women are difficult, how do you manage them?' I asked.

'If she doesn't obey me, then I get rid of her or something.'

'And if she disrespects you?' I asked.

'I give her a smack, I punish her. The next time, I punch her in the face. Sometimes it's necessary to shoot her in the leg or arm for warning. When I talk to someone in a situation like this, I'm always calm and polite. But when it comes to some bitch getting on my nerves, then I'm not so nice,' he said.

*****

In the months before we opened our establishment, our researchers visited over a hundred brothels, masquerading as concerned brothers looking for their missing sisters who they believed had been trafficked. Using this ruse, the researchers explained that they just wanted to talk, in the hope that the young women would open up about their predicament.

The girls were reticent at first and found it very difficult to trust a man after what they had been through. But after a number of visits, many revealed the horrific truth of their circumstances.

As we trudged from saunas to massage parlours – brothels in all but name – we were hoping to find women who felt able to accept our help to escape this world. But we were not naïve, and understood the complex psychological chains that keep these girls in this terrible life.

Eventually, one of our undercover team reported that a dark-haired girl of about 19 or 20 had been opening up to him about being forced into prostitution by a group of Albanians in Manor Park, North London. A blond fifty-something Madame introduced her as Eni from Greece.

'I'm not Greek. I am Albanian; I swear to God. I am in college,' she told the researcher. She said that she had been smuggled into the UK and was being forced to have sex up to five times a night and then to hand all the money over to her pimp. 'I have nowhere to go but I can't call the Police, because I have just one brother and he is smaller than me. If I go to the Police, [my pimp] said he will kill my brother.'

The Albanians work in clans: families, cousins and friends from the same village create a kind of network and they operate together.

Eni's pimp was also her boyfriend and he was forcing her to earn cash for him by working in the sauna. According to Eni, many of his friends were doing the same.

We waited outside the sauna to watch her pimp pick her up. We noticed that his car was for sale, so the next day we phoned him and arranged to meet up on the pretext that we were interested in buying it. Over a drink, he introduced himself as Zamir and we chatted for a while.

We casually dropped into the conversation that we were opening a sauna in Camden and his eyes lit up. 'We are the same. I am [here with] four brothers and one cousin and we each have working girls,' he said. 'We are looking for a new place for work.' He took out a photograph of Eni from his wallet and showed it to us. We asked him how much she earned for him. '£300 a night, sometimes £200, sometimes nothing,' Zamir said, laughing. We didn't buy the car but we kept in contact with him.

After that, Eni went missing from the sauna for over a week. When she eventually came back to work, she explained her absence: 'My boyfriend hit me. I told him I not working any more, and he hit me,' she said, pointing to her face. She seemed at her wits' end.

She didn't know that we had already met her boyfriend.

It took a number of visits before our researcher felt able to reveal who he was and what his true intentions were. When he finally told her the truth and asked her if she wanted help, she said that she needed to think about it. We gave her the number of a solicitor to call for advice and hoped that she would call us after she had spoken to her. In the end, the solicitor contacted us and told us Eni had decided that she wanted to get out of the situation she was in.

She packed her bags and left the home she shared with Zamir. We had her under surveillance and followed her as she made her way to the Tube and on to the arranged meeting point.

I first saw Eni coming towards me with Stratford Tube station behind her. She passed through here every day on her way to the sauna. We were tracking Zamir's movements, worried that he would scupper the rescue plan. I went over to her after she talked to the lawyer and introduced myself. She was very vulnerable and nervous but brave enough to trust us.

On the way to the safe house, we drove past the sauna. 'I don't want to look,' Eni said. 'He punched me many times. [He said,] "I kill your family and your brother." Some who do sex are nice with customers. But after I have sex, customers go to maid and say, "She is pretty but she is no good." The maid says, "Sorry. Next time chose another girl."'

She tried to talk more, but was too upset. It was awkward being a man in these circumstances and I couldn't help but feel ashamed of my sex.

We phoned Zamir, pretending to be from the UK Border Agency, and told him that Eni was being held in custody pending deportation proceedings. We kept the cover story short and kept conversation to a minimum, hoping that this would buy us some time. Within half an hour he had called Eni 31 times.

Her new home would be on the other side of the city, away from Zamir and his brothers. I hoped she would settle down and be able to get on with her life.

*****

With Eni safe, we continued with the preparations at our own brothel in Camden. The traffickers were excited to have a new customer and were eager to do deals with us.

'Ron' entered the brothel with a swagger, bringing two young Russian women with him. He was dressed all in black and had Michael Bolton-style hair that did him no favours. He and his sidekick sat down on the red sofa and the women were directed to the room upstairs while negotiations took place.

'One is a brunette. She is going for £7,000. We can barter. And the other is blond and £9,000,' he told us. Ron said that we could rent the girls, but that it would be better to buy them outright. 'You feed, you clothe – they work.' He also offered his own girlfriend for rent. Naturally, I would pay the rent to him and not her. He gave me some advice about their diet: 'When they work, they have no time for cooking. Maybe buy a burger, or if you want to be more nice, take to a cheap restaurant. Don't

Like the Queen and Margaret Thatcher, Johnny 'Mad Dog' Adair talks about himself exclusively in the third person.
© David Wootton Photography

Adair adds yet another tattoo to his collection. *Factum non verbum* – Actions not words.
© David Wootton Photography

The usual suspects congregate for a photo shoot for the *MacIntyre's Underworld* series. L to R: Johnny Adair; Newcastle's most notorious gangster, Paddy Conroy; me; suspected cocaine king, Andrew Pritchard.
© Robin Culley

My worst disguise ever. Jonathan Ross said I looked like an elderly Italian accountant.
© David Wootton Photography

Gary Booth, my friendly mugger. 'You were lucky I mugged you. Some of my friends would have stabbed you.'
© David Wootton Photography

The Haitian Voodoo Mafia, or Zoe Pound gang, strut their stuff when I meet them in Little Haiti, Miami.
© Five TV

One of the leaders of the gang, 'Blind', shares his wisdom with me.
© Five TV

The best of enemies. Face to face with Wayne Hardy ten years after I exposed him as a drug dealer, for *World in Action*.
© *Robin Culley*

Wayne has not had a conviction in over four years – he has either gone straight or got smarter.
© *Robin Culley*

The Insect Tribe of Papua New Guinea welcome me to the Sepic River and the village of Swagup. They taught me how to hunt wild boar and crocodiles.

Chief Joseph of the Insect Tribe in his traditional headdress. He stole the show when we attended a charity ball at The Dorchester.
© Dare Films

Enjoying the open air while filming *Wild Weather* during the monsoon in Goa, India.
© David Wootton Photography

Florentine Houdiniere and me dressed in spandex and sparkle for the launch of *Dancing on Ice*. We skated to REM's 'Everybody Hurts', or 'Everything Hurts' as it became known after I dropped her on a number of occasions.

With Katie Derham on my first day as an anchorman. She made sure that I survived my debut without any major hitches.
© Niké Komolafe

Family – my greatest adventure!

Ameera and me getting hitched.

At home with Ameera, baby Tiger (3) and Allegra (8).

worry: they don't take much feeding,' he assured me.

'I'll bear that in mind,' I said.

Later I went up to speak to the women alone. They seemed completely lost and confused. We chatted about nothing in particular for a while, but they were clearly nervous and aware that they were being traded.

'I have never done this before. I have no money,' one of them said.

'How many punters?' the other girl asked, looking concerned.

'Five,' I told her.

'OK,' she replied, downcast.

We told Ron that we would close the deal as soon as we were fully open for business. Instead, we handed the information over to the Police and Ron and his cronies were investigated for prostitution, assault and trafficking. We never saw the girls again.

*****

Salvation proved to be a lonely place for Eni and she was left with many issues to sort through. She contacted me to say that she wanted to meet her pimping ex again, to confront him over what he had done to her. I called Zamir and we arranged to meet at a café in Chiswick.

'You beat her and made her work as a prostitute. Why?' I asked.

'I am jealous for her,' he said, shrugging his shoulders and taking a drag on his cigarette.

'Why don't you get work as a rent boy?' I asked him.

'I never heard of such a thing,' he said.

'I haven't come to put you in jail. I just want an explanation.'

It was a bizarre situation: I was caught halfway between journalist and marriage counsellor.

'Where did you hit her? In the face, the head, the back?' I asked him.

Zamir's head dropped.

'I sometimes slap in the face and punch.'

'How can you behave like this?'

'They can put me in prison for 15 years. I accept everything,' he said.

Eni was relieved to at last hear some kind of admission of guilt, but if she had been expecting contrition, she would be disappointed.

'I am what I am,' he said.

He put on his knee-length black leather jacket and walked onto the high street alone. Thankfully, Eni refused to go with him.

Over the next couple of years, Eni managed to eke out an existence for herself away from the sex trade. She was fighting to stay in the country and I was called to a final immigration appeal at an office near Heathrow, to give evidence about her life as a sex slave. I told the officials that she had gone through hell. By breaking away from her boyfriend and telling her story, she had given courage to other sex slaves and she would be in grave danger of retaliation if she were to be repatriated to Albania. There are some days when you feel proud of your work, and this was one of those days.

Against the odds, Eni was reprieved and was granted leave to remain in the country on humanitarian grounds. After that we met up occasionally for coffee and I was always delighted to hear about the progress she was making with her new life. She would send me cards every now and then and congratulated me when I got married. We had a trust: I was someone she could rely on and I was happy to support her in whatever way I could.

About three years later – five years after the programme was made – I received a call from the Police in relation to the investigation. The officer said that he wanted to talk to me regarding a murder inquiry and a person he thought I had interviewed for my sex traffickers documentary. My first thought was for Eni: by telling her story to us, she had made a fistful of enemies.

'Oh, she's alright,' the officer told me. 'The victim is a 24-year-old male. He was stabbed in a hostel for vulnerable tenants.'

Eni had been staying at the same hostel as the murdered man. The victim was a manager at a health-food store and was well liked, by all accounts. They had known each other for some time and had become close, according to the officer. He said Eni had been doing some cleaning work and studying English part-time.

'But how is Eni involved?' I asked

'She has been charged with the murder.'

'What?' I said. 'That can't be.'

'Well, she has already confessed to it.'

'She is no murderer,' I said.

'We don't believe it either, but we need her to tell the truth, and that's where we believe you can come in.'

It was like something out of *Crime and Punishment.*

Apparently, Eni was having sex with the victim when her brother walked in on them. He became incensed that she was with a black man and stabbed him before fleeing the scene. To this day her brother has not been found and remains on the run. Eni had gone on the game to protect him from her pimp who had threatened to kill him and he had repaid her by killing her boyfriend and disappearing.

I was told that Eni was in Holloway Women's Prison and the Police felt that maybe I could persuade her to change her story and stop protecting her brother. The prison that once held Oscar Wilde and Constance Markievicz now held my friend, Eni, remanded in custody for murder. I was stunned.

I contacted her lawyer immediately but was told that Eni did not want to speak to me. I wrote to her, but still she wouldn't engage. Then, after about three months, she called me from prison, in tears. 'I am so sorry. It's a mess. It's all my fault,' she said. We tried to arrange a visit but the governor of Holloway wouldn't give me permission because, he said, of an investigation I had done into corrupt prison officers at Wandsworth Prison the previous year. The Home Office refused to intervene, despite the fact that the Police knew that I could help to persuade Eni to tell the truth.

In the end, after much cajoling, she took my advice and that of her legal team and told the Court what had happened, admitting that she had lied to protect her brother. The murder charge against her was dropped, but she was convicted of perverting the course of justice. Her brother was convicted in absentia of murder. Eni was released after serving 11 months of a 16-month sentence.

'Her one enduring regret is that a decent man lost his life because of an engagement with her that night,' her lawyer told the Court.

The judge said that the victim was a totally innocent man whose family may have been deprived of justice because of Eni's actions. He said that DNA and fingerprints might have been on the blood-soaked weapon that she had wiped clean.

'He was a hard-working, well-respected man who had done nothing wrong.'

After Eni was released, we met over coffee near the *Cutty Sark*, in the shadow of Tower Bridge. She talked about going to college and starting a new life, but she still blamed herself for everything. I tried to convince her that she was wrong to do this, that she was another victim who had become trapped in a destructive series of events.

'It's like waking from a bad dream. I wish I could turn the clock back,' she said. I was devastated for her. She was broken and distressed over the tragedies that seemed to follow her through life.

The journey that started with choosing wallpaper for our bordello had ended with a horrific, racially motivated murder. We followed the story of a single sex trafficking victim in one city, and had seen the devastation that had cascaded tragically through the lives of many. People like Eni deserve our sympathy and protection, and the sorry truth is that she is just one of the thousands of hidden victims of this industry in Ireland and Britain.

Eni's view of the circle of violence she found herself caught up in is soul-destroying in its sense of resignation: 'That's life sometimes,' she said. 'That's life.'

13

How to Get Mugged – in One Easy Lesson

With the A40 White City flyover to my right and the BBC buildings behind me, two hooded men appeared out of nowhere and jumped me. They wrestled me to the ground, grabbed my belongings and left me sprawled on the tarmac. As the robbers ran off, I spotted one of the BBC postmen looking on. He was shocked and came over to assist me. He had just seen one of his colleagues getting mugged outside work and was visibly concerned for my well-being. Then I saw his shock turn to terror as the muggers doubled back and returned for seconds. They approached me and slapped me on the back, saying: 'Well done, Macker. That's the rehearsal; let's see if you've got the balls for the real thing.'

The plan was simple: go get mugged! I was to do my best not to get killed, and had to make sure that the camera was on and that every gruesome detail was recorded. Naturally, there was another Irishman behind this dastardly plan – producer Stephen Mcquillan. If it wasn't a Maguire getting me to throw myself out of aeroplanes, it was a Mcquillan telling me to go and get mugged. We were filming a BBC special investigation into the epidemic of street crime that had hit London and the rest of the UK in the early 2000s.

Mcquillan had the air of a man on a serious mission but

there was always a hint that the whole thing was a long drawn-out practical joke, the punch line of which would be delivered at knifepoint. I wondered if I wasn't just the victim of his quirky sense of humour.

The plan was to walk three well-known mugging trails in Brixton, in Lambeth, South London, and over a period of three days, see if some unlucky crim would dare to mug me. It seemed like the right place to carry out our very unusual experiment. At the time, this part of London had the highest rate of street crime in the country, with nearly 6,000 reported muggings in the previous year. The streets of London appeared to be out of control, and Tony Blair had declared combatting street crime a top priority.

The point of all this was not to get me attacked but to track the stolen goods to the middlemen, fixers and fences who sell on stolen property in the UK and abroad. There was even the hope that we might get the property back (our budget was tight!). But first we had to get it stolen.

At this point, I was the county's best-known undercover reporter (something of an oxymoron, I agree), so it was decided that I would have to be in disguise to get mugged. After three hours in the hands of a make-up artist, I was ready for the streets. I had a greying, itchy goatee; a fetchingly swept-over fringe; salt-and-pepper hair that made me look about ten years older; a pair of stylish Italian glasses; and a tan overcoat that covered my covert equipment effectively enough. The three hours of handiwork gave me a terrifying glimpse into my fat, middle-aged future. I resolved to give up Mars bars and never to grow a beard. Added to all this was a stab-proof vest that left me looking a little like the Hunchback of Notre Dame from behind.

When he had me on his show after my report was broadcast, Jonathan Ross said I looked like an over-weight 50-year-old Italian accountant, albeit with an Irish accent. Naturally, this was always going to provide ample fodder for him to abuse me. I had little choice but to take it on the chin.

I was suited and booted, wired to the gunnels and ready for a kicking. In my ear, I had one of those earpieces that the secret services use. I had trackers in my pocket, on my mobile phone and in my laptop bag, so that the team could follow me and my possessions as I walked the streets. We even fitted my phone and my laptop bag with special acoustic technology, so we could hear the culprits speaking after they had stolen the goods.

We were using high-tech military technology. A two-way communication system would keep me in contact with the filming vehicle, where my safety and the footage I captured would be monitored by the team. My microphone relayed my voice directly to Stephen in the van 2 km away, and he would be directing my movements around the Brixton area. We had a London taxi on standby to pick me up when my feet gave in or if I was injured.

In keeping with the military technology, I was given a battlefield call sign – 'Delta Mike' – my initials. This was going to be fun – a military operation run by civilians. What could go wrong?

It was early in April and while there were no showers, a cold wind blew through the streets. Brixton has always had an edgy attractiveness about it, from the crumbling grandeur of the Victorian architecture to the vibrant markets and trendy nightspots. But there are parts of the area that provoke a genuine nervousness among outsiders. Groups of junkies and dealers hang around in the shadows and there is a tense undercurrent surrounding them.

I was dropped off at eight o'clock in the evening and walked down the A23, along the route of the old Roman road, up Brixton Hill towards Streatham. I thought I looked so vulnerable that I may as well have had sign on my back saying, 'Please mug me'. But it is harder to invite a street robbery than you might think.

Just before 10 o'clock, I was waddling down the street when it became clear that a group of six young men aged between 17 and 24 was following me. I went into a small newsagent to gather my thoughts. They young men crossed the road to congregate near the shop and I could hear them laughing outside. Maybe I was reading more into it than was there – but maybe not. I bought a can of coke and made sure all the equipment was on and working, hoping that the young men would do their worst as I left. In truth I was a little apprehensive about that explosive moment when the threat would become a reality; there was no predicting exactly how events would unfold. As I was about to leave, the shopkeeper, an elderly Indian gentleman, said: 'Be careful.' I nodded to him, half-distracted, playing the lost stranger in town, but he became very insistent, nearly admonishing me.

'Look, be careful: they want to rob you,' he repeated, pointing to the lads outside.

'Oh, I'll be all right, thanks,' I told him.

I hoped he was right.

The equipment was heavy and sweaty, and sometimes the batteries leaked acid in places that cannot be politely scratched in public. I walked out of the shop and turned left, away from the main streets and into the darkness. I could hear the mob getting closer and closer. 'This is it,' I thought. They came right up to my back; I could hear them breathing behind me and could sense the threat in the air.

And then they turned away down a side street. The Police presence in the area was huge but that wasn't what had deterred them. The shopkeeper had left his shop and was very conspicuously following behind the gang. They had obviously become nervous and decided I wasn't worth the bother in front of a witness. I cursed my Good Samaritan friend. Trust me to find a concerned citizen to watch out for me when all I needed was a good shoeing on camera so I can go home to my warm bed.

I walked the streets for a further two uneventful hours and then called it a night, so that Mcquillan could go home to his partner who was over eight-and-a-half months pregnant and worried that my mugging would interfere with the birth.

The next evening it was pretty quiet on the streets. I was dripping with sweat with all the protective clothing and the heavy disguise. The false beard was beginning to shift position as my perspiration dissolved the glue.

As I walked down Loughborough Road, a female voice

attracted my attention. 'You got a fag?' the girl asked. It was nearly a whisper. She couldn't have been more than 19 or 20 and was clearly homeless. I gave her a cigarette and lit it for her.

She was wearing a huge parka coat that swaddled her from head to toe and that I suspected and acted as her sleeping bag. Pointing to my phone, she's said, 'You better put that away, there's dangerous people about.'

I put in some more hard yards that night – over three hours on known mugging routes, and still there was no hint of threat. The mugging capital of Europe was proving to be very benign. It looked like we might have to rewrite the script.

After four hours on the street, I was hungry and I eventually succumbed to the lure of the Kentucky Fried Chicken on Brixton Road. This was a hang out for crack heads and shots (drug dealers). As I entered the fast-food joint, I felt someone brush past me and I knew immediately what was happening. He was heroin-skinny in his white Umbro top and had a few teeth missing. His jacket was draped over his arm and he was so close that he was breathing my oxygen. Getting pickpocketed was not part of the plan. The extra buffer of his jacket allowed him the space to get into my pocket and help himself to its contents. 'There goes the remote for the secret camera,' I thought. 'And there goes the fiver from the other pocket.'

What was I to do?

If I called the Police on this minor matter, I would have been toxic in the area and any potential muggers would have given me a wide berth. I had to just suck it up. Besides, I was still hungry.

Half an hour later I was back on the beat and was again on the precipice of being robbed. There was a guy following me and I could tell he was sussing me out. 'About 50 yards behind you, a young man wearing a red top is looking at you. You are a target. Turn on the camera,' Mcquillan told me. He counted me down through my earpiece: 'Twenty metres, ten metres; be careful, Donal, prepare.' I could hear the guy's footsteps pick up pace as he closed in on me. For a while he slowed down and kept a steady distance. Then he passed me by on the other side of the street, all the while watching me, before disappearing into the shadows. He had given me up as prey. Did he feel sorry for me? Did I smell like a set-up?

After one more furtive walk around the area, we decided to call it a day. It was just after midnight and I returned to our hotel a couple of miles away to de-rig and debrief. Something had to change. My disguise had to go – we would have a new plan tomorrow. Mcquillan went home again to his pregnant partner, who by now was more upset than anyone that I hadn't been mugged.

On the final night, we decided that I would play the lost Irishman in London. This is a role I naturally play well, as my sense of direction is useless and I can often be found driving around entirely the wrong part of the city just trying to get home. It was a dry, mild night and I was ready as ever to be a victim – if only I could find a perpetrator.

It seemed to me that if I was going to get robbed, it would simply happen and there was little I could do to expedite the situation. If I didn't get mugged, we knew that there would be no programme and that the project would be shelved, meaning we would have wasted our time. We always take risks like this; sometimes they pay off and sometimes they don't.

This last night started out as badly as the others. As I walked down a back alley towards a group of layabouts, the situation looked encouragingly dodgy. I could see one of the group feel for something in his pocket – maybe a cosh or a knife, I couldn't tell. Suddenly, a drug dealer in a wheelchair broke away from the group and sped towards me, shouting and screaming. The rest of his crew followed suit, eager to be in on the action. 'Here we go,' I thought.

'He done undercover,' he shouted to the rest of his gang.

'Oi, Oi! That geezer's done undercover. In the white jacket – he's done undercover!'

It looked like I was in trouble for all the wrong reasons.

'He done the football programme,' the dealer told his friends.

My goal was to be targeted as a normal punter, so this was off script and not welcome at all. 'Grass, grass!' they shouted. They had obviously been offended by some of my previous work. I whispered into my microphone: 'I've been clocked.'

I was laughing at the surreal nature of this turn of events but the risk was ever present as the rowdy group approached me, shouting and jeering. At this stage, though, I didn't really care who mugged me or whether they recognised me or not.

Just when I thought my number was up and my mugging was imminent, a homeless runaway prostitute rushed to my rescue. She grabbed me by the arm and said: 'Just say you're my friend. I'm a known face round here. We'll walk around the other way.'

Why would nobody leave me to get robbed in peace?

I chatted to my rescuer for a while and she told me a familiar tale of drugs, prostitution and homelessness. But for all she had been through, she still had enough kindness in her heart to help out a complete stranger. I wanted to hear more but there was work to do, so I gave her a tenner and some fags and we parted ways.

The security team could hear everything that was going on, and they were becoming impatient. Time was running out and Brixton was proving to be a haven of do-gooders and saints, contrary to its (obviously undeserved) reputation. To me it felt like there was an element of the downtrodden looking out for the downtrodden. Maybe the vulnerable were subconsciously looking after their own – as an Irishman lost in town, I fitted that mould in their minds.

Very bored and tired by now, I continued on my desperate quest. As I rounded a corner, I was spotted by a group of young men. They raced towards me but they had no intention of mugging me – they just wanted to sell me drugs. At the time, Brixton was running an experiment that had more or less decriminalised the sale of cannabis on the streets. This controversial scheme meant that policemen could be found standing beside drug dealers openly selling marijuana.

It was like an Indian spice bazaar as the gaggle of small-time dealers crowded around me, each trying to outdo the other with a better deal. This had nothing to do with our story, but, as there was little else going on, I decided to amuse myself.

'Want some marijuana, bro?' they asked, thrusting ready-rolled spliffs into my hand.

'No, no,' I said.

'Ten pounds, ten pounds,' they chorused.

'I'm not interested in dope,' I told them. 'Can you get me some charlie?'

At least five of the mob were crowding in on me now, desperate for business.

'Skunk, do you want some? Whatever you want.'

I had my camera rolling just for the hell of it. I could hear Mcquillan in my ear, saying:

'What's up? Are you in trouble?'

'All cool,' I said to the dealers, knowing that the same message would be relayed to the team.

One of the dealers got so close that he hit the computer board of the camera on my shirt. He was startled. His face fell and he started to back away as the others continued pitching for business. Then he shouted out:

'Camera, camera! You got a camera!'

Initially, I tried to deny it.

'He's a cop,' he shouted.

The others stood back, suddenly looking at me suspiciously.

'No, I'm not,' I protested.

'What's that? What's that? Camera! And he's Police.'

For some reason, probably boredom, I simply said: 'Listen guys, you know what this is: it's a camera, and it's rolling. I'm not Police.'

'Buy the skunk. Give me £10 if you not Police,'

Half of the group was backing away and the other half was nudging forwards, eager to make a sale.

I was laughing at this stage.

I had no fear of these men, and perhaps that should have concerned me. I was alone on streets I didn't know, in the company of nervous drug dealers and I couldn't care less. I think they could sense my indifference, and that scared them. A man without fear is to be feared.

I wandered off, away from the cannabis dealers and put in a request to be picked up. I had been compromised and needed to get out of the immediate area and change my jacket, so as not to be easily recognised. I met with Mcquillan and the team and we decided that I would give it one last attempt before we gave up altogether. I got rid of what remained of my disguise and just wore my stubble and my own clothes. I would walk as myself and hope that that the poor light would keep me from being recognised. We hoped that my comfort in my own skin would make those who wanted to rob me more comfortable in their task.

I took my final stroll down Brixton Road just after midnight, walking away from the train station towards central London. There was plenty of traffic on the streets and the footpaths were still lively and bustling at this late hour.

Down a side street to my left, I heard a promising commotion. A group of 15-year-olds was approaching: they had spotted me. I stopped and tried to engage them.

'Sorry, excuse me; I'm looking for Stockwell Tube,' I said.

'Eh,' one of them pretended to think about directions and held my attention, while another made a dive for me, snatched my mobile phone and darted off triumphantly, with his accomplice close behind him.

'Help! Help!' I shouted. 'Someone has stolen my phone.'

Job done! I was delighted. There was a sense of achievement, but also of anticlimax, after three nights of effort. It seemed to be over before anything even happened.

We later traced the phone to Accra in Ghana and it was returned to me six weeks later. I was amazed that a stolen mobile phone could make such a long journey and even more amazed that we got it back.

At that stage I thought my work was done. But the night took a bit of a twist. As I was retreating, I was approached by a handsome young man, who appeared to be very concerned about my predicament.

'I can get your phone back for you,' he told me. 'My cousin took it, and if you give me a tenner, I'll get your phone back. It's my little cousin. Clearly, I should do it for free but I'm kind of broke.'

He told me to follow him into a nearby estate where he would make contact and then do a cash trade for the phone. 'What the hell,' I thought. It would make for an interesting chapter in the phone saga – another Good Samaritan comes to the rescue.

In my innocence, I genuinely thought that he would get the phone back for me. I considered it to be part of the adventure, and, after the unremarkable mugging, I decided to continue where wiser people might not. There was also a vulnerability about this guy that suggested to me that he meant no harm. I was slightly bigger than him, taller and broader and maybe I felt that if the worst came to the worst, I could take him in a fight.

He told me his name was Gary and we chatted amiably as we walked towards the estate.

'If I had known he was going to do it, I'd have told him not to bother, but obviously he did it on impulse. But I know where he lives,' he told me.

The estate carried a hint of eerie malace at this hour, and I should probably have been more aware of that than I was. The flats were like military bunkers and the walkways could have been designed by street robbers to facilitate attacks rather than prevent them. I can see why old estates like this are torn down to be replaced with more open, community-friendly architecture.

Meanwhile, the team were becoming concerned. Mcquillan called the surveillance guys, wondering if anybody knew where I was. They were monitoring me on the GPS systems but had lost me in the concrete jungle of the flats complex.

Gary was, naturally, slightly suspicious that someone would so willingly go with him at midnight into an estate with a bad reputation, especially just after being robbed.

'What are you doing here?' he asked.

'Ah, sure I'm just over here for the weekend and I'm up for the craic,' I said.

'The crack?' he asked, startled. The Irish-ism was lost on the young crack addict.

He marched me to a nearby balcony and kept me there while he went to look for his cousin. Even this didn't worry me. I simply was not thinking about the danger and was just going with the flow. I was, however, aware that I had lost contact with the team. All radio communications were down. It's something that can happen at any time, but, as luck would have it, they went down just when they were really needed. The comfortably familiar crackle and hiss were absent and I knew I was on my own, without the comfort blanket of Mcquillan's soothing voice or the ability to phone for back-up.

When Gary came back, he was twitchy and nervous. I thought he was distracted and that something was wrong. We chatted a bit more. We had been together for nearly 30 minutes now, and he was becoming difficult and belligerent. He asked me for more money.

'I thought you were one of the good guys,' I said to him, suggesting that he was fleecing me. 'I would rather believe in the Good Samaritan than think the worst of you.'

'I'm not being funny, but you look like a cop,' he said.

'Not many Irish cops around here.'

'You sure?'

'I am from Dublin. You know the history of the blacks and the Irish.'

'No blacks, no dogs, no Irish,' he said.

Then, in the blink of an eye, he pulled out a 7" blade and screamed: 'Look, no more fucking about! Give the bag to me, or else.'

I hadn't been expecting this. I turned and ran and ran until I had the flats well behind me. The team had lost me and I had never felt so vulnerable – ever. One second I was toying with drug dealers and the next I was crying like a baby and sprinting away from the scene.

I had wanted to get mugged, but as soon as it happened for real, it took me by surprise and I was a blubbing wreck. I think I had become so inured to danger that I didn't respond appropriately to it anymore. It dawned on me that if I didn't stop doing this kind of work, it would leave me for dead.

Later, I tracked down Gary and we became friends. I was

keen that this violent meeting wouldn't be our only connection. I wanted to follow up on his story and discover what he was really about. At 23 years of age, he was a crack addict and a father of one. He had been in and out of prison all his life. He was doing his best to beat his addiction, but on the night of our first meeting, it had got the better of him. He was not used to his victims wanting to re-engage with him, but he rolled with it.

We were both aware that our meeting was the conclusion of a strange series of events and an odd collection of motives. I was, after all, the only person in the country *trying* to get mugged that night and he had had the bad fortune to rob someone who happened to be wearing a secret camera.

'You were lucky you were mugged by me. I would never have stabbed you, but plenty of my mates would have. There would have been a show,' he said, 'but you might not have been in it.'

I wondered afterwards why I broke down. I had been shot at, beaten up, threatened, bombed and kidnapped, and still held it together. But when Gary pulled the knife on me, I had had enough. I had to stop pretending I was invulnerable and I had to accept that danger posed the same risk to me as to anybody else. Mcquillan was worried about me and about my state of mind, but his partner was delighted that I had finally been mugged, and that she could get on with having her baby. Shortly afterwards, she gave birth to a beautiful little girl.

These days I try to avoid getting mugged, just like the rest of the sane population. There are some jobs that place you in the path of danger, and they are seductive and fun – but sometimes you have to realise when your days are numbered. I'm just glad I was given this stern lesson in life by Gary and not by one of his mates.

14

Calpol and Kidnapping

Occasionally, terrible events can enrich and enlighten. The horrors of one of my recent journalistic assignments did just that – in ways that I could never have predicted.

I was in Mexico City working on a project very subtly entitled *World's Toughest Towns*. Despite the tabloid-sounding name, it was quite an in-depth exploration of the dark side of some of the world's most iconic cities, from Washington to Istanbul.

On the night in question, I was meeting up with the journalists, radio hacks, and photographers whose job it is to get to a crime scene faster than flies to a corpse. It was as close as you could get to the crime paparazzi of 1930s Chicago without watching *The Untouchables*. This is a trade fuelled by the Mexican public's fascination for violent crime and a seemingly unending rise in brutal murders and kidnappings.

We were at the Monumento a la Revolución, Plaza de la Republica, a memorial to the country's dead heroes and a meeting place for snappers on the hunt for dead drug dealers and other victims of violent gangland crime. Photographers and journalists meet here every night and chain-smoke Mexican cigarettes in the menacing shadows of the streetlights. These men of the night work the 'dead beat' – and there are no shortage of corpses on these streets, as drug-related killings in Mexico have escalated to record levels; 6,587 people were murdered in

2009 alone. These hacks wait around for news of a murder or an accident and then race to the location, in pursuit of the front page and a big payday.

The neon signs of late night bars and the bark of wild dogs on the streets created an appropriate atmosphere for the night ahead. 'Let's go!' The off was sounded by one of the photographers when he got news of a possible drug shooting across town. The motley crew scurried like rats into their cars and dispersed into the night. The destination was revealed en route through the whispered crackle of a radio scanner. I was a terrified member of this posse as they careered through the insane city traffic at over 100 mph. Red lights are a matter of opinion here, and none were observed in the mad dash across town.

I had no clue where we were heading, but had a fair idea of what we would find at our destination. The adrenaline was clearly addictive. Among the pack there seemed to be a primal enjoyment of this vulture-like behaviour.

This is a dangerous job, and not just because of the Formula 1 dash: often the press pack arrives in the middle of a gun fight and has to duck and dodge the violent action before they can start doing their own shooting.

Dead bodies are the currency of this ambulance-chasing set. Drug mayhem and kidnap victims are the spit and sawdust of their trade. In Mexico, grizzly images of victims of the nation's war between rival drugs barons are devoured by city folk. Crime is the staple diet of the media not just because of the public's appetite for the macabre, but also because it is so prevalent that it touches everyone. Dead bodies crowd the front pages of the papers and this can pay bills for the men who hunt out the pictures of the fallen and the slain.

The little dignity that remains is reserved for their own. Veteran journo, Valente Rosas, told me that, essentially, the brotherhood of newshounds is afforded a dignity in death that is denied to others: 'If one of us gets killed, we have a golden rule: we never photograph one of our own.' With his full beard, soft plump cheeks and full belly, he could easily have passed for Santa Claus, were it not for his dark hair.

Photographer David Alvardo is top dog in this press pack and told me that he has been 'covering death' for over 20 years. He looks more like a teacher with his NHS-style glasses, brown Hush Puppies and dark blue chords. 'The majority of people here go first to the murder pages in the papers, look at the photos and stay there .... We love our blood,' he said.

This is not a country for the faint-hearted. Mexico is fast descending into lawlessness, evolving into a so-called narco-state, in a mirror image of Columbia in the 1990s. As it stands, whole swathes of the country are ungovernable because of gangland bribes and gun-barrel intimidation.

Screeching to a halt, we arrived at the scene with the first Police officers. It was an ordinary suburban street with a mix of restaurants and houses that wouldn't have been out of place in comfortable West London, but the emergency lights cast a new, more sinister hue on this part of town. The killing was over and the scavenging had begun. A young man in his early thirties was lying crumpled, half on the pavement, half on the street. He was dead, and yet there were only smiles among my colleagues. I was still high on the thrill of the car chase, but the reality of the situation was beginning to hit me. I felt like I had stumbled onto the set of a Quentin Tarantino movie.

The man had been dead a little over 20 minutes. He had left a local bar with two men chasing after him. As he turned the corner onto a side street, a gunshot had rung out and the hunted man fell where he was shot, according to one local snoop who scuttled around the aftermath of the execution, enjoying the attention that his eye-witness status earned him. There were squinting windows on both sides of the street, but no one else was brave enough to talk: it can be a dangerous pastime in these quarters.

I walked over to the body to gawk like the rest of the pack. The victim was wearing black trainers and jeans, and had ended his days as he had begun them, in the foetal position. There was blood on the collar of his jacket and on the beaten-up road. His eyes were open and appeared to be staring into nothingness. My gaze was drawn to the gap between his trouser hem and his socks. The exposed skin of his shin seemed somehow vulnerable and out of place. I was somehow more affected by his bare shin than the horrific wound in the back of his head.

Here was a corpse still warm to the touch. He was likely a husband, a father, and was certainly someone's son. And yet I was embarrassingly nonplussed. All I felt was a kind of numb confusion. A dead dog on the street would have moved me more. None of the assembled cast of journalists and paparazzi showed any human response to the sight either. Nobody blessed themselves and not a prayer was uttered; no one even seemed shocked.

I heard the clink of metal skidding along the ground. My foot had kicked a stray bullet sideways, but the Police seemed unconcerned that I had contaminated the evidence; they were well used to the press overstepping the mark. The casing of the bullet that killed the man was later found by David, the photographer. The Police made half-hearted efforts to clear us from the scene, but they allowed the photographers time for their snaps and shared some locker room jokes while everybody got their work done. This lenient attitude further underlined the banality of this kind of drug-related murder here, and to me was a clear sign that the authorities had nearly given up the fight.

Ultimately, it appeared that the business of death was more important than the life of the victim. This was no way to die and no way to be found dead.

One of the press pack told me that the forensics would be minimal at the crime scene, but I really needed to take a CSI look at myself. I took a breather to consider my own reaction. I felt like scum. I felt that there must be something seriously wrong with me, if my only reaction to this scene was the occasional smog-induced cough. Was my work allowing my humanity to slowly ebb away into the gutter? I had worried for some time that I was becoming inured to such scenes and now I feared that I would end up like the hacks I saw in front of me, seeing only opportunity in the pain of others.

'Let's get out of here,' I said to the crew.

*****

We were here in Mexico to report on the kidnapping and murder epidemic in the country and I was being forced to examine a side of myself that I did not like. Images played through my mind of the bodies of the victims of genocide I had seen in Rwanda, the emaciated refugees of the Congo, and the terrible sight of the slum dogs of Bangalore selling their kidneys so they could buy food. I had flashbacks to seeing disabled children chained to their cots in India, baby orangutans being packed into tiny wooden crates in Indonesia, lines of refugees in Bosnia and bullet-ridden bodies shot by the Burmese Army in the Golden Triangle. My work has taken me to many dark places over the years. I had seen horrors that night and was shocked by how unmoved I had been by the sight of a dead body.

But in my kids I have a refuge from the worst that life could throw at me.

Back at the hotel baby Tiger was running a temperature. It was three o'clock in the morning and she had been out of sorts all evening. Calpol was not doing the trick and all Mummy's cradling had been to no avail. Tiger's saucer-like blue eyes were rheumy and her cheeks were ruby-red and hot. This was during the gestation phase of swine flu in Mexico, which, apart from drugs, is its most famous recent export. The hotel doctor was called in a panic, but he just said, 'Do as you are doing and double the dose of Calpol' – the parents' best friend in such circumstances.

When I got back from work, I took over the night shift. This was daddy and daughter time. I held her limp limbs to my chest and drizzled water over her hot brow. The thermometer had shown 103°F. By 4 a.m. she was stable. I caressed the fawn curls that fell down her tiny neck and tapped her bottom. She tapped my back in return and then set about walking around the room. She stumbled over suitcases and pillows, regaining some of her spirit.

Unfortunately, baby Tiger's temperature soared again. I

bathed her again and washed the water over her dimpled, chubby body. She played with her mermaid and her wind-up frog and I fished and hooked little plastic minnows for her amusement. As the heat evaporated from her blue-white skin, her mood rose again and I felt a kind of relief I never understood before I was a parent. It was five in the morning now. I was jet-lagged, war weary, and life felt fragile.

Just before dawn, Tiger seemed to have turned a corner. At the time she was not really speaking, but was eloquent enough to make herself understood. 'No! No way,' was my favorite phrase, and one she had perfected. At eight months we thought we heard her say 'daddy' but she never uttered it again. Months on and she had yet to complete a full sentence, until at that moment in our Mexico City hotel, when out of sorts and out of the blue, she suddenly said, 'Dada, I love you.'

A wave of emotion washed over me. Tiger turned her head and teased her curls with her tiny fingers, unaware of the significance her words held. For her the moment was over. As for me, I burst into tears.

This was a special moment for a father, especially for one who grew up without a dad.

I am determined not to repeat the sins of my own father, and to be a constant presence in my kids' lives. My mom brought up five of us single-handedly, and every day of her hard life was a small reminder of the dad deficit. Because of that, I take the gift of fatherhood very seriously and I relish my role as daddy to my beautiful girls.

As the tears fell, I thanked God there was still a place in my heart for meaning and a home for unconditional love. I was caught halfway between the potential of a life yet to be lived and the smell of death still in my nostrils. The tears told me that I was at least not completely dead to the world.

Considering the kind of stories that I had covered, it was perhaps inevitable that my empathy switch would be turned off at some stage. With a few simple words, my daughter had flipped it back on again. It was five months before she spoke a full sentence again. But I think she knew what I needed to hear that night.

*****

Such an emotionally-charged state of mind is not necessarily ideally suited to engaging with Mexico City's disturbed underworld, but that was my day job and there was work to be done. With just three hours' sleep, I set out to meet a man whose only daughter who had been tortured, raped and murdered. This would no doubt mean a car crash of emotions and I was not looking forward to it.

Kidnapping is endemic in this part of South America. It is not only the rich and famous that are targeted: the crime has percolated down to all sectors of society. It is so prevalent that cases of neighbour kidnapping neighbour have become increasingly common. In one case, a young boy from one of the city's poorest districts was kidnapped for a ransom of $200. When his parents could not find the money to pay the kidnappers, he was killed with an injection of battery acid to his heart. His suffering is unimaginable. The boy was just five years of age; his abductor was a 17-year-old friend of the family.

My assignment that morning was to meet Eduardo Gallo, who once had a little girl just like mine. His story was a devastating contrast to the picture-postcard scenes of Mexico that entice millions of tourists there on a regular basis.

Eduardo is a handsome man in his fifties. He sported a thick goatee and his welcoming smile expressed a warmth that belied his pain. He had the confidence of a man who has been to hell and back, and is wiser for the experience. It was a strange and disconcerting confidence that seemed to say: 'Do your worst: nothing you can do could hurt me more than I've already been hurt.' I understood that perspective and I could see that there is a certain liberation to be had from it.

Eduardo wanted to share his story, to offer hope to those who think that justice is beyond them; to kick the judiciary and the Police into more honest practices; and to tell fathers that love, not revenge, is what must be born out of the kind of tragedy he has suffered.

Where I have hopes and dreams for my daughters, he is

left with just memories. At the age of 23, with her whole life ahead of her, his little princess, Paola, was kidnapped, raped, and brutally murdered, despite the ransom having been paid. During the delivery of the ransom, three of his daughter's kidnappers had themselves been robbed and killed. When the ransom failed to materialise, the other members of the gang shot Paola in the neck.

She was found beside the dead kidnappers. Initially, the Police believed that Eduardo had arranged for the kidnappers to be shot during the handover of the ransom. They blamed Eduardo for Paola's death and said that the kidnappers had shot her because he tried to intervene.

'I lost my head and started shouting at them and telling them where they should go. They were saying I killed my daughter. I said that they are not only stupid but also corrupt.' At that stage he realised that the Police would not pursue the investigation. As he told me the story, he leaned forward, his hands tightly clasped in anger.

Photographs of raven-haired Paola sit on the mantelpiece in the family's sitting room. 'She was a very happy girl, who always loved to play jokes. We found out she was shot with a .45 mm calibre gun. At least she died immediately,'

Having buried his only daughter, he was determined to find the remaining kidnappers. Using all the resources he had, he set out to bring the men responsible for Paola's murder to justice. It took him three years before he finally rounded them up.

'I started collecting information on the dead kidnappers, like photographs, information about their brothers, fathers, cousins ... I knew who I was looking for and what I was looking for. I tracked down every lead. I had the leads from the dead kidnappers, of course, which gave me a head start. This was the job of the Police, but they didn't want to know,' he told me.

Eduardo brought the evidence he had gathered to the Police. His determination and perseverance finally paid off, and the culprits were brought before the courts and convicted. Since then, he has been offered the opportunity to exact revenge on Paola's killers. This is common in Mexico, but he has steadfastly refused to contaminate his daughter's memory by sinking to that level. I'm not sure that I could I maintain such dignity, faced with what Eduardo has been through. I would almost certainly want revenge, but he is a better man than I. But Eduardo knows that the death of the kidnappers would do nothing to ease the pain in his heart.

On the fourth Sunday of every month, he goes to the prison just to make sure that the kidnappers haven't bribed their way to freedom. 'I like to go to see them, just to be sure they are still there. This is Mexico after all,' he said.

I asked him if he felt a great satisfaction knowing that he tracked down the kidnappers and brought them to justice. 'Well, it's not a matter of satisfaction: it's just justice and it's a way of telling Paola, even if she cannot hear me, "I love you."'

I reflected on just how lucky I am to be able to say these simple words to my own daughters.

With tears in his eyes and pain etched in every facial muscle, he told that for him there is no future, only a past.

'Do you have children? Any daughters?' he asked.

'Yes,' I said. 'I have two girls.'

I told him about my baby girl and the words she had spoken to me just a few hours previously. This was heavy stuff between complete strangers. But emotion came easily to Eduardo; he had nothing to lose and he gave me a permission of sorts to reveal my own feelings. There was a painful connection between us as we lived and relived that indescribable bond between father and daughter. As he looked into my eyes, I could see the hurt in his soul that would never heal. I could see how he carries that pain with great dignity and expresses it with true eloquence. Both overcome with emotion, we cried together and allowed the moment to happen.

The scene of two grown men crying bewildered the production crew. But none of them had children. They weren't daddies, and were perhaps too young to understand the tragic difference between a father's dreams and his memories. Either out of politeness or discomfort, neither the cameraman nor the producer ever mentioned this moment after the event. But it will stay with me for the rest of my days.

15

Best of Enemies

It was July 1988. In the shadow of Nottingham County Hall, an array of national flags fluttered in the breeze one hundred metres from the Trent Bridge. Behind each flag stood nervous and hungry athletes making their last minute preparations for the World Canoeing Championships. The River Trent gushed by, over-laden with rainwater.

In the Irish team, was a very excited 22-year-old – me. The city of Nottingham is the home of the National Water Sports Centre at Holme Pierrepont, and a canoe and rowing course that I had attended since I was aged 15 and was a junior international on the Irish team.

That day I raced to eleventh place in the world, and this city and this result came to signify the pinnacle of my canoeing career.

Seven years later I was standing outside the Imperial Bar in Nottingham just off the main square. I spotted two friends coming down the street. Rupert and Peter were paddlers I had known for over 15 years from my days at Holme Pierrepont. They had stood on the banks of the River Trent on that windy day in 1988, supporting me in the World Championships. I am a convivial sort of chap and this chance meeting should have delighted me, but these were different times.

I was living a different life and going by a different name. Tony Hearns was my 'nom de guerre' and I was dressed in an Everlast bomber jacket, black jeans, black t-shirt and black steel-capped shoes. Lee, who in his spare time sold me whizz (amphetamines), and another Tony, a grumpy Italian, shared the door with me. Had I known that he would have the same name as my undercover alias, I would have chosen a different one. Across the road my white Mitsubishi Shogun was illegally parked. There was a sports bag with a remote control micro-camera strategically positioned to capture a wide shot of the nightclub entrance and us three bouncers monitoring the revellers entering the venue on this Friday night.

Earlier that evening, the bar staff served coffee to the doormen as we arrived. Nupi, one of the bargirls, approached me and asked: 'What will you have, Tony, tea or coffee?'

'Coffee, please,' I said.

When she brought it to me she asked where I was from?

'Here and there,' I said. 'What do you do?'

'I'm a media student.'

'Really? What would you like to do – films, PR?'

'My ambition is to work in documentaries. I'd love to work for a programme like *World in Action*; that's what I'd really like to do.'

I thought that was a little too close to home for comfort, as that was exactly who I was working for.

'Really? Why would you want to do that?' I asked, taking another sip of coffee.

'That's where they really dig deep into the story.'

'Be careful what you wish for,' I tell her. 'It isn't necessarily all it's cracked up to be.'

About eight years later Nupi and I met up again. She is a TV producer and was interviewing me for a Channel Four film she was directing. We had a good laugh about just how close she came to finding me out that day. It wasn't funny at the time, though.

Now I could see my canoe club buddies approaching, but thankfully they couldn't see me – yet. They had no idea of my undercover job, but they did know that I was a journalist and they could be relied upon to say entirely the wrong thing at the wrong time: 'Times must be hard in the world of television,

Mac!' or something equally certain to reveal that I had no business being a bouncer at a club in Nottingham.

In front of them was a posse of about 15 women in various states of undress. Nottingham is famous for having three times more women than men. Groups of men would come from Leeds, Coventry, Derby and as far away as Liverpool and Hull to take advantage of the man deficit. This was Friday night, when women and men travelled in single-sex packs. Saturday was couples' night and Sunday was family day.

The small of my back was hot and sweaty against the nylon belt that held my recorder. The appearance of my two friends could spell the end of the operation. I had finally got a job on the doors after four months undercover, and had been taken under the wing of the city's biggest drug dealer. He got me the job and his reputation was protecting me, a *World in Action* reporter. I was scratching the criminal underbelly of the city and I had forgotten that this was regatta week, when canoeists from all over Ireland and the UK converge on Nottingham. It looked like my real life was about to collide with my undercover one.

I was not allowed to move from my post or to go inside to avoid my friends. I tried to hide my face by smoking a cigarette with my hand cupped over my mouth but I couldn't try too hard, because odd behaviour would provoke too much interest from my fellow bouncers. Every stride my old pals took towards me was a step closer to a serious beating, or much, much worse.

I was trying to work out if I could get across the street to my jeep in one piece if my cover was blown. I would have to get out of the city immediately. Despite having spent a great deal of time here as a youngster, I had naively failed to factor in this scenario.

At *World in Action* we had all the undercover toys and gadgets but we had little idea of how to manage a long-term undercover operation in these dangerous waters. I was a rookie getting by on my enthusiasm and a lot of adrenalin. My training for this deep-infiltration role had consisted of a Police briefing and a cup of coffee with the editor. 'Don't get in too deep and don't use drugs,' was the extent of the advice I had been given.

Rupert and Peter were coming ever closer. Rupert is a photographer and has an eye for detail. I could see him in my peripheral vision, scanning the street ahead of him. He had never seen me with a shaved head and I would be completely out of context, but I still felt sure he would recognise me at a glance.

I tried to hide behind Lee, my fellow bouncer, but he moved and leaned his back against the wall, making him useless to me as camouflage.

'Do I have Rupert's number?' I asked myself. In my panic I had forgotten this get-out-of-jail-free card. I took out my phone and searched through the phonebook. Nothing under Rupert; nothing under Peter. Suddenly I found Rupert's – under 'The Dude', of all things. I called the number. They had stopped just 25 metres away to look in the window of restaurant. I could hear his phone ring and saw him pull it out of his pocket to answer.

'Hey, what are you up to?' he shouted into the phone. I could hear his voice carrying down the street. Then he turned around towards me. Before he had a chance to look directly at me, I dashed over to him and was ready to punch him in the smacker and explain later. Suddenly, he and Peter turned again and started walking in the opposite direction towards the market square. I breathed a sigh of relief and ended the call, pretending we had been cut off.

'What the fuck was that about, Tony?' Lee asked.

'Thought he was a c**t who gave me gip last week. I was going to sort him out but he's fucked off.'

The greatest dangers are often the random ones that there is no preparation for. The gods were with me that day, but for how long?

*****

'Would the guy with the biggest shoulders in the office please stand up?' This was how the longest undercover operation ever conducted by a television broadcaster had begun. The editor knew I was the only bloke in the office and the only one with any kind of undercover experience: I had been volunteered in 1995 to investigate the increasing epidemic of ecstasy in clubs throughout the UK.

'Have you done any security work?'

'Yes,' I fibbed.

It sounded like a challenge that was just up my street, but I think the real reason I agreed to do it was that it was Nottingham. It had been a lucky city for me on the water and now I hoped it would hold up for me in the back streets.

I set about building up a false background and personal life that would be appropriate to a Nottingham bouncer. To shortcut some details, I rented the identity of a very good friend of mine, Tony Hearns, who had emigrated from Ireland to the US a few years previously. I figured that he wouldn't need it anytime soon, and he was far enough out of harm's way if anything went drastically wrong. Tony is still in the US and I still owe him the £500 rental fee. Of course if it had been MI5 instead of ITV, I might have had an army of helpers, but this was journalism and I was very much on my own.

It wasn't just a case of following these bouncers and becoming friendly with them – I had to become one of them. Within a month or so I was a Shogun-driving, Marlboro-smoking Irishman, apparently on the run, who might have an interest in drugs and definitely hated students. My reading habits were reassuringly tabloid and my haircut determinedly short. I adopted the uniform of bomber jacket, black jeans and tight t-shirts and attended the gym as if it were the office. The transformation was complete.

We chose Nottingham because it was perceived as an average British city – it didn't have the gun culture of Liverpool or Manchester, yet the violence and drug-dealing were almost as serious. The target was initially the doormen: the intelligence we had indicated that that the city's drug lords were using the bouncers to peddle drugs.

I joined a gym that was known to be a popular hangout for

doormen and drug dealers. On one of my first days there, I approached a man for advice on bodybuilding. My task in this gym was to blend in as a stranger and to get to know the guys working in the city's clubs and pubs. There was no shortage of bodybuilding types so I approached the most affable-looking one, thinking I'd start chatting him up, so to speak, for a bit of practice. He was bald shaven and fitted the stereotype of a bouncer: squat, heavy-set and square-shouldered.

I took a subservient role and complimented him on his muscles and his physique. He offered to spot me for a couple of weights and gave me some bodybuilding advice. In the showers we compared each other's muscles in the mirror and we both suggested areas of improvement. It struck me that this world had a touch of the homoerotic about it, but I kept the thought to myself. I left feeling pleased that I had had a bit of practice. I wanted to settle in and get the cylinders firing before I jumped in the deep end. My new best friend and training partner, had given me the perfect opportunity to get the lie of the land and ease myself into my new world.

A few days later, I received a briefing from the Nottingham Drugs Squad. They gave me a rundown of the major players – characters I could expect to bump into about town. The big players were a 'no go zone', and I was told that on no account was I to attempt to get close to The Hardy Boys – Wayne Hardy and his brother Dean – in particular. I was told that they were serious criminals and Wayne was described as 'a major cross-border drug trafficker'. This was big boy stuff and the detectives wanted a rookie undercover reporter to steer clear of him. My job was to get to the doormen, and we all agreed that anything else would be outside the scope of the investigation.

They showed me a photograph of the city's biggest kingpin.

I smiled.

'You know him?' one of the drugs officers asked.

'Yeah, that's my new mate, Wayne,' I told them. There were a few shocked faces around the table. The last thing the Police wanted was an undercover journalist on their patch. They had no control over me and rightly thought of me as inexperienced and as a bit of a loose cannon. Our Police contact had been under the impression that this would be a quiet foray into the world of drug-dealing doormen, but now it was developing into something very serious indeed.

By accident I had befriended the number one target of the Nottinghamshire Constabulary. It was a bit of luck that could change my life and would certainly change Wayne's.

*****

My Irish accent was a blessing: no one could tell what area or class I was from. When I was asked what I did before, I'd say that I had done 'a bit of this and that'. I dropped hints around the gym that I had worked in security, bodyguarding and that kind of thing. It was code that indicated that I was up to no good. I told Wayne that I was laying low after a bit of trouble at home in Ireland and he politely chose not to push me for details.

Wayne took my story at face value. I wasn't a threat to him and, as long as I didn't intrude on his business, I never would be. For months we just hung out, had a few drinks and trained together. Intuitively, I felt that the slower I took it, the more he would ultimately reveal. If I tried to move too quickly, I would arouse his suspicions and would immediately be excluded from the inner circle.

So, for the first few months I didn't discuss drugs with Wayne – in fact we spoke about anything but drugs. We talked football, girls, muscles and weights; we even discussed education.

His daughter, Kylie, was just 14 at the time and she was struggling at school. 'Tony, you kick with the left foot. I hear those Catholic schools are good for discipline; what do you think?' he asked me. 'She's going off the rails.'

Other times he would complain to me about snouts or grasses. Nottingham was rife with police informants and the criminal fraternity referred to it as the Whispering City.

'No one could keep a secret in this town,' Wayne would say. If only he knew who he was telling his secrets to.

My relationship with Wayne was paying off and others were beginning to open up to me.

'There's a lot of money to be earned in this town,' Scott, once a promising apprentice electrician, told me. 'But it's a whispering city, so it's a bad city to do business in. The coppers know nothing that nobody hasn't told them.' He is 6 ft 1", with the obligatory cropped hair and broad shoulders. Pointing to his mouth and gesturing with his finger, he went on: 'If everyone kept that shut, coppers wouldn't have a fucking clue.' I nodded in conspiratorial disillusionment. 'It's a terrible world where you can't trust anyone,' I said. Nearly inconsolable at this stage, Scott continued his rant: 'If everyone kept their mouth shut, we would be making a lot more money.'

But he was a small player who talked big but wielded little power. He had come to my camera-ridden little flat in one of the nicer parts of Nottingham to sell me guns and Amway products. 'Well, it'll cost you a whack for the 9 mm but I can throw in some really good deals on my Amway products,' he told me, deadly serious. He was offering me gallon containers of washing-up liquid and 10 kg boxes of detergent to sweeten the deal for a 9 mm pistol. It felt like something from *Monty Python*.

'This is Wayne's town, not my town. I am a nobody,' Scott lamented. 'I'm a little piece of shit compared to Wayne – a very well-respected man.' Indeed, Wayne was earning £250,000 a month from his illicit dealings and had all the trappings of the successful gangster: fancy cars, motorboats and a £90,000 watch on his wrist. 'We talk about Wayne in terms of his empire,' a drug squad officer had told me.

Wayne was a man who got things done, and he got me my job as a bouncer. 'This is Tony. He'll be working with you,' was all he had to say. Scott, Lee and Tony were my fellow bouncers, and I figured that they posed a greater threat to my safety than any drunk patron. Most of them were on gear of some sort and steroid use was rife. Another bouncer told me: 'You know you are losing it when you lose your temper and you're kind of enjoying it in a way and you wind yourself up and up. Do you do the same – you are winding yourself up and you are getting off on it?'

'Yeah, I know exactly what you mean,' I agreed, lying.

'You know when your missus winds you up and for a split second I can see myself demolishing her. I try not to get violent with her. I say 'try'. Sometimes, you are in bed and her skin touches you and you could just knee her out of bed, but you can't,' he said, explaining his steroid rage. The local steroid dealer worked at the club before I arrived but had to leave because he 'battered someone'. Nice guys.

There was a lot of stress involved in dealing with these people and keeping myself safely undercover. Sometimes the loneliness got to me. I would retreat to my flat with a tube of Pringles, crackers and some sandwich spread, and curl up on the sofa to hide from the stresses of the street. These moments would pass quickly, but they were an intense reminder that this was a one-man operation. My closest support was the production team in London and I would occasionally meet with producers from the Manchester office. But this simply wasn't enough and weeks could pass without me seeing anyone. If I was an undercover policeman, I would have had support 24/7. Later, when I led undercover teams, I would do my best to ensure that they would never feel so isolated.

*****

One Saturday morning, I was brought to a gym for a rite of passage that turned out to be much more than I had bargained for. I was supposedly going for some training with the lads, but the poorly-disguised sniggering when I arrived gave me the impression that I was in for something much more challenging.

In fact, I was expected to step into the ring with a contender for the British heavyweight boxing title. I watched as monster after steroid-fuelled monster was bashed around by this Goliath. I had arrived at the gym with a mini camera in my bag and another in my t-shirt. I dashed off to the toilet to change and get rid of the t-shirt with the hidden camera. I had to take my bag with me, which looked a little odd, but I had no choice. I came back into the spit-and-sawdust gym, hoping that if I was killed in the ring, I would at least capture it all on the camera in my red sports bag. I placed the camera where it would get a clear shot of the entire ring, made a mental note of where to fall and went to get my punishment.

The producer described what happened next as my finest nine minutes. I was pummelled to pieces. I hit the deck three times in each round and by the end of it, I didn't know my real name, never mind my undercover one. I could barely lift myself off the ground, but when I did, it won me more brownie points with the boys. At least every time I crashed to the floor it was in line with my bag and the camera, so I had the shots and the producer was happy.

This episode bought me street cred and earned me kudos with Wayne, too. 'I heard you took a pounding,' he said. 'And I heard you kept getting up for more.'

As I gained the trust of these people and got deeper into their world, I was discovering how the mechanics of the drugs underworld operated. The doormen decided who could sell drugs in the clubs. If you were found selling drugs without permission or without handing over a cut of the takings, you had a choice – either give them everything or be turned over to the Police. 'Some [dealers] get a bit cocky, but we soon bring them down when we get our hands down their pants looking up their arsehole and that. They don't like that,' one of the bouncers told me. Eventually, I was able to demonstrate that everyone, from the lowliest drug couriers to those closest to Hardy, was making money out of the drug business. Evidence that directly linked Wayne to drug dealing was harder to come by, but eventually I got him on tape, conducting business.

After months of skirting around the issue, I was confident enough to talk to him about drugs. I told him that a mate of mine could get some charlie from Amsterdam.

'Would you be interested?' I asked.

'How pure?' he wanted to know.

'Good stuff, about 90 per cent at £30,000 a kilo,' I bluffed.

'That is good,' he said.

'How much do you want?'

'As much as you can get,' he said.

Hardy wouldn't normally do business with someone like me, but after nine months, he considered me a friend, so he was willing to cross a boundary he otherwise would not have. This was the breakthrough I had been craving and it was all on camera. The long days and months circling this shark had finally paid off.

*****

The shark had teeth but he did look after me and had taken me under his wing. As long as you weren't his enemy, he could be very charming and likeable.

Although he is not formally educated, Wayne is a smart man and occasionally he even revealed a spiritual streak.

'I have been reading about Nostradamus. It's frightening, mate. You don't want to read it, mate; you don't want to know. His prophesies about the future are terrifying,' he told me. Although he didn't know it, Wayne's immediate future involved television stardom. After nearly a year in his company, I put away my gym kit and put on my reporter's suit. I had changed uniform. I knew where Wayne was parking his car and I was ensconced in a van nearby with a TV crew. For a year he had known me as a pal and now I was about to reveal myself as his nemesis.

'Mr Hardy, for the last year you have known me as Tony Hearns, but I am Donal MacIntyre, a *World in Action* reporter. Can you tell us how you earned your fortune over the last year, Mr Hardy?' I asked him. His face dropped. He was visibly shaken. But he held his grin as he tried to fathom it all. At that moment, I was very glad he wasn't armed.

I packed my bags and left Nottingham immediately. Wayne fled to Jamaica and waited for the heat to die down. I had caused ructions in the city's underworld: no one knew what they had said or could remember how much they had compromised themselves. All they knew was that all would be revealed in a two-part special on *World in Action*.

When Wayne returned to the city, the Police stepped up the pressure and he was eventually jailed for three years after he was found with a load of cannabis in his car.

If the documentary changed Wayne's life, it certainly changed mine, too. Many underworld gangsters were upset by my investigation and as a result I ended up with a £50,000 price on my head and had to live under constant protection, continually looking over my shoulder. Both of us had got much more than we ever bargained for from Tony Hearns.

*****

Ten years later, I felt driven to contact Wayne Hardy again. He had been on my mind for years. Why? Well, when you work undercover, there is a feeling that with every world you enter and with every identity you assume, you leave a little of yourself behind and take a little of your alias with you. You can't spend a year as someone else and not be affected by it. And when you go to your twin's wedding and forget your real name (which I did), you know that something is wrong.

After working in so many fields and living so many roles, I had a fear that there was little of the real me left. I was having a real crisis of identity. I felt I was becoming the sum of the parts of my undercover roles and that my own identity was slipping away from me. I seemed to be caught halfway between the person I was and the people I had become, and that worried me. My drive to revisit my first major undercover target was an attempt to collect some of the pieces I had left behind.

It was a kind of therapy for me, but not one that had been sanctioned by any psychologist or security expert. I was at the end of my undercover career and I think I needed some kind of resolution. I was willing to risk my life to get some peace of mind.

Perhaps there was also an element of guilt – I knew that

Wayne wasn't all bad. Yes, he was a drug dealer and a criminal but he was also a loving son, a good brother, and a caring father. But reporting on these characteristics was outside my remit.

The picture I had painted of Wayne in my investigation was rightly that of a criminal – but it wasn't the whole story. The truth was, and is, that there is more to a man than just his criminal record and there is more to me than just my CV. He is not Attila the Hun, and I am not Judas Iscariot.

After three years of trying to make contact, Wayne and I came face-to-face again, and this time I got to be myself. My producers had made inroads, but he was not keen on the idea of us getting together. However, following the death of his brother in a freak accident, he decided that a reunion might afford him some time to reflect on his life. The years of negotiations had paid off. When we finally met on camera, Wayne gave vent to his anger over my exposé a decade earlier.

'You see you, you c**t? You don't know how long I've waited to meet you – ten years! You come into my town and take the fucking piss out of me. I wanted to knock the fucking life out of you. You don't know how close you was to getting a proper pasting.' Actually, I had a fair idea of how close I came.

A decade on, Wayne wanted to say that he was more than just a convicted drug dealer, that there was a different film to be made about him – one which would tell the story of the man rather than the gangster.

Talking to him then gave me a unique insight into the aftermath of the investigation. My investigation ultimately cost him his liberty and nearly cost me my sanity but we had both done some growing up since then.

'Time is a great healer but it's not nice being put on film undercover. I mean I got surveillance, now I got coppers, Customs and now a fucking reporter – that's all I need. My life was paranoid as it was – and then you,' he said.

We watched the *World in Action* documentary, *Wayne's World*, in an effort to air the issues and put them behind us. He hadn't seen the film since it had gone out and as he watched it, I could see the anger and pain that it caused him. He had trusted me and I had betrayed that trust. Whatever he was guilty of, the betrayal still affected him on a very human level. He winced as each sequence was shown and I began to worry about the fallout. The programme ended with my confrontation with him, when I revealed myself as a reporter who had spent a year fooling him so I could get my story. Wayne gave me a running commentary of those moments from his perspective. This is a side of the story you never hear and I was fascinated to know what was going on in his head.

'My mind was racing. [I was thinking:] what is he? A copper? And then I saw the camera and I twigged. You got yourself into a situation and you were lucky to get out alive. It was reckless of your employers to put you there. One part of me was saying, "Whack him!" and the other was saying, "Get into the car and go."' Which is what he did.

The meeting proved to me just how fortunate I was to get away from this situation unharmed. Luck is the most important commodity in my line of business, and Wayne's too, I dare say.

He surprised me as he opened up in spite of our history. This was new ground for both of us.

Wayne revealed his most private thoughts about his family to me, and there were poignant echoes of the friendship that we had briefly shared 10 years previously.

He said that although my investigation had upset his mother, Rita, she was pleased with one thing. 'I don't give a fuck what they say about you, son, but I brought up my sons proper. When they was filming you, at least when you opened the door, you wiped your feet,' she had said. The vivacious 65-year-old has great charisma and it's easy to see where Wayne gets his charm.

I discovered that he is the father of a learning-disabled son, Jordan, who may not live into adulthood. He changes his nappies, does the school run and fervently defends his son's rights.

He told me about the recent tragic death of his brother, who fell in the way of a bin lorry on Trent Bridge and died in Wayne's arms.

He revealed the painful memory of the loss of his first child, Sunny, and his partner, who died while he was in prison. 'She called me and said, "You know Sunny loves you."'

Later that evening the prison chaplain knocked on Wayne's cell door. 'I couldn't imagine what he wanted. He sat me in my room and told me that she killed my daughter and then killed herself.' Sunny was just 10 months old.

Wayne is torn apart by the havoc his criminal career has wreaked on his family life. He professes to have left that career behind, and is now dealing in shares and currencies online. For the last five years he has had no serious convictions. Either he's gone straight or got smarter.

Kylie, his daughter whose education he had been so concerned about years earlier, is now addicted to heroin. She is working as a prostitute and has suffered rape and abuse as a result. If anything has rescued Wayne from a life of crime, it is her addiction. I got close to her, when Wayne accepted me as a friend again after our unlikely reunion.

As the father of two girls, I cannot imagine the pain he has gone through watching Kylie descend into the hell of heroin. Today, it is touching to see how close they remain despite everything.

'I may be a hypocrite, but heroin has changed this town. I should know how hard it is because my daughter is on it. Kylie has been in and out of prison for the last eight years. I have to admit that I bear some responsibility for this,' With a deeply-felt anguish that I had never seen in him before, he revealed much more about the real Wayne than my year-long undercover exposé could ever have unveiled.

'Sometimes, I am relieved when she is in prison, because I know she is not on the game, used and abused. I have a cross to bear for this life.' He turned to Kylie and said. 'If I wasn't in prison, I could have been there for you.'

'I couldn't blame you. You just did your best for us,' Kylie reassured him, and turning to me, she said: 'He loves me so much.'

Wayne has even paid for his daughter to attend The Priory to try to beat her addiction. She is on a methadone programme but is finding the going hard. At one point Wayne turned to the camera and spoke directly to the dealers: 'If you are watching this, please don't go up to my daughter with heroin or drugs, because if I find out who you are, I'll chop your fucking hands off.' And he meant every word.

I am still touched that they opened their lives up to me like this. The more Wayne let me back into his world, the more I felt I was rebuilding my own in a way that I still don't fully understand.

This was a reconciliation that nobody had recommended. Betrayal, threats, humiliation and fear had been the legacy of our professional relationship, but we turned it around and, in the end, salvaged a friendship that is genuine. Only two men who had nothing to lose – who had done their worst to each other – could travel this road together. The brave decision was Wayne's, and, despite the advice of those around him, he extended the hand of reconciliation.

Today, I feel I could trust him with my life. Once the best of friends, and now the best of enemies.

16

TRIBE SWAP

We were entertaining our new houseguests over tea and biscuits and their conversational gambits were proving to be somewhat unusual.

'How much did you pay for your wife?' Samuel asked me coolly.

'I, er, well, I didn't actually ... ' I spluttered.

'Do you mind if your husband has a baby with another woman?' Christina asked my seven-months-pregnant wife, Ameera, who almost choked on her tea.

'Who is the boss?' asked Samuel, casting a knowing glance towards Ameera.

I think it's fair to say that these crocodile-hunting polygamists from the Pacific Island of Papua New Guinea would add a certain frisson to any polite Wimbledon soirée.

Samuel and Christina are members of the 250-strong Insect Tribe of hunter-gatherers who are just a generation away from cannibalism. They hunt crocodiles with spears and stalk wild boar with bows and arrows. They speak their own language, Ngala, and worship their glassy-eyed totem of the praying mantis. Polygamy is accepted in the tribe and dowries are often, rather poetically, paid in seashells. One tribesman has 12 wives, and another is said to have 112 children scattered among several local villages.

Family planning comes in the form of a potion, the manufacture of which involves spiders' webs and numerous incantations to the ancestors of the tribe. They claim that it has a one hundred per cent success rate. I'm not too sure the incantations would leave me in the mood either.

I first met the tribe in 2007, when I travelled the world to observe how ancient cultures and tribes were engaging with the ever-encroaching modern world. I spent time with the nomadic Bedouin of the Arabian Sands, the Sea Gypsies of Borneo and the llama traders of the Bolivian Andes. But it was the Insect Tribe that stole my travel-weary heart. I lived in their remote village of Swagup, ate their food, shared their homes and mined the secrets of their culture.

I had arrived by canoe to a cacophony of noise and song. Everyone was painted with a kaleidoscope of colours and dressed with feathers and animal skins to represent the trees, mountains and the bird-spirits they worship. They welcomed me with a 'sing sing' – a celebration of the rain forest and jungle that is their home, their life, their everything. The witchdoctors and the village elders in ceremonial dress hailed me as a visiting head of state. A more welcoming people I have never met. They captivated me with their friendliness and generosity of spirit.

The centre of village life is the Haus Tambaran (spirit house) where the magnificent carvings of the animal spirits for which the tribe is renowned are on display. This is also where young men are initiated into manhood by having intricate designs of crocodiles carved on their bodies with a combination of wooden needles and hot branding irons.

The life force of the area is the mighty Sepik River, one of the great river systems of the world. It is 1,126 km long and its flood plain extends beyond 50 km. The rhythm of life there works in concert with the ebb and flow of the river. It is a beautiful marriage between man and nature.

There is no major settlement within 800 km and the nearest hospital is a two-day canoe trip away. The river, the surrounding countryside and the gods provide those who live there with everything they need. Fish, wild boar, fruit, building and hunting materials are all gathered from nature, and the village witchdoctor provides them with medical assistance and advice. The tribespeople think of their home as a land of plenty, a paradise that has provided for them for thousands of years.

They have robustly defended their culture against all comers, from intrepid Christian evangelists to Japanese soldiers during World War II. Their one concession was to allow the missionaries to teach them basic English. Wisely, the elders recognised that they could protect themselves better if they could speak the language of the settlers. The village school still teaches them English today.

They showed themselves to be as curious about my world as I was about theirs, and bombarded me with questions about London and the 'Chief', or the Queen as she is more commonly known. As Papua New Guinea is a Commonwealth country, Her Majesty is also their chief. She is regarded with a mixture of fascination and awe that I never expected of people so far removed from British culture. The tribe's own Chief, a rather colourful character called Joseph, was elected by a majority vote for a five-year term. Once in power, the Chief commands supreme authority and is the most respected member of the community.

Sitting in his wooden three-storey palace, Joseph and I got to talking. I wanted the opportunity to return the overwhelming hospitality and kindness that they had shown to me, so I invited him and his kin to undertake the 20,000 km journey to my home in Wimbledon, South West London.

It wasn't any great anthropological experiment or an outrageous idea for a new reality TV show, it was just old-fashioned good manners. I had studied them and their lives and now I wanted them to have the chance to examine the way we live.

The tribespeople had never before travelled beyond their local stomping ground; the furthest they normally go is a few kilometres downriver, to trade with other villages or settlements.

Making the journey were Joseph, Samuel, Christina, James,

Steven and one of his two wives, Delma. Together they comprised the 'Swagup Six', a party of 'Ancient World' travellers coming to a microchip world. The Papua New Guinean government had to specially authorise their passports because they couldn't tell when they were born and had no identification documents. After a multitude of inoculations and much praying to the spirits, they began the four-day journey to London. 'I don't know what magic they have in Britain but we are about to find out,' Joseph declared to his people in a pre-departure address.

The Swagup Six arrived at Heathrow's Terminal 4, with spears on their backs and bows over their shoulders. There was a little explaining to be done as they brought their hunting weapons through customs and airport security. Eventually, the letters of invitation and the antiquity of the implements convinced the officials to let them through. 'They were not going to refuse me,' said Chief Joseph, convinced the authorities wouldn't dare to prevent a man of his standing from entering the UK.

In Arrivals, every escalator was met with terror and every lift with suspicion until one of the group, usually Steven, an expert crocodile hunter, would venture forth. The rest of the tribe followed, slightly in awe of his bravery. A revolving door inspired wonderment. 'It is an invisible hand that moves this. I can't believe it,' Samuel said.

As a culinary introduction to Britain, I gave the troop porridge and a fry-up for breakfast. Hunters who can't simply go to the fridge for their next meal tend to have insatiable appetites and a profound appreciation of food. But they were wary of processed British fare and scathing of the airline food they had been served on the 'bird with engines'.

My guests were fascinated by everyday objects and situations to which we wouldn't give a second thought. They believed the leafless winter trees were dead and that the ice dispenser in the fridge was some kind of sorcery. The battery-powered cries of my daughter's doll drew shrieks from the women. But James was thrilled by the shower; he had never before felt warm water on his skin.

Delma was bemused to see me cut my daughter Allegra's

lunchtime sandwiches into shapes to encourage her to eat them. She told me that if her children didn't eat, they went hungry. 'They soon learn,' she said.

When Delma and Christina accompanied Ameera to her seven-month scan, they were ashen-faced at the sight of the image on the screen. 'The spirit of the baby is in the machine,' Delma shrieked. Despite their terror, they stayed to share the experience with her.

Samuel and Christina, themselves a couple, were interested in how Ameera and I related to each other. They seemed to suspect it was Ameera who wore the trousers, a situation that would be unthinkable in their village. There, the men dominate everything from politics to hunting. The women bear all the responsibility for cooking and childcare but command none of the power. Women in the tribe who challenge the male dominance of their society risk the wrath of the masali (evil spirits). 'It may be by lightning or disease, but women who break the law, die,' the village witchdoctor had told me in no uncertain terms. Such transgressions include standing up while paddling a canoe, or entering a spirit house – rights that are reserved exclusively for men.

In the MacIntyre household, I am merely the deputy. Ameera is the chief exec, and I'm not going to say any more, lest I get into trouble. 'In Swagup, the man is indisputably in charge. He is the boss,' we were told. But whatever Samuel and Christina secretly thought of our unorthodox marriage, they maintained a public front of diplomatic broad-mindedness. The Chief's guiding principle was: 'When in London...'.

When I stayed with them, I had done my best to adopt the same approach. My bed was hung from the eaves of the reed house, which was built on stilts in the middle of the Sepik River. It was communal living: in one corner were the two kids snuggled up under animal skins, and Samuel and his two wives slept together in the opposite corner. Occasionally, my eyes drifted in the adults' direction and thankfully they were all asleep.

Once in London, the Insect Tribe were cautious about some

of the city's tourist attractions. At the London Eye, the tribe held congress in the shadow of the huge wheel. 'It's not meant for humans,' was the general consensus. But Delma urged them on, shouting: 'We've come this far, haven't we?' Released from the patriarchy of the jungle, she took it upon herself to push the tribe to braver heights. Eventually, the Chief decided that they should try to enjoy the bird's-eye view of London. 'As we were on the wheel, all our hearts were hanging,' Samuel told me later. 'I couldn't believe I was so high above the land. All the buildings were joined up, and they were huge. They looked like trees, with branches. There's no end, no mountain, only buildings. I was wondering how the wheel goes round, what gods make this turn.'

When our capsule reached the summit, Joseph asked me to point out our 'spirit house'. He found the great dome of St Paul's Cathedral remarkable, not for its grandeur but for its diminutive size next to the other great buildings of London. 'In our village, no building can be bigger than the spirit house. Nothing is more important to us than our gods and spirits,' he said.

His remark highlighted how our values have changed over the centuries: how the architecture of business and commerce now towers over our places of worship. It was a point worth noting. We went to visit St Paul's and the Chief gave the women special dispensation to enter. This was perhaps in deference to his host but I think it was also an expression of his firm belief that our gods are simply not as powerful as theirs.

But everyone was impressed by Sir Christopher Wren's work. 'This building must have formed with the earth. It could not be made by man,' said an awestruck Delma. When we showed her the magnificent statues in the cathedral, she said: 'The people must have just frozen by magic. Maybe they will get up and walk when we are not here.'

In stark contrast to what its daily passengers think of it, the London Underground also inspired awe. Astounded by the enormity of the network, James was mesmerised by the Underground and was convinced that the Tube was built first, and that the streets were added on top later. 'London is a double city. The first city is underground and the second city they built on top of the first city.'

Unfortunately, the underground adventure was brought to a shuddering halt when the train driver announced that a passenger in another carriage had defecated on the seats. I had never expected London to be a civilising influence and I wasn't proved wrong.

Spirits were raised by the prospect of a visit to Buckingham Palace. For the Chief it presented the possibility of a meeting of minds. As a tribal leader in a Commonwealth country, Joseph regards himself as the Queen's representative in Swagup. She was his head of state and he was a visiting dignitary. We dutifully put in a request for a meeting, but regretfully, it was declined. 'Why can't I go in there?' he asked in an injured tone as we stood outside. 'I will return to my village and I will get old and die. I will never return to London. She should show respect.'

In his part of the world, he is a king. Here, sadly, he was just another tourist.

As we walked away, the group's attention was diverted when they caught sight of a grey squirrel in St James Park. They chased it through the park and up the trees. 'I like it so much I want to put it on my head for the sing sing,' James said with a beaming smile. Their version of pest control may yet catch on. There was even a suggestion that we might bring one home to Wimbledon to cook for dinner.

Not being a huge fan of squirrel, I suggested an Indian takeaway instead, For the Insect Tribe, 'takeaway' means fishing and then cooking their catch on their canoes. They ate the spicy food and I think they enjoyed it – certainly very little was left behind. But that may have been due more to their abhorrence of waste than to a newfound love of tandoori chicken.

After our tour of London, we spent some time in Wales, where the Swagup Six were introduced to falconry. They were aghast that a bird would be trained to hunt in such a way. 'Hunting is for humans,' Steven said, as if his own job were under threat.

It was here too that the group encountered snow for the first time. 'It's like the sand on the river bank but the colour is white and it falls from the sky. When will it stop? It is very very cold,' Joseph said. As six inches of snow covered the Welsh countryside, a world that had become a little familiar was now alien again. But after a tentative start, they were soon throwing snowballs with pinpoint accuracy.

When I was in Swagup, they brought me out to hunt wild boar, so I brought them to a pheasant shoot in Norfolk to meet some Brits who live off the land.

Before hunting in Papua New Guinea, incantations to the spirits are said; in Norfolk spirits of a different kind herald the hunt. The hunter-gathers had left their bows and arrows behind but took to the rifle with impressive ease. The Norfolk landed gentry and the men of the forest soon found common ground as they bemoaned the price they get for their produce – farmers are the same all over the world!

Back in London, the Make-A-Wish Foundation, a charity dedicated to helping fulfill the wishes of terminally ill children, had invited Ameera and me to a fundraising event at the Dorchester Hotel. We took Joseph along, resplendent in his ceremonial headgear. The Chief waltzed past the snapping paparazzi unfazed, and walked straight into the arms of Melinda Messenger and Simon Cowell. Comedian Mel Smith came bounding over to find out about the man who had upstaged Jude Law's grand entrance.

Joseph, meanwhile, was working the table like a pro. He quickly charmed two lottery winners into volunteering to travel to Papua New Guinea and bring medical and educational supplies with them.

Much of what the tribespeople said gave me pause for thought. It was enlightening to see through their eyes how far from our own sense of community we have drifted. When they visited a sheltered housing scheme for the elderly, they were distressed that the 'elders' in the UK are not taken care of by their children. 'It is not right,' said Steven, shaking his head. 'They brought you up when you were naked. They cared for you, and when they are old you must care for them.' James told the elderly residents: 'You make me worried because your sons and daughters are supposed to look after you.' Living apart from your parents is something that the tribe cannot get to grips with.

For all the luxuries he was temporarily enjoying, James was not tempted by our lifestyle. 'If I stay in England, I have to pay for everything; if I stay in my own village, everything is free … You have such busy lives. Do strangers talk to each other, or even have time to breathe? I think you need too much money to stand still.'

Their openness and enthusiasm highlighted for me how jaded we have become, and how indifferent we sometimes are to the wonderful sights on our own doorstep. They embraced their experience of our culture, without renouncing an ounce of their own.

The goodbyes at Heathrow were emotional.

'It was the first time I saw the white man cry,' James said. 'We come from the same pot.'

'What do you miss most from home?' I asked.

'My second wife,' Samuel said, without a blink. He was standing beside his first wife, Christina.

And so they left, convinced that it is they who have it right, and we who are primitive. I don't think they would swap our world for their own, where everything they need is free and plentiful, where everything is shared and where the only things treasured are the values of family and community.

Since their visit, Chief Joseph died while hunting crocodiles. I suspect that is how he would have liked to have bowed out.

Back at my home, a carved praying mantis stands on my mantelpiece and a beautifully crafted spear stands in the corner, reminders of our friends who taught us a lesson in simplicity.

17

Miami Ice

I once told a fellow journalist that he had permission to shoot me if I ever took part in a show with the word 'celebrity' in the title. It was a firmly held conviction and I was confident that I could escape such indignities with ease. I hadn't of course counted on the persuasive powers of my wife, Ameera, our two daughters, Allegra and Tiger, and the Haitian Voodoo Mafia.

In the sultry heat haze of Miami, members of the most dangerous and violent street gang in the US were hanging outside the crack houses of Little Haiti, smoking weed and doing deals to a soundtrack of Police sirens and homemade hip-hop from their own backstreet studios.

The previous evening Miami's finest drug squad officers had taken me on a tour of the neighbourhood and we had driven past the very same drug den. These hoods were threatening a fresh wave of killing and vice in a city with no shortage of either. They were the new pirates of the Caribbean, using new drug trafficking routes into the US via their lawless homeland.

I leaned into the window of a battered car occupied by a man my own age and his eight-year-old son. The man told me he was a hitman and wouldn't think twice about ending my days with 9 mm bullet to the head.

'Why would you do that?' I asked.

'The colour of your eyes; I might not like the way you smell today,' he answered.

This man was the real deal. I had every reason to be terrified.

'How many do you think you have killed?'

'By the time I was 21, I had lost count.'

I believed every word of it.

'Eat, shit, sleep, kill: that's what I do best,' he said.

His child, eyes wide, held his gaze on me throughout. He didn't utter a word or move a muscle. Daddy spoke again: 'There is nothing more exciting than watching someone take their last breath,' he told me.

I asked him about his son.

'He knows what I do.' The boy just looked scared.

I was sweating profusely from my armpits to my groin, and for good reason: another street soldier, nicknamed 'Blind', had lifted his shirt to display a small firearm tucked into his belt. He took it out and waved it about. 'With my record, if I'm caught with it, I am inside for life,' he said. Under the 'three strikes and you're out' rule, Blind would get no leniency from the Miami County Sheriff. He had earned his reputation the hard way and had already served time for murder as a juvenile. He knew the stakes were high.

Blind was keen to explain to me that the Haitian Voodoo Mafia were much more than just a drug dealing gang – they were a community action group, social workers, business facilitators and now artists, with their own music label and pirate radio station.

A new wave of Haitian immigrants hit American shores in 1991 after a coup d'état overthrew President Jean-Bertrand Aristide. It was said at the time that the black, poor Haitians were at the very bottom of American society, and that hard-working Haitians were treated worse than any previous immigrant population in the history of the US.

Small wonder then that the second generation, armed with youthful confidence and firearms, had fought back with such ferocity. The Zoe Pound gang gave as good as they got, and then some.

Today though, the Voodoo Mafia wanted me to hear their

music and admire their guns – in that order. After an hour of mindless evasive driving and counter-surveillance, moving from safe house to safe house around the Zoe Pound's neighbourhood, we pulled up outside a suburban detached house. The banal exterior gave no hint of the madness inside.

The smell of weed alone was enough to get anyone high. The TV blared McCain and Obama in the midst of election fever. At the back of the house there was a sophisticated music studio with hundreds of thousands of dollars' worth of equipment. The music didn't quite live up to the quality that the expensive equipment promised, however. But there was no disputing the quality of the guns on display: shiny new AK-47s, often referred to as 'widow makers', were the killing machines of choice.

The motley crew of killers, drug dealers and wise guys presented their guns, wearing the obligatory balaclavas. 'Vote Obama,' they shouted, randomly. It wasn't exactly the kind of endorsement the soon-to-be President was canvassing.

And then my phone rang. In such circumstances, I would normally have the phone turned off during filming, but the health and safety issues involved in dealing with madmen and guns meant that it was wise to keep your phone about you - and switched on!

'Hello, Daddy. I lost the moon in the sky, Daddy,' said my daughter, Allegra. Well, that was a call I had to take, particularly as there was a chance that it could be the last I would ever take. Allegra told me about her wobbly tooth and said: 'Freddie at school says that he has *Hannah Montana 15*, the DVD, at home. That's a lie Daddy, isn't it?'

'Of course it is, gorgeous. Can I talk to Mommy, quickly?'

It had to be brief, because there was more urban hardware to peruse and I wanted to get the hell out of there as soon as possible. I am a coward at heart and am finely attuned to appropriate departure times when there are loaded guns about.

'Hi, babes. I know you have issues with it, but me and the girls have decided you are doing *Dancing on Ice*,' Ameera began.

'Honey, can we talk later? I'm a bit busy now,' I said, smiling at my gun-toting friends.

Taking advantage of my precarious predicament, she asserted herself in no uncertain terms.

'No chance. The deed is done,' she said. 'Don't be angry. It's for the best, and the kids will love it.'

'But honey –'

'You'll be trained by Torvill and Dean!'

'I don't care if I am trained by a thousand virgins,' I said, feeling like I had already lost the battle.

I wasn't angry – I was terrified. Terrified of the humiliation, of the skin-tight spandex on my 42" rollover waist, of the fake tan, of the public vote. Oh, and let's not forget that I couldn't skate and I don't dance – ever.

Just then, the leader of the Zoe Pound, Mac A. Zoe, phoned from Dade County Jail on a contraband mobile phone. He had been remanded in custody on suspicion of being involved in four murders.

His henchmen were watching me, nervous that I might be talking to the Police. I said to Ameera: 'Put baby Tiger on the phone,' and I put the call on loudspeaker. 'Nooo, no way ... Elmo poo,' said my eighteen-month-old daughter, talking about our puppy sausage dog, for whom the JCB pooper-scooper was invented. She then launched into a rendition of a song from *Mamma Mia*. It's the girls' favourite movie (they suffered badly when they gave it up for Lent).

Immediately, the nervous twitches abated.

'Got to go. Love you,' I said.

And that is how I was surrendered to the sequins.

Suddenly the guns in front of me held no danger. This was a world I could relate to. The whiff of cordite, the balaclavas, the drug dealers and killers – I was used to them all. Sequins, red carpets and spandex were another matter entirely.

Later, talking to Ameera on the phone, I said: 'At least it'll be nice to do a show that isn't preceded by the warning: "Some viewers may find the following scenes disturbing."'

'I wouldn't be so sure,' she shot back.

*****

Back in London it was time to decide who should be included in the shortlist for the 2009 series of *Dancing On Ice*. Every year, 50 or so celebrities are canvassed and tested for their level of interest, aptitude and enthusiasm for the slippery tasks involved. In spite of my own good sense, I found myself in that motley collection of possibles, probables and highly-unlikelies. In truth, I thought that I would be so bad that I would fail the selection process and I took some comfort from that, thinking that I might get the better of my girls after all. As it turned out, however, the downright useless were more likely to be selected than the moderately good, on the basis that bad skating makes for good television.

I had always steadfastly avoided shows like this. From *Celebrity Wife Swap* to *Strictly Come Dancing*, I had turned them all down. As a journalist I prefer to be recognised for my work, rather than to be known for being known. I figured that there are only a few reasons for doing such shows and the most common one is that your career is in a cataclysmic downward spiral. I was pondering this as I tied up my skates for the trials and took awkwardly to the ice for the first time.

The former world number two, Karen Barber, who still coaches and mentors Torvill and Dean, was going to assess me for the show. My trial by skates followed that of double Olympic gold medallist in sailing, Sarah Dempsey. Sarah didn't recognise me but did her best to pretend that she did, which I thought was very polite of her. Thanks very much to the producers for putting me on after the Olympic gold medallist!

To Barber's credit she gave the same level of concentration to us as she did to Torvill and Dean. If I had been her I would have thrown me on the ice and let gravity do its worst.

Karen had a chart and a clipboard to record my ineptitude. First she held me by one arm and insisted that I place my hand on the side of the rink. My feet were not moving; my muscles were frozen with fear. In two generations, no MacIntyre has broken a bone and I didn't want to be the one to end the lucky run just as I lost my 'celebrity virginity'.

'Please let me be rejected and let me get on with my life,' I prayed.

So, there was Sarah Dempsey elegantly gliding across the ice, having done no more than a bit of Christmas ice-skating. The natural sports star in her shone through and she was rewarded with admiring nods from Karen. And then there was me: the fat bloke with the muffin belly spilling over the elasticated waist of his tracksuit bottoms. The running order was not designed to make me feel good.

'I should have stayed away from the ice and stuck to broadcasting,' I thought to myself. I was suddenly craving a warzone or the company of a dangerous gangster.

In the end, Karen ranked the 50 celebrities who were brave enough to try out. I came second lowest in terms of ability (no surprise there!) and highest in terms of enthusiasm. Apparently Todd Carty and I were the poorest skaters they had ever come across, and Karen had clearly misinterpreted my terror as eagerness. She did note in her report that I had the potential to be reckless, and, in her words, I was 'not risk adverse'. Like a misbehaving puppy I was out of control, snappy and not house-trained, but with discipline and training, some progress might be possible.

* * * * *

Sunday, 28 September 2008

As an undercover investigative journalist, my office has typically been the mean streets, and my wife has long complained that I have never been able to take our two daughters to work to show them what I do. But taking part in *Dancing On Ice*, in which 13 celebrities partner professional skaters, try to learn how to figure-skate and compete against each other, is my opportunity to finally impress them. So far the full extent of my skating experience has been a session at a rink in Richmond one Christmas more than 20 years ago. Nothing like a challenge!

Thursday, 20 November 2008

Today I met my professional partner for the show, the brilliant French international skater, Florentine Houdiniere. I proudly told her that I'm slowly getting to grips with the basics, apart from going forwards. 'Hmm,' she musesd. 'In many respects going forwards is quite important.' Florentine is a wonderful mix of Parisian flair and Foreign Legion discipline, with a heavy French accent on the discipline and a little domination thrown in for good measure. Some celebrities pay good money for that kind of cocktail, but it never attracted me until today, when Flo became my no-nonsense trainer, determined that I wouldn't make a loser out of her with my inability to skate forwards.

Thursday, 27 November 2008

Christopher Dean and Jayne Torvill, who choreograph the show, are the only pair ever to be awarded a perfect score in a free programme, which they received for their 'Bolero' routine at the 1984 Winter Olympics. My wife has a long-standing crush on Chris, and even blushes when he comes on TV, so when I introduced her to him in person she did nothing but stare and giggle. Chris, presumably used to swooning maidens with fluttering eyelashes, was the perfect gentleman. He confirmed his reputation as having both a profound understanding of his sport and also a mastery of understatement when he pointed out that I am 'not a natural skater'.

Wednesday, 10 December 2008

Met the other celebrities at an ice rink in London's Lea Valley today. I instantly hit it off with former *Grange Hill* and *Eastenders* star, Todd Carty. I quickly discovered that he is to figure skating what Mike Tyson is to embroidery.

I also bonded with ex-England footballer, Graeme Le Saux, who was paying close attention to my skating technique. 'I hope you don't mind me saying,' he offered, 'but you look as if you're recovering from a serious car accident.' He softened the blow by adding that he looked as if he had been my passenger.

The women are far more impressive on the ice. Zoe Salmon, the former *Blue Peter* presenter, is enthusiastic and very good, and so is the graceful Jessica Taylor, who used to be in the pop band, Liberty X.

Meanwhile, presenter Coleen Nolan is witty and funny and threatens to monopolise the John Sergeant vote, though we all think Todd will run her close.

Before we left, Todd came over to me and pointed out my ample lovehandles. 'They're not lovehandles,' I said. 'They're airbags, and I'll need them.'

Sunday, 11 January 2009

My first performance in front of the judges on live TV! This week, just the seven male contestants were competing. I skated resplendent in a sky-blue silk shirt with glitter down the front: positively macho compared to the pink wraparound effort worn by actor Jeremy Edwards.

Florentine and I performed to Nickelback's 'Rockstar'. I managed to pull off what I think was a fairly impressive lift. I'm filled with admiration for Florentine, and indeed all the female professionals. These women rely on their fantastic looks and physical wellbeing to make a living – and now they are being thrown around by idiots like me.

Unfortunately, my lift didn't impress the show's five judges. We scored a total of 13.5 out of a possible 30, although Jason Gardiner, the judge with a splinter of ice where his heart should be, said I was not as bad as he was expecting. I'm told it may be the nicest thing he has ever said to anyone, which cheered me up.

When the judges' scores were combined with the audience votes, Graeme Le Saux and I were the bottom two and had to take part in a skate-off. Last time I was this nervous, a Liverpool crack addict was pointing a gun at me. My head dropped momentarily and Florentine urged me to 'snap out of it'. This was the moment when my 'F-list' celebrity embarrassment gave way to my competitive drive. 'Jesus, don't let me go out in the first round. I swear I'll go to mass and give up drink – just get me through to week two,' I thought.

I gave it my very best effort in the skate-off, which looked hysterically inept, but clearly the judges saw something at the outer edges of my ability, as they elected to keep me in and boot out Graeme. I suspect I got the marks for effort rather than style. I was sorry to see him go, but rather him than me. I started to feel a little more confident about the whole thing, until my twin brother took the wind out of my sails by telling me I had looked like an elephant dancing.

Monday, 12 January 2009

Not only was I not the most popular contestant with the audience, I wasn't even the most popular in my own household. Ameera tells me she was backing Graeme, and the two girls were supporting Roxanne Pallett from *Emmerdale*. I'm working hard to chase their votes. I'll be checking the phone bill to see who they've voted for.

Wednesday, 14 January 2009

At the practice session today I asked Andrei Lipanov, the Russian professional who partners actress Gemma Bissix, to lift me up so I can get a sense of what it's like for the women. Lipanov, who is built like a T-34 tank, raised me above his head and spun me round like a helicopter blade. It felt like being trapped in an out-of-control washing machine and left me terrified, nauseous and unable to stand up. That was quite enough of getting in touch with my feminine side for one day.

Monday, 19 January 2009

Each day I spend about two hours on the ice with Florentine and then I try to do an extra hour by myself. I have lost almost three stone since I started training. The worse you are at skating, the more weight you lose because your movement on the ice is so inefficient. I must be pretty bad!

Unfortunately, this is something of a disincentive to improve. All the MacIntyre boys are what we like to call 'big-boned'. No MacIntyre has been under 15 st for about 15 years. Now I'm hovering just over the 12 st mark. 'Are you sure you've not got worms, Donal?' my Mum asked. My previous weight-loss programmes have usually depended on food poisoning. Now I've become one of those annoying people who can eat whatever they want and not pile on weight. Today I've already had two chocolate bars and a generous fried breakfast. When I get kicked out of the show, I figure I'll have a beach body for a couple of months. So before I start tucking into the beer and pizza again, I'm going to commission a set of photographs on the beach. Sadly, I have no fitness DVD to promote. What a waste!

Tuesday, 20 January 2009

I have received, via ITV1 and my agent, nearly 50 affectionate fan letters from Her Majesty's prisons. They are exclusively from male prisoners, some of them in high-security installations. Many are addressed to 'The Iceman' or 'King of the Ice'. Some of the most dangerous men in the country have surrendered to the sequins, it seems. A prison warden told me that he couldn't remember a family-orientated show ever attracting such a following in the wings of a high-security prison. Go figure.

'I'm delivering a whole new audience for this show,' I boast to Ameera.

'It's nothing to do with the gorgeous, super-fit girls in the skimpy costumes, then?' she says.

Wednesday, 21 January 2009

I've been working on my killer move, the Hydroblade, which involves crouching low and skating backwards with one leg extended. In the metrosexual world of ice dancing, this is the nearest you get to masculinity. It requires a kind of rugby strength in the legs and thighs, and lots of flexibility.

I'm told it's a move even some professionals can't pull off, but, thanks to some freak accident of genetics, I can do it. The show's organisers and the pros are mystified, as am I. It's a filthy, trophy-hunting trick that I am hoping will raise a cheap cheer.

Florentine remarked the other day that I might benefit from ballet lessons. As my daughters go to ballet every Wednesday, I tagged along with them to the Fairy Footsteps For Tiny Tots And Kids class and even wore a pink tutu at the request of the girls, though I declined the fairy wand that Tiger offered me. On second thoughts, a magic wand maybe just what I need!

Thursday, 22 January 2009

Note to self: A couple of glasses of white wine before skating is not a great idea. I was feeling stressed and decided to have a couple of liveners before going for an extra practice session. I spent much of it falling on my backside. At least it didn't hurt as much as usual.

Sunday, 25 January 2009

It's my forty-third birthday and they had me in navy-blue this week. Florentine and I skated to the Otis Redding classic, 'Dock Of The Bay'. I love the song but I don't like skating to it. Of course we told everyone that we loved it and smiled our brightest smiles. Our pièce de résistance was to be our entry onto the ice from the judges' table. I slid down one side beside Karen Barber and was supposed to slide across the table and chill my way to Flo. I was trying to be cool, but it was clunky, ugly and embarrassingly amusing. It was like watching a teenager take their first puff on a cigarette.

Each week there is a required element in the routine and this time it is toe steps, which I mess up royally. However, I did pull off two big lifts, including the Reverse Pencil, in which Florentine was upside down, and, of course, the Hydroblade.

We got a total score of 15 from the judges: an improvement of sorts, but still second last, which actually means last, if you discount Todd – which, if you'd seen him, you would.

Tonight, during his routine, Todd careered off the rink and out of camera shot, arms flailing, legs akimbo. When it happened, Sharon the physio bolted towards him, but he was caught by a couple of burly assistants and shunted back onto the rink.

I now call him Vera. Just as Vera Lynn helped keep up morale during World War II, so Todd is helping to keep people smiling during the recession.

Despite our low standing in the table, Florentine and I were voted through by the audience. The country's generosity knows no bounds. My mum tells me people in Ireland are getting their friends in the UK to vote for me because they are not allowed to vote themselves. If the Irish could vote, I could sit back and pick up the trophy later. We do like to support one of our own.

Monday, 26 January 2009

One of the lifts we did last night was the Swan Stand (we make the names up ourselves!), in which Florentine faces me, I go into a crouch, she rests a foot in my lap and then stands up like a swan, so to speak. I have found that having nine inches of cold, sharp steel in one's lap while skating at high speed does nothing for one's peace of mind, no matter how well one gets on with one's partner. Indeed, I've been coming home with cuts and bruises that are perilously close for comfort. To avoid any further potential damage, I've started wearing a cricket box.

Sunday, 1 February 2009

Tonight I was in a glittering pinstriped suit and a tie. My suit was so sparkly with its £3,000 worth of sequins that there were complaints from ITV transmission that it was interfering with the quality of the picture. It might have started all sparkly but I did my best to dull things down with my performance.

Florentine has been pushing me hard, trying to get me to relish the limelight and tonight we performed our routine to the Blues Brothers track, 'Everybody Needs Somebody'. It was pretty tricky, and disaster struck when I fell trying to do three jumps in a row. This was a little over-ambitious as I was clearly struggling to do a single jump. I picked myself up and got going again immediately but I knew it was going to cost us.

Incredibly, we got a score of 16 – our best to date. One judge gave us an impressive 4.5 out of 6, although Jason awarded us just 2.5.

As he delivered his caustic comments, the audience drowned him out with boos – the first time this has happened. I did catch the word 'pathetic', however.

As usual, the only team below us was Todd and his partner, Susie. Once again Florentine and I were protected by the public vote. The thought does cross my mind that, if it's mostly women who phone in, the cricket box might be something of a vote-winner.

Monday, 2 February 2009

Ironically, several contestants struggled to make the training sessions because of the ice and snow blanketing the country!

My waist measurement is now down from 41" to just 33". 'Chubby hubby' has disappeared. No more elasticated waistbands! In fact I'm now frenziedly eating as much as possible to keep my weight up.

Tuesday, 3 February 2009

While attempting a high lift during practice today, I dropped Florentine onto the ice from six feet in the air. Thankfully, she is absolutely fine. The only thing I bruised was my ego – and my shins, knees, thighs, stomach, chest, back, arms, shoulders and neck.

I have played rugby, skied, shot rapids in a canoe; I have climbed the Matterhorn and parachuted out of a plane in the Arctic, but I have never before had as many bruises as I do now.

If anyone ever again suggests to me that ice dancing is a little bit girlie, I will strangle them with one of my spangled shirts.

Friday, 6 February 2009

I have been having physio since the accident but I feel OK. I know I've done well to stay in the contest this long, given that I'm two parts testosterone and one part shambles. If I can limp on for another couple of weeks, I will have got much further than I ever dared to hope.

I'm just thrilled it's taken me so far outside my comfort

zone – the world of drugs and murder – and given me a chance to show my girls what I can do.

Sunday, 8 February 2009

The required element tonight was the Change of Edge: shifting the weight from one side of the blade to the other. Skating to Sam Sparro's 'Black and Gold', wearing a black shirt, I managed to raise Florentine into a shoulder lift and we scored 17. 'Better musicality,' Jason said. 'Very solid partnering.'

We were all shocked when Todd Carty was kicked out. We thought the public would be happy to hang on to his hilarious coat tails for a couple of weeks longer. There are now just eight of us left.

Saturday, 14 February 2009

I like to include a really difficult move every week. This can, of course, result in over-ambition. This week I was trying to perfect a sort of American baseball slide that ended up with me flat on the ice, spinning round and then stepping out of it. It looks terrific when it's done by a professional. But I still hadn't mastered it by Saturday evening and I said to Florentine: 'I don't think this is working. It looks as if I'm just falling over.'

She tried to reassure me but I wasn't convinced. The 10-year-old son of one of the production staff was watching us rehearse.

'What do you think?' I asked him.

'Looks like you're falling over, mate,' he said.

We took it out.

Sunday, 15 February 2009

Tonight we skated to 'Addicted to Love', with me in a pink shirt and white suit; it was very *Miami Vice*. The judges award us 18, commending our 'intensity'. We're the only couple who have improved their score every week. Every time Coleen and I get through, we exchange a wink, but I noticed Florentine shoot a look at Stewart, Coleen's partner, that said: 'How on earth have we managed to propel these buffoons through to another round?'

Ray Quinn, who was runner-up to Leona Lewis in the *X Factor*, achieved the first perfect score of the series tonight, but my buddy, rugby star Ellery Hanley (I can honestly say he is all the human being I would want to be but am not) was sent packing. I am the last 'real' man standing. Let's face it, Ray Quinn is a dance god and cannot be considered mortal.

Monday, 16 February 2009

After choreography class with Chris and Jayne (now known to the celebrities as 'The Icons'), I was straight off to a disused RAF base in Lincolnshire to blow up a car for my gangsters show. Having blown any ambitions of being a dancer in the morning session, it was my mission to blow a car to smithereens in the afternoon. We were demonstrating the use of pipe bombs made from plastic explosives. From spandex to Semtex in one day! With help from Tony Lewis, a military expert, we took a steel tube and packed it with homemade explosives. We capped both ends but placed a detonator in one of them. In an instant, we had a deadly pipe bomb that we could use to devastating effect from 300 metres away. I have to admit that blowing up cars on old military bases was much more exhilerating than skating badly – no matter how wonderful Torvill and Dean are.

Wednesday, 18 February 2009

During rehearsals there are people who sit in for the real judges and give scores after we run through our routines. Today Florentine and I achieved all sixes – a perfect score, the holy grail of the ice skating universe. Unlike the real judges, these stand-ins are open to bribery and susceptible to pleading.

My progress is now wearing thin with my daughters, who weren't banking on me staying in the show this long. They want me around in the morning and to pick them up from school. I'm trying to skate earlier in the mornings so I can spend time with them in the evening, but work on my other shows is piling up.

Sunday, 22 February 2009

Tonight our music was REM's 'Everybody Hurts' or 'Everything Hurts' as we appropriatly renamed it. I wore a royal-blue V-neck top. I stumbled and clipped Florentine's ankle with my skate and she yelped in pain. We scored just 17. Thankfully, we still got through. Melinda Messenger was booted off by the judges. We're down to the last six.

Wednesday, 25 February 2009

This week is 'prop week'. All the contestants have to include some sort of object in their routine. My prop is a broom and I've been carrying it around with me everywhere. Ameera says this is the closest to housework I've come in years.

A cab driver studied me carefully in his rear-view mirror today. The show is regularly topping nine million viewers and clearly he is one of them. Finally, the penny dropped with him: 'Here, you're that bloke off *Dancing On Ice*,' he said. I considered telling him that I'm an investigative journalist, war correspondent and documentary-maker. Instead, I nodded in quiet resignation and just thanked God he didn't ask about the broom.

Sunday, 1 March 2009

On the show tonight, I revealed the shocking black bruise the size of a doormat that extends from my hip, right across my buttock and down my leg. It is the result of repeatedly falling over and landing on the same side. Whenever I drop Florentine or trip her up, she picks herself straight up and gets back to work without a word of complaint. So I feel I have to do the same, however much I'd rather hobble to the side of the rink and weep.

We scored 23 – our best so far – for the routine we performed to 'I Guess That's Why They Call It The Blues'. Roxanne Pallett was voted off. As she skated off the rink, she threw her bouquet to Allegra to thank her for her support. Allegra has now switched her allegiance to Ray Quinn rather than her Dad.

Monday, 2 March 2009

Many people have stopped me in the street to comment on my bruise, including a squaddie, who said: 'Jesus, Donal! My mate got bitten on the arse by a camel and it didn't look half as bad as that.'

Friday, 6 March 2009

This morning I was on GMTV talking about the show. I noticed that in the script it said: 'Donal drops his trousers and shows us his bruise.' However, in order to allow the nation to enjoy its breakfast, the MacIntyre apparel stayed firmly in place.

More fan letters arrived and Ameera sorted through them. She handed me one with an enclosed photograph showing a jolly-looking lady of middling years. This lady claimed to be a member of the Women's Institute and suggested we meet to engage in a number of exotic activities one does not readily associate with the WI.

'So that's what they do with all the extra jam,' said Ameera.

Sunday, 8 March 2009

Skating to Roxy Music's 'Let's Stick Together', I manage this week's required element, an unassisted jump, without mishap. Of course, 'jump' is defined simply as both feet leaving the ice at once. I think I might have managed the dizzy heights of about 2 ½". Nevertheless, our score of 22 was enough to see us through.

Zoe Salmon was kicked out, so that leaves just four of us: Coleen, Ray, Jessica Taylor and me. If anyone had told me six months ago that I'd be in the semi-final, I would have laughed out loud, and so would everyone else.

Friday, 13 March 2009

This week I've been wearing a large, flattened silicone patch to protect my bruise. 'What do you call this thing?' I asked one of the medics.

'An incompetence pad,' he said.

Coleen Nolan, however, really has been in the wars. Despite sustaining a rib and back injury this week, and nursing a broken bone in her wrist, she is determined to skate in the semi-final. It would be a brave man who'd bet against her doing it.

The music Christopher Dean has selected for Flo and me is the Bond theme, 'Live and Let Die'. 'It was the closest thing I could think of to your proper job,' he said. To be honest, I'm beginning to think this is more dangerous than my proper job.

Sunday, 15 March 2009

This was a strange night. The producers have always said that the audience knows when it's time to go. I was praying it was not my time. My 007 performance reminded me of what Justice Patwell had said to me in Tipperary County Court 16 years previously: 'I am sure Mr MacIntyre will admit that he is no James Bond.' After my performance with Flo tonight, I expected to be arrested for crimes against choreography – if not the style police, for my sleeveless top. A man over 40 should know better.

In the event we scored really good marks, but were left in a skate-off with Colleen. Stewart, Colleen's partner, is also Flo's professional partner and we were about to challenge each other for the final. We both knew we had come further than we thought possible. When the judges gave their final decision, I had survived the first and last skate-off in the show. That is simply ridiculous. In the end I did it for the girls, my sweet princesses and my wife. Daddy was no longer just dad but a daddy in touch with sequins and shiny things. And for a daddy, it doesn't get better than that.

Sunday, 22 March 2009

I was strangely relaxed for the final today. Happy to be there, I had no expectations and I wasn't going to be disappointed whatever happened. The male professionals tried to rattle me by stitching together the legs of my trousers and, moments before I was to go on, they hid my boots. I tried to stay calm and just before panic set in, they were found. Never was a man happier to come second. My joy tonight was the opportunity to wire-fly to Elton John's 'Rocket Man'.

My baby daughter, Tiger, is eager to tell her pals that her daddy can fly. If there was ever a reason for doing a reality show, that was it. Ray Quinn was crowned the Ice King, but I was surprised and delighted to be his very decrepid understudy. It was a long way from Little Haiti, but skating on thin ice has always been my stock and trade.

*****

My daughter's drama teacher, who doesn't watch television, came up to me recently. She looked me up and down and stared at me strangely as if something didn't quite fit.

'Allegra tells me you are a professional dancer,' she said, doubtfully.

'Not quite,' I said.

Well, I don't want to ruin the fantasy for Allegra just yet.

18

AND FINALLY...

That early evening of 6 April 2010, the London Eye undoubtedly gave us the best view of politics that the capital had to offer. The sun glistened on the River Thames and the Palace of Westminster looked impressive from the top of the wheel. Earlier that day, Gordon Brown had met with the Queen to request the dissolution of Parliament. Eight hours later, as Big Ben struck six o'clock, I was about to make the transition from feral journalist to prime-time anchorman as I joined Katie Derham live on the Eye to present *London Tonight* for ITN.

I had no stubble, no leather jacket, no secret cameras or wires strapped to my body. There were no stealth vehicles and there was no hiding in bushes. Yet still I didn't have a pot to piss in – literally! In fairness, Katie and I had been warned that there would be no toilet breaks, outside or otherwise, because the wheel wouldn't stop for us, no matter how desperate our needs became. We would simply have to hold it in.

I was wearing a crisp new white shirt and a new suit. Before today, suits only made it onto my back for funerals and weddings, so wearing one to work felt decidedly uncomfortable. The pantomime cougars of *Loose Women* had chosen my tie, and had threatened to hunt me down if I didn't wear it as promised in my virgin broadcast as an anchorman. My shoes were cheap and shiny – and off camera.

I had been thrown in at the deep end. There had been no rehearsals and I hadn't even done a screen test. These had been diligently planned, but somehow fell off the radar as external events consumed everyone's time. If I messed up on screen, my days as an anchorman would be over before they had even begun. So no pressure! Oh, and thanks for starting me on a big news day with a live outside broadcast! Some practice would have been nice, but I suppose the chaos and my utter lack of preparation at least provided some degree of continuity between this and my previous career.

The God of television news, Alastair Stewart, had wished me well as I left the ITN building on Gray's Inn Road to fill the vacancy that he had created when he went to read the national news. 'Don't worry if you make a mistake: the public will love you for it,' he assured me. I wasn't so sure.

It was five minutes to air when one of the cameramen turned to me and said:

'It's very brave of you to kick-start with an outside broadcast, and at the start of the election, too.' Well, it wasn't exactly my idea.

'How does it feel to be Ron Jeremy, anchorman?' the soundman asked.

'I think he's the porn star,' I said.

I was going more for Ron Burgundy, but if I blew this gig, porn might be the only television work left for me.

Katie Derham smiled at me and said, 'Enjoy! You'll do great.' I could get it wrong on other days, but not today. The last time I had been on the London Eye was with the Insect Tribe of Papua New Guinea. If they could get over their fear of the wheel, I figured I could swallow my nerves and present the news from it.

It seemed like an age since I had been at the *Irish Press* in Dublin in 1990, being shouted at by sub-editors over my appalling spelling and even worse grammar.

I had defended myself robustly: 'That's not bad spelling – It's fucking job creation.' You had to be tough to survive in there. It was an old-style newsroom, where the air was coloured blue by the choice language and the thick cigarette smoke.

Opinions were shouted rather than discussed and occasionally a typewriter would be thrown across the office to emphasise a point. It was gritty and loud and real. Computers lay idle on our desks because the union had not agreed to allow us to use them, and we had to get permission from the management to use the photocopier.

It was eccentric and sometimes very fraught, but you knew you were alive. I was part of a group of young journalists who had joined the paper at the same time and were christened the 'Zodo Club' after the children's cartoon strip that ran every day.

It was a put-down from the old guard of the paper and we probably deserved it. On my first day, Eamon De Valera, the owner of the paper and the grandson of the founder, came to welcome us aboard. There were some words in Irish that I didn't quite catch and then I spilled coffee all over him.

Twenty years later, I avoided coffee as we counted down to the broadcast from the London Eye. The bongs of Big Ben announced the start of my new career, and, with a lot of help from Katie, I managed a clean broadcast. I breathed a sigh of relief as I ran for the toilet after we came off air and off the Eye. The next day, Boy George was on the sofa in the studio welcoming me to my new job. 'I only remember you from *Dancing on Ice*,' he told me.

For all my covert journalism and warzone reporting, from Burma to Beirut, the only thing I am remembered for is sequins and skating. 'How random life is,' I thought.

There were fluffs and stumbles and the occasional howler. The best was when I read 'crack in the ice' as 'crap on the ice'. 'Don't worry. There'll be plenty more where that came from,' Katie consoled me.

My first ever reporting job in London was to cover the annual Bloody Sunday commemoration march in the centre of London for the *Sunday Tribune*. That day 400 right-wing activists from Combat 18 and the National Front attacked the marchers. I reported that it was the worst attack on the march in recent memory.

Seven years later, I attended the same march as a BBC

journalist, this time undercover and in the middle of a group of far-right hooligans and racists who were attacking the parade in the most aggressive assault since I had first reported on it.

As I surveyed the city skyline that day of 6 April 2010, at the start of another London adventure, I couldn't help marvelling at the serendipity of life. Where in God's name would I be seven years from now?

Your guess is undoubtedly as good as mine.

*****

POSTSCRIPT

Within six months on the Sofa, I had Hollywood legends Carrie Fisher and Jeff Goldblum mimicking my accent, clownishly pronouncing Doo-naaaaal like a character from *The Quiet Man*.

'It's kinda Donald without the 'D',' I proffered, trying to assist.

'Onald?' said Jeff, slightly perplexed.

'That's a much better name,' I said.

Onald the Anchorman certainly has a ring to it, but not one that my mother had intended, I suspect.

On one occasion, I was sent out by ITN to camp with peace protesters in Parliament Square. They taught me how to use a straw bail as a latrine under the shadow of Big Ben, in full view of a thousand CCTV cameras and a group of Police officers. Life as a journalist on the most desired piece of real estate in England is usually more glamorous, but I felt strangely at ease with this raggle-taggle band of eco-warriors, homeless and anti-war protestors, eating out-of-date food scavenged from dumpsters and sleeping under tarpaulin.

Just a few weeks later, I was dispatched on an assignment

to Egypt and found myself reporting from a huge rubbish tip that 65,000 people call home. In the distance, beyond the City of the Dead, I could see the Great Pyramid of Giza, and the majestic River Nile was just about visible from where I was standing. My attention was drawn, however, to a more startling sight – that of a herd of goats on the rooftop of a five-storey apartment block.

The occasional sharp shard of sunlight that caught my eye gave a hint to an inspiring and extraordinary way of life that has developed in of the most impoverished ghettos of Egypt. There were heaps of rubbish in every living room, in every corridor, on every staircase – indeed, everywhere I looked. This, however, is not a testimony to their poverty but to their ingenuity.

This area is home to 7,000 families, collectively known as the Zabaleen, Cairo's garbage collectors. In the shadow of the Coptic Christian church cut into the sandy rock face, lies Moqattam, or 'Garbage City' as it is known. Here, an entire community is dedicated to recycling 4,500 tonnes of rubbish daily from Cairo. The refuse is delivered in trucks and distributed among the Zabaleen for processing. Some families specialise in recycling leather, others in electrics, others in cans or plastic bags. Everything from food to furniture is recycled. Fathers, mothers, children and grandparents all join in the industry of turning waste into a resource that will clothe and feed them. Huge mounds of papers, textiles, metals, even light bulbs are slowly and methodically sorted, compressed, washed, and then packed into huge grey hessian bags to be sold as raw material. Glass is collected and sold to factories; copper and other metals are melted and sold to dealers; plastics are reused in the manufacture of toys, and textiles are shredded and made into mattress filling. Certain shampoo bottles carry a premium because their manufacturers pay a little for every returned container to prevent them from being refilled and sold as counterfeits. Head & Shoulders and Pantene are among the first words students are taught in literacy classes. Donkey-drawn carts trundle along the potholed streets, over-laden with the valuable detritus. This hole in the ground is the recycling capital of the world.

Gazing on this in wonder I found my vast reservoir of war-weary cynicism melting away as I learned how the poorest of the poor have found a way of eking out a living in the worst of circumstances – with the best and most remarkable of consequences. Never again shall I grumble about the selection of bins and recycling containers that clutter my doorstep.

The flashes of sunlight across the skyline that had caught my eye came from the solar panels that are part of an initiative to supply the district with hot water. I shared a cup of tea with a young man called Hanna, his wife and their new baby. The tea was all the sweeter for being the fruit of their ingenuity. In the shadow of an ancient wonder of the world, the Great Pyramid of Giza, I was witnessing a very modern miracle.

I could see how one community, one person can make a difference and how that difference can multiply and grow into a movement that changes lives and moves mountains. All it takes is one seed – and I never expected to find such inspiration in 'Garbage City'. There was a time when I was beaten down by the worst that life had to offer – a time when I was so shot by fear and war wounds that I was nearly dead to the world around me. With the pungent aromas challenging my senses, and surrounded by the detritus of human existence, I was immensely grateful to inhale every breath of this uplifting experience. The Zabaleen have reminded me that hope springs eternal, even from the most unlikely of circumstances.

Life on the edge suddenly seemed more comfortable than life on the sofa.